RETURN TO STAR JUNCTION

LEGENDS OF STAR JUNCTION

SERRA WILDHEART

Scribe Hive
Publishing

Return to Star Junction

Series: Legends of Star Junction

Serra Wildheart

Copyright © 2023

ISBN Paperback: 978-1-962112-04-8

ISBN Ebook: 978-1-962112-05-5

Cover design by: Medeiros Creative

Published through Scribe Hive Publishing LLC

Pueblo, CO

www.scribehivepublishing.com

A women-owned publishing cooperative driven to share great stories that want to be told.

PRAISE FOR RETURN TO STAR JUNCTION

"Return To Star Junction is more than a story of family, returning home, and community. It's a story about remembering who we are. Who we came here to be, and what we came here to do. It's a beautiful tale of a woman rediscovering herself in those she loves. This tale will stay with you, and if you're lucky will find it's way into your dreams." ~ E.L. Winters

"A brilliant, lovely tale woven with characters that ooze magic and seem surreal—part human, part angel. This book got personal for me. Helped me open up to a part of myself I misplaced. To me and for me a great book is one that allows me open up and feel my hidden feelings. This a book for more than one reading—-each reading has yielded more knowledge and healing. Thank you to Serra Wildheart for providing a vehicle for healing woven into a powerful story of love, family and going home. A marvelous story of hope." ~B.R. Maryse

"As the title suggests, *Return to Star Junction* is a return through and through. But not just a return to place— it's a return to home, a return to community, a return to family, a return to self. This incredible debut book from author Serra Wildheart follows Val, a savvy California-based businesswoman whose life gets thrown upside down when she finds herself in charge of her two nephews and back in her childhood hometown on the Colorado Plateau.... As the web of interconnectedness is woven, both Val, her nephews, and even the reader, find themselves set onto a journey into self, pausing to reflect on what the landscape and all the life it holds has to say to us, showing us how to return to a deeper humanity of our own. This book is a beautiful work of art that stays with the reader long after the last page has been turned." ~Rebecca H

A foggy mist made it hard to see. Val walked toward the flickering light, where she felt something was waiting for her. The mist began to clear as she approached, and the fire burned brightly. The wind stirred the flames, launching sparks that became stars. Enchanting music carried by drums played in her ears. It appeared that a young girl was dancing with the fire with the music and the drumbeats. When Val reached the circle, she could see the girl was a woman, aging right before her eyes.

Others were present, but she couldn't stop watching the dancing woman. Val tried to see her face but couldn't. She closed her eyes to feel the music and suddenly felt as if she was the one dancing.

"Picaflor." It was William's voice. "Picaflor, it is time to return."

She opened her eyes and saw her father there, looking as he did when she was the child who adored him. He was with Grandmother Flor and many elders she didn't recognize but knew somehow.

Then Grace appeared and said, "Valerie, bring them home."

Children and others appeared before her. A boy around ten with curly dark red hair. An older boy, tall and intense, maybe fifteen. A young girl *with long golden hair holding the older boy's hand. The people multiplied too fast. Val couldn't see all the faces.*

Then, all the voices spoke, "It is time. Bring them together. Bring them home."

Val awoke with a start. Her eyes open but still dreaming. The starlight filtered into the room, revealing the figures from her dream. Her father, William, looked upon her with great love before dissipating into the soft light. Each loved one from the dream did the same. Though her heart raced when she awoke, she remained still while the people of her memories had their quiet visit. When they had all disappeared back into the starlight, her eyes found the clock. 2:22 a.m.

Val let her head fall back onto the pillow. *"What am I supposed to do?"* she asked into the quiet void. But her mind raced, and she heard no answer. She knew the boys in the dream must be her nephews. Her brother Cade's son Alex was ten, maybe eleven. The older boy in the dream was likely Jake, their half-sister Sissy's son.

Her mind was busy doing mental math, counting back the years since she had seen any of them and trying to put names to the faces before they faded. *Eight!* Her mind found the answer. It had been eight years since she had seen her family. Eight years since their mother's funeral. *But who is the girl?* Val closed her eyes and let out a deep breath, knowing sleep was done for the night. Sleep had become unreliable, and she was weary.

Val opened her laptop at the breakfast nook in her Palos Verdes home. She told herself she would work if she couldn't sleep, but her mind was on her dream. No, her mind was on the people in the dream—the family she hadn't seen in far too long.

Her brother had stopped talking to her, and she'd tried so hard not to miss him. Her half-sisters Sissy, who mostly played phone tag, but whose turn it had been for longer than Val could remember and Melanie, who blamed Val for most of her problems. She didn't know the nephews but sent birthday cards and gifts to them most years.

"Bring them together," whispered in her mind.

She stared out the window for the answer, watching the moonlight kiss the leaves of the oak and walnut trees as they softly flickered with the breeze. "Bring them *home*." She heard it again. *But whose home?* Val wondered as she watched an opossum move slowly through her yard.

Her email sat open but untouched until her alarm went off at 6:00 a.m., and her body jumped to action. Her routine was as automatic as the coffee maker—thirty minutes on the elliptical, fifteen minutes on core and arms, and then stretch. Shower. Juice. Toast. Coffee while answering emails. Drive to work at 7:30. But today Val's phone rang at 7:14 a.m. as she was gathering her laptop and files for work. She didn't look, just tapped the button on her earpiece.

"Hello?" she answered.

"Val? This is Cade." Val sat down and texted her assistant. *On a call. Cancel meetings. Will connect when done.*

Her brother Cade was ten years old when Val left home at seventeen. He was the only boy in the family and her only remaining connection to her father and memories so distant they felt like they belonged to someone else. He hadn't spoken to her in almost three years, not since his wife Karen died in an accident and Val missed the funeral. It didn't matter that Val was out of the country. It didn't matter that flights were canceled and layovers long. It only mattered that Val was the family member he had always depended on, and she wasn't there.

Even though it shook, Cade's voice was so pleasing to her ears, like a favorite song that soothed her tension away and nudged her heart to open. So shaky, it was almost a whisper.

"Val, I need your help—and so does Jake. Sissy's dead."

Val heard the tears in his words. Her mind raced to understand his meaning as a lump formed in her throat and a sense of dread washed over her. Cade paused, waiting, until she rallied.

"I'm here, Cade," she said softly. "What can I do?"

Val listened to her brother reveal his troubles and confess his mistakes. She had tried to reach him many times after Karen died, but he stopped returning her calls. Eventually, she stopped trying but never stopped thinking she should try again. It was an internal dance of guilt and justification. She felt her heart fluttering as he opened up, only to have it quickly stop when he told her about Sissy.

She stopped her breath as if to unhear his words and turn back time to when their sister was still alive. Questions and self-recriminations swirled around her as she was flooded with years of guilt, but now wasn't the time for that. She wrote notes to herself as they spoke: *Contact attorneys, Exton? Find Jake, get answers, bring them home.* Her dream came back. *Exton!* And she suddenly remembered why the name sounded familiar. Exton was the nearest city to their home town. *Had Sissy gone back to Star Junction?* Val wondered.

The estranged brother and sister talked for hours, both transported back in time, revisiting their roles, and Cade let everything spill out of him. The grief of losing Karen and not knowing how to be a father alone. Feeling incapable of being whole enough to care for his beautiful son Alex. They talked about the girlfriend Nancy, the accident, and how desperately he wanted to find his way back to being a good father and being whole again. During the conversation, he realized that Val didn't have to be convinced or cajoled into helping him. Still, he had a script in his head that he had practiced before calling.

"Sis, I know you are crazy busy with your business, but maybe it wouldn't be too much inconvenience if Alex came to stay with you for a few weeks? You wouldn't have to leave work, and Alex could see Southern California." Val smiled at Cade's pitch.

"I think I have a better idea, Cade. I had a dream last night, and now I understand it better."

Cade knew about Val's dreams. They'd had many adventures as kids because of those dreams that helped Val navigate life with their stepfather, Emmet. "I'd like to take Alex to Star Junction until you can join us there. I'll find Jake in Exton and bring him, too."

"Yes," was the only word he could get out. It was more than he could have hoped for.

"Great! I will be there tomorrow morning. The sooner we can find Jake, the better."

Val got to work. She contacted her attorney with the information she had, asking them to find Jake and make arrangements for her to take custody ASAP. For the rest of the day, she juggled CEO duties for her two companies: high-end corporate design and artsy product development for use in interior design and retail markets. Video conferences, emails, reviewing project briefs, and significant rescheduling of meetings took much of her day.

She invited her assistant, Elliot—who she hired six years ago as her VP of operations and had come to rely on for far more—to help her close up the house and rework her schedule for the next week, shifting in-person meetings to video, postponing anything not urgent, and addressing any potential fires. He also booked her flights, arranged a car, and prepped the GPS on her phone for her drive from Phoenix Sky Harbor Airport to Cade's and then to Star Junction. He would also take care of her houseplants and, of course, her cat.

Cleo, a remarkable looking white and tortoiseshell tabby with green eyes, watched intently, purring as Val packed for warm and cold, driving comfort and versatility. Jeans, sweats, T-shirts, two blouses. One suit. She never liked wearing suits, but they had become her uniform and battle armor. She often wondered how she had done this to herself. Nevertheless, when the suit was on, business Val was too. Val looked at her closet, wondering if she should be taking more clothes, more business attire. Cleo decided it was a good time to sit in the small suitcase. "Ha! You're right, Cleo." She scooped the cat onto her shoulder and closed the suitcase with the other hand.

Early the next morning, Val waited in her garden for the car to the airport. The early morning light was just beginning to illuminate the day. Sitting under a giant English walnut tree and looking over a multitude of colorful flowers, she wondered how it came to be that she spent so little time sitting in her garden or enjoying the walnuts.

The hummingbirds darted from flower to flower, in and out, chasing each other away. She smiled as she watched them and heard her father singing, "Picaflor, my little picaflor," in her thoughts. A hawk launched from its perch and let out a long call as it flew overhead. Val found herself taking a deeper breath than usual. It seemed her breath was always so shallow.

"Are you ready?" Elliot peeked around the corner of the house from the driveway, his tall frame hard to miss. He'd decided to be her chauffeur instead of hiring a service. Val looked at him and smiled.

"You mean to take on two kids I don't know and return to a place I haven't been in thirty years?"

"Yeah. You ready?"

She took in a breath and nodded. "Yes, somehow, I am."

"Don't worry. I'll take good care of Cleo," he assured her.

"I know you will. She loves you."

Elliot picked up her suitcase and carry-on bag, complete with laptop, work papers, documents from the attorney, and a map that could at least point her in the right direction. She could leave the house and be away from the office, but work still must get done. "Elliot, thank you for all of your help with this. It's way above and beyond. I appreciate it."

"Nonsense. All due respect, boss, there is no 'above and beyond' when it comes to friendship."

Val was uncharacteristically sheepish. She was used to being the one who held the light and gave the support. She hadn't been the one to receive it personally in ages. At this moment, she became acutely aware of how much she had come to rely on Elliot and how much she would miss him.

"Hey, boss," he said playfully.

She met his gaze.

"You are doing the right thing, and you will be great. No question." He put the suitcase in the trunk and opened her car door for her.

As he put his seatbelt on and started the car, he added, "And you will tell me more about it, or I quit!" They laughed.

Val did her best to keep herself occupied on the short flight from Los Angeles to Phoenix. She looked over the information the attorneys had sent—papers to retrieve Jake from foster care and an appointment time with children's services. She couldn't bring herself to think about Sissy while on the plane. If Val stayed in business mode, she would make it through. But her heart hurt as she wondered about Jake; she hoped that being a teenager somehow made it easier than if he had been younger and questioned if he would understand why nobody had been there to claim him before now. She wasn't even sure he would remember meeting her years before. She couldn't stay focused. Instead, she found herself drifting off to another time and place.

Forty years ago—Star Junction, tucked somewhere in the high desert mountains between Arizona and Utah.

"Daddy?"

"Yes, picaflor."

"Where do we live?"

"What do you mean, young Valerie? You know the name Star Junction, yes?"

"Yes, but where are we and why?" She gestured with her arms sweeping outward.

"Why? Because the stars are here."

"Can we find it on a map?"

William smiled at his daughter. "Hmmm, well, we can come

close." He retrieved an atlas from the shelf and found the pages that would best show a location. "Do you see this area on the edges of these two states? Arizona is here. Utah the one above. If you follow this line, it is a highway. It comes through Star Junction, continues to Exton, and then goes further southwest."

Valerie scrunched her face, trying to see. "But I don't see us."

"Because we are a very small town," he responded with a smile. "Do you want to know a secret?

Her eyes lit up, "Yes!"

"We really don't mind not showing up on the big maps. That way our community stays one of friends. Other places have lots of traffic and people and noise."

"Have you ever been to one of them?"

"Yes, I was born in a big city before coming to Star Junction. And I traveled with your uncle when we were young. We were glad to return here where it is quiet and we can listen better to the magic."

"Will I ever go to a city?"

"Yes, my picaflor. You will travel and experience many people and places. But one day, you too will return home to the mountain to once again talk with the stars."

"And dance?"

William beamed. "Yes, to dance with the fire."

***

Present Day

Val was lulled back to the present with the pilot's announcement to prepare for landing. She smiled at the memory of her father and Star Junction. After thirty years away, she was finally seeing her father's words come true. Thoughts of her family took over. She last saw her siblings eight years ago at their mother's funeral and somehow, they all went back to living separate lives. Why? She was beginning to understand the words in the dream *"Bring them together"* and hoped it wasn't too late.

Cade had been a single father to Alex since his beloved Karen died in a car accident almost three years ago. Alex, now going on eleven, was a kind, introverted kid with endless curiosity and a deep sense of empathy. Though he used to express every thought and ask questions constantly, his focus had shifted to quiet. His curiosity channeled to intense, intricate drawings.

It wasn't that he didn't want to ask the questions. Just no one was there to answer them anymore. Cade struggled in his own paralyzing grief and failed to be present for Alex. Looking at his son only reminded him of the pain and loss. He had been afraid to breathe or blink or talk to anyone who might trigger the grief he held inside. Three years without Karen's light. Three years since his heart had stopped wanting to feel and died with her. He knew he had cheated Alex out of his presence, out of a father who could help him feel safe and loved and not alone. Cade numbed the pain by working extra, drinking more, and filling the void with the attention of a woman who wanted to own him.

When Cade met Nancy, he buried himself in her attention as if she was his lifeline. Nancy was well-packaged in designer clothes and exciting stories. They met at a work event—one that he had to attend because he was the lead on the building project—and her eyes never left her target. Her words were well-honed invitations to escape his world; he was hooked.

Nancy wanted her trophy: successful, attractive Cade. She had no room in the picture for a kid. In the year that Cade and Nancy had been dating, Alex spent most of his time at home alone, either in his room or in the backyard. His grades at school remained okay, but his teacher expressed concerns about his change in demeanor and affect.

At times Alex sought Cade's attention, he even attempted to get Nancy's. He'd quickly discovered that any attention she gave him was false at best and generally venomous. She would often criticize his drawings and imply that he needed some sort of special help because he must be delayed or have some other issue.

"Normal boys don't just sit around drawing all the time."

Eventually, Cade found himself fighting to spend time with his own son but ended up becoming a broken record of excuses to Alex. "I'm sorry, bud. I'll make it up to you soon. I know you understand."

Too much time had passed without him realizing it, and suddenly Cade felt like he had lost touch with everything that mattered. He felt like he was constricted somehow and simultaneously, like everything he had been working so hard to numb and avoid was pushing its way out. His heart ached again—for what had been and for his son.

Nancy's spells had become less alluring, and they had begun to fight. She didn't tolerate dissension. If he didn't want to do things her way, she pushed him until he gave in. Nancy had mastered the art of pushing his buttons and handing him a drink all with a sweet smile, a peck on the cheek, and an "Oh, honey, don't be so difficult. You know I'm right."

But two nights ago, Cade left her place angry and intoxicated because he knew she wasn't right. His heart was speaking again, and she ridiculed him for it. He woke up in the morning in the hospital, banged up, bruised, and feeling clearer than he had in months. And he had a mess to clean up. The good news—his was the only car involved in the accident. The bad news—he would likely face DUI charges. All he knew for sure that morning was that he had to fix things with Alex and for Alex and get their life back.

Cade spent the day with Alex, reconnecting and cleaning up while trying to get in touch with Sissy. He knew he would have to deal with the consequences of the accident, but he also felt strongly that Alex needed some time with family—and hopefully some fun with his cousin Jake.

When Cade couldn't reach Sissy after hours of trying, he knew something had to be wrong. It wasn't like her not to respond. He tried the hospital where he thought she worked. He tried his other half-sister, Melanie, hoping she could connect him with Sissy. But Melanie was a flight attendant who often flew international flights and could be unreachable for days, if she wanted to be reached. His curiosity led to panic and an ache in the pit of his stomach. Cade started internet searches and found what might be an obituary. His fear rose, his heart frantic.

"Dad, is everything okay?" Alex asked.

Cade stopped for a minute and hugged Alex.

"I'm not sure, bud. I'm having trouble reaching Aunt Sissy. But don't worry. We'll figure it out." Cade tried to reassure Alex and decided to reach out to his detective friend, Thomas. He didn't hear back until the morning.

"Cade, I'm sorry I couldn't get back to you sooner. I wanted to make sure the info was correct." Thomas's voice was kind and careful.

"Of course...just tell me that she's okay."

"I wish I could. Unfortunately, I found a death certificate from the town of Exton, Arizona. Cade, I'm sorry. It looks cancer related. Just over a year ago."

Cade shook his head as if to shake the news away. He felt as if the words were being spoken to someone else. He closed his eyes and focused on his breath, willing himself to stay present and find the words.

"What about Jake?"

"Who?"

"Jake, her son. He's fifteen, I think. Where is he?"

There was a pause on the line.

"Okay, found him. It looks like the children would be with children's services, like foster care or other housing. Also in Exton. Cade, on a personal note, let me know what else I can do. I'm sorry about your sister."

"Thanks, Thomas. I'll be in touch."

Cade sat alone in the kitchen with his eyes closed after hanging up, trying to find the answers. Alex hadn't come down from his room yet. It didn't feel possible. Another member of the family lost. Why didn't he know? He wondered why she was all the way in Exton when he thought she still lived outside of Phoenix. He wondered if her ex had come back, or if they were on a road trip. *"Ahh, Sis, I'm so sorry I didn't know."*

Alex and Cade waited in their kitchen for Val's arrival. Alex had been up since before dawn, his dreams having summoned him awake again. The dreams were filled with people he didn't know and landscapes he had never seen before, yet he traveled in them without hesitation. His sketchpad filled with every detail he could draw.

Usually, he stopped drawing only long enough to eat his dad's magic pancakes. That was their name because when Alex's mom was still alive, Cade won the best pancakes contest in the house, and he became the sole maker of pancakes. They were Alex's favorite breakfast for reasons beyond the pancakes themselves. They were magic because when Cade made pancakes for Alex, the rest of the world seemed to stop.

He made Alex a part of the process, telling stories, making jokes that only they found hilarious, and creating pancake art with surprisingly intricate designs, considering they were pancakes and meant to be devoured. Karen would tease that it was a lot of work for something so temporary and only Cade could turn making pancakes into a performance piece. She loved that he did, and she loved how much Alex soaked his father in fully, never taking his eyes off of him. This morning, the performance didn't disappoint, even though both of them knew that Val would soon arrive to take Alex on an adventure to Star Junction while Cade put some pieces back together.

With the pancakes eaten, all became quiet in the kitchen as Cade cleaned up and Alex returned to his sketchpad. Cade couldn't help but watch Alex's deep focus on his art. It felt like Alex embodied a pure presence, and Cade was overcome with inspired determination. He pulled out the stool next to Alex and sat, looking at his beautiful son. Alex looked up to Cade.

"Alex, I love you. You are the best and most important thing in my life. You know that. Right?"

Alex put his pencil down and looked at Cade with tears that turned to pure love and adoration when he smiled. He hadn't felt that in a long time. Alex had felt helpless to reach his dad, to bring him back from the dark haze and the girlfriend, to bring him back from a guy he just didn't recognize and felt alone around. Alex had felt like Cade wasn't even in his body anymore. Alex's eyes had pleaded so many times to find his dad again, and now, here he was. The father he'd been missing.

"I'm so glad you're back," Alex said as he hugged Cade as tightly as he could. Cade forgot his bruised and banged-up body and wrapped his arms around Alex to hold him.

"I am back. Alex, I'm so sorry I was gone. I'm sorry that you had to go through that. I won't let it happen again." Alex held his dad tightly enough to last. Cade's eyes closed as he took a deep, slow breath. "Thanks, bud. Hey, show me what you're drawing there."

Alex's eyes lit up. He cocked his head playfully as he picked up the sketchpad, pulled it to his chest, and looked at his dad. "Umm... Okay!" he said as he turned it around to show the picture. "It's you."

Cade looked in amazement at the intricate drawing of himself, eyes bright, looking better than he had looked in ages and wearing a T-shirt that was more like a superhero uniform. The emblem was a complex and detailed almost three-dimensional geometric design whose lines extended past the shirt and through the whole page.

"Wow, Alex, this is amazing! How did you come up with this?" Alex looked perplexed.

"What do you mean?" Alex asked. He looked at his father with so much love that Cade felt like he could dissolve into it.

Cade hoped Val got there soon because he suddenly felt like he might lose his composure. He wasn't sure why he didn't want Alex to see him cry. Cade never saw his stepfather Emmet cry. In fact, he had never seen Emmet as anything but hard and mean. But he wasn't Emmet. Cade's eyes soon revealed him and the tears fell.

Alex responded to the tears softly, as if speaking to a child. "It's how I see you." Cade pulled Alex to him again and let the tears flow.

Val pulled into Cade's driveway and put the car in park. She'd kept her internal dialogue at bay by listening to an annoying morning show on the radio followed by a quick work call with Elliot. She sat in the car fidgeting and checking all the instruments over and over, pretending it was because it was a different car than she was used to. Finally, she stopped and took a deep breath in, holding it for as long as she could. Val wasn't used to being nervous. She prided herself on being cool. In control. Always composed. She scoffed at the thought and chuckled at herself.

"Here we go," she said to the universe and got out of the car. Cade and Alex were already at the front steps, trying not to seem like they hadn't been watching her. She looked up at her brother and smiled, realizing just how much she had missed him and his boy. This was a day for the laying down of armor. Too many years of distance, guilt, and resentment were enough. Val looked at her brother as she headed toward him and couldn't see any of that. All she could see was the love she felt. They met in the middle.

"Cade," she said as they hugged tightly, holding each other as the barriers and years apart dissolved between them. It felt like an excruciatingly long hug for Alex, who was eager to meet Val and a little anxious about it all.

"Dad?" was his version of "Ahem." Cade and Val let out a little laugh and let go of the embrace.

"Val, meet Alex," Cade said playfully.

Alex stepped forward with his arm out to shake hands like he had learned from Cade. Firm grip, three solid shakes, let go. Val gave him a huge smile.

"Hi, Alex. I am so happy to meet you in person." Val opened her arms and invited him into a hug. Alex smiled and accepted. He liked how she felt.

They did what people do with a short time to visit after long gaps between. Cade and Alex showed Val the house, the leftover pancakes, and Alex's room with his posters of galaxies and natural wonders, like the Grand Canyon. A picture of Karen holding Alex as a toddler sat in a frame by Alex's bed. Cade gave her the information he had about Sissy and Jake, just in case she still needed it.

They loaded Alex's bags into the back of the white SUV. Val noticed the sketchpad with his daypack and looked to Cade for confirmation. Cade beamed. "Oh yeah, he's really good!"

Cade opened the door for Alex. "Okay, bud…it's going to be a long drive. So you have to get going." He picked up Alex in a bear hug. "I'm going to miss you so much, but I want you to have the best time. I will join you there when I can."

"I know you will. I feel it!" Alex smiled and got into the back seat.

Val hugged Cade again. "You, take care of you. Get it sorted out quickly and then join us there. Soon."

"I will." He stepped away slightly so she could get in the car. "Thank you, Sis." Val smiled and nodded assurance to Cade.

Instead of getting in the car, she leaned in and whispered, "It will be okay. You can do this." She cupped his face in her hands like she had done when they were kids and leaned her forehead into his when she spoke. Then she turned and got in the car.

"You ready?" Val asked Alex with a playful tone.

"Yep!"

Val backed the car out of the driveway. She and Alex waved to Cade. Val smiled with an assuring nod. Cade watched them drive away with a mix of hopeful resolve and pending dread. Two smart things he scheduled for today: an appointment with his attorney, and a run with Thomas. It wasn't a good day to be alone.

Alex fidgeted in the back seat. He would normally try to sketch, even in the car, but there was too much to look at. He opened every compartment, door slot, console, and examined all the buttons and controls that he could reach. Val noticed and watched with amusement.

"This is a cool car, Aunt Val."

She smiled at him. "I'm glad you like it. I thought we would try it out and see if it would be comfortable for us."

"Well, so far, it is nice. Our car is kind of beat up." He realized he wasn't sure it even ran anymore after Cade's accident. He changed the subject. "I've never really been away from home."

Val knew it wasn't just a statement of fact. There was anxiety there. Alex had fear and uncertainty about leaving his dad and whether things would ever truly be okay again. He needed reassurance of safety.

"It's a big thing, leaving home for a bit. And maybe kind of confusing, like you are part excited and part uneasy?" Val was careful not to say afraid.

Alex nodded and glanced at her, making eye contact in the rearview mirror, relieved that she somehow knew.

She continued, "Let's make a deal. No matter what you feel, you can tell me—even if you think it is crazy or embarrassing or stupid. Okay? I mean it. Safe zone. You can tell me, and I will listen."

Alex considered the offer and smiled. "Okay, and you can tell me things and I will listen!"

"Deal?" she asked.

"Deal!" They both smiled. "So are you kind of nervous, too?" he asked.

She raised her eyebrows playfully, as if it were an absurd notion and shook her head no as she admitted, "I am absolutely, totally nervous!" She laughed, which made him laugh. Then she asked him "Are *you?*"

"Yeah," he said, looking down briefly. Val had the thought he hadn't wanted to hurt her feelings. *Wow, this kid.*

"That's good. We can be nervous together. At least until we aren't nervous anymore." He reminded her so much of Cade when he was a child. Caring. Paying attention to every detail like a sponge absorbing water. "Okay, Alex, I have a really important question for you now." Val's tone was grave. Alex looked at her with a questioning uncertainty. "What kind of music do you like?"

Alex smiled. "My dad says it is called Classic Rock. But I kind of like to listen to a lot of different things. Like songs I haven't heard before."

"Okay, well, you can be in charge of the music, but I hold veto power."

Alex's eyes lit up as he reached for the stereo controls. "Deal."

———

Alex watched the outside go by with the time, mesmerized by its enormity. He started off trying to count the saguaros until his imagination was ignited by the sometimes strange and contorted shapes they formed, stretching, curving, twisting, and leaning over to find the best position in the sun. They were huge. He wondered if they were hard like trees or squishy since he had heard that they store water inside. Maybe when they moved, they made sloshing sounds like a water balloon. He wondered what the splatter would be like. He knew he would try to draw this later.

"What are you imagining back there?" Val had been watching him daydream from the rearview mirror. She recognized the look.

Alex smiled sheepishly, as though caught in a grand scheme, and paused to find the right words.

"I didn't know it was so big."

"What part?"

"All of it—the world. I didn't know."

Val smiled. She had forgotten the endlessness of the desert. The way it seemed to expand beyond the edges of the world we know. It had always held a certain magic for her to open beyond her own perceived edges and disrupt convictions of what *is*.

"It gets even bigger. And better," she whispered the last part.

They'd been driving for almost three hours. Val felt it was about time for lunch, gas, and a break from the monotony of driving and her thoughts that had started to take over. What would she do when they got there? *What would Jake be like? Would he be angry? Was he sitting in foster care, wondering where his family was and why no one had come yet?*

She hoped to send the message now. *"Hang on, Jake. We're coming."*

Her mind turned to Star Junction and the people she had known as family and had called grandmother and uncle. *Will any of them still be there thirty years later? How did I get so far apart from everything that shaped my early world?*

"Aunt Val?" The words pulled her back from the thought abyss. "Can we get something to eat?" Saved by the kid.

"Yep. Let's check out the next stop. Okay?"

Alex had an affinity for burgers and fries. This wasn't particularly surprising for Val since Cade declared them his favorite food when he was a little younger than Alex. Not that they got to have them often as children. Val enjoyed the memory but noticed that Alex was eating slowly.

"How's your burger?"

"Great!"

"Yeah?" Val eyed him with playful suspicion.

Alex stopped himself just before his next bite. "Are we really going to where you and Dad are from?"

"We are. Has he told you much about it?"

"Just a little. He said he was younger than me when he moved to Phoenix. But he said that it was a magical place and you would remember more."

Val hadn't considered how young Cade was when they moved away. She had tried to fill their father's shoes and show Cade the magic of their hometown. Still a child herself, she tried to teach him the lessons their father had taught her, but she had had limited freedom or power to do much with their stepfather around. Emmet changed their world.

Val suddenly found herself filled with gratitude—for her memories, the lessons of her father, the life so full of love she remembered before Emmet and this call to return. She hoped it was still as magical as she remembered and hadn't been ruined by the decades. She could picture Alex soaking it all in like he was seeing the vastness of the desert for the first time.

"Do you think I'll like it?"

Val stopped eating and looked Alex in the eyes. "I feel you will love it there—and find it just as mysterious and magical as I did when I was your age."

Alex's eyes lit up, and he began to devour his food so they could get on the road.

"You might want to slow down just a little," she teased playfully. "We will get there right on time."

***

It had been too quiet since Alex dozed off, mesmerized by the endless landscape passing by. This same terrain was triggering floods of memories for Val. The memories of her father filled her with love and longing. She hoped Alex would wake up soon and distract her from losing herself in those memories... and the much darker ones of Emmet. The reason they left Star Junction. The one she blamed for her losing her home, her family, and her childhood.

Alex began to stir and stretch. Val noticed a rest stop up ahead and decided to pull over for a break, and a breath. Their journey took them north and higher in altitude. The saguaros had been replaced by yucca, sagebrush, juniper, and occasional pinyon pines and oak trees.

"Why are there more trees here?" Alex broke the silence.

"We are at a higher elevation. The high-desert looks a bit different. More trees, more plants, more water," she answered.

They walked and explored the viewpoint to stretch their legs. The terrain included red and brown rock formations, buttes, mesas, and spires speckled with shrubs and trees.

"Why is that mountain red?"

Val smiled. "Iron. The dirt has a high iron content, which makes it red."

Alex's mood seemed to shift from excited and full of wonder to pensive and sad.

Val watched as he processed something and then paused before asking, "What's up?"

"We were going to go to the Grand Canyon. All of us. Dad, me, and Mom. But—" he paused as he picked apart a twig. "Why do people die?" Val sat down on a bench overlooking the valley they had just passed through and gestured for him to join her.

"That's a big question. I'm not sure I have an answer that will make you feel any better." She searched the horizon, quickly considering her next words. "My father used to tell me that we all come here for a certain amount of time. To play parts in each other's dreams. It is all a precious gift. And it really sucks when they have to say goodbye because it hurts and we miss them so much."

"I didn't get to say goodbye." He dropped his head and fidgeted, not sure if it was okay to talk about, to share, to feel. Val rested her arm on his shoulder to reassure him.

"I'm sorry, Alex. I know your mom would have stayed if she could. A parent never wants to leave their child." In that moment, Val felt the words didn't come *from* her as much as *for* both of them. *A parent never wants to leave their child.* She sat in silence with Alex, allowing that truth to settle in her heart. Together they looked at the view, the landscape sculpted by wind, rain, and time. The layered colors offered mesmerizing salve for weary hearts.

"Do you still talk to her?" Val quietly eased back into conversation.

Alex's eyes got huge, and he wondered how she knew.

She smiled at him and answered, "I was nine when my father died. Your grandfather. You would have loved him. You remind me of him. He was kind of magical." She nudged his shoulder playfully and shared the information like it was a long-lost secret. "Before he died —in fact, most of my childhood—he taught me how to communicate with my heart. He taught me that I would always be able to find him there, in my heart. When things got hard, if I listened, I would hear him saying, '*I am always with you.*' Just like your mom is always with *you.*"

"Do you still talk to your dad?" Alex asked.

"You know what? Honestly, I forgot to do that for a really long time. Or at least, I forgot to listen. But this is helping me to remember."

Alex felt good around Aunt Val. He didn't know why, but she was easy to talk to. He had felt so alone since his mom died. When Alex began having dreams with Val in them, he began to feel hopeful again.

Star Junction wasn't its official name. To the world, it was just another small, remote town without much to offer in the way of financial opportunity or convenience. "Out in the middle of nowhere" would be a popular comment, and the locals wouldn't have it any other way.

That was precisely why some had made it their home for many generations. The bordering towns grew larger with the space to build factories and burgeoning industries. Star Junction chose simplicity and interconnection. They shared resources and valued time spent together.

It had always been called Star Junction, but for most, the reason why was lost to legends and magical stories told around a fire about a constellation and how people came to be here. The heart of the town was protected by the mountains. In many traditions the mountains and rivers were the guardians of the land.

In Peru, the Quechua terms "Apu" and "Ñusta" mean "spirit of" the mountain, river, or lake. Here they were regarded as protective friends whose counsel could be sought during times of difficulty or change. Grandmother Flor had always said, "The mountains are full of wisdom for the heart open to learning."

The roads were no longer flat and straight. They wrapped around and wove through the high desert mountains and included well-shaped formations that delighted Alex and perked him up again. Val didn't remember this part of the road; she had been a passenger on this road only once before—a sixteen-year-old unwilling, resistant, and full of swallowed rage the day Emmet moved them away from Star Junction.

Now, as they got closer, she noticed an uneasy feeling beginning in her stomach. As much as she believed she was doing the right thing, she still had no idea what she was doing at all. It had been three decades since she'd seen Star Junction, and questions plagued her mind. Why didn't she come back here when she left Phoenix? Or when she sold the first business? What kept her away? And, most importantly, was the town she knew still there? All she knew was that a town existed in its spot, and she had a hotel booked for a week.

"*Wow!* Look at that!" Alex's exclamation startled her out of her depressing thought loop. She looked up just in time to see a pronounced and distinct eye formation in the mountain.

"Did you see it, Aunt Val?"

"Yes, I did." She smiled at his excitement.

"What do you think it is?" he asked.

It was a simple question. Her mind wanted to answer that it was a formation caused by water erosion, and it was very cool looking. A whisper in her thoughts told her instead, "*Remember.*"

Alex kept searching through the trees to find it again. She shot the question back to him, "What do you think it is?"

Alex gleamed. "It's the eye of the mountain! Or a giant dinosaur. It's watching us; we have to get closer to it!"

The road wound around and the Eye went out of view. Alex was confused by where it could have gone and lost track of direction with all the curves and winding of the road. He was not discouraged, though, and was determined to find it again.

Val was ready for a break. It had already been over twelve hours of travel since she left her house and she was tired. The doubtful thoughts had found a way in and worn her down, and she knew she would have work to catch up on once they settled in for the night. She thought they should be getting close but hadn't seen any road signs in miles.

"Let's look for a place to stop," she said out loud, as much for her own benefit as Alex's awareness. The roads must have heard her and began to level out and have longer straight sections. As they rounded a corner, they came to a small gas station and mini-mart. "Great, let's stop."

The gas station was an older one with just two pumps. A vintage soda machine sat to the left of the mini-mart entrance and an even older ice freezer to the right. Alex was fascinated by the soda machine. Unlike the modern ones, it wasn't immediately obvious how it worked, and it had glass bottles instead of cans with a bottle opener on the front. A milk crate still sat to the left of the machine with empty bottles in it for those who wanted to leave them.

"Look, Aunt Val!" Alex pointed at the antique machine.

"I haven't seen one like that in ages," she responded. Not since the day they had left Star Junction.

Val and Alex entered the market where the inside was brightly lit, clean, and well-organized. Val felt an immediate sense of relief. The owner, a tall man with graying black hair and kind eyes watched patiently and nodded to Val when she made eye contact. Alex fingered all the brochures and local maps on the rack before turning his attention to the shelf of animal totems carved by a local artist.

"Wow, Aunt Val, look at these!"

"Yeah, I see, nice," Val responded encouragingly but without attention. She was more focused on getting water and figuring out how to match the new landmarks with her old memories.

The owner spoke for her, "Those are very special." Just as Val started to tell Alex to be careful, the man continued, his voice full of kindness and mystery, "Which one speaks to you?"

Alex's eyes lit up. He, too, was expecting to be told not to touch or to be careful. With permission granted, his focus grew. He slowly examined each totem; the bear standing upright, teeth bared, the rabbit with ears perked, the owl with eyes wide open, the flying hawk, the wolf. Ahh, the wolf.

As Alex was examining each totem, Val approached the counter and asked which map would be better. The old man's eyes shined so brightly she had to look away.

"Welcome home," he said in that same, kind voice.

She looked back into his eyes, searching, "Do I know..."

"The wolf! The wolf speaks to me!" Alex exclaimed.

Both Val and the man looked at him.

"That is a good choice for you. Very good." The man returned his gaze to Val to save her question. "You look like someone who has been gone from home for a very long time." He smiled and pulled out and opened a map for her.

Alex ran up to the counter asking, "What about the eye. Can we get to the eye?"

"The Eye?" The man looked at Alex when the boy spoke.

"Yeah, when we came here, a huge eye in the hillside was watching us. It was awesome!"

"He is talking about a formation about three miles down the road from here—through the pass."

"Ahh, so you both saw the Eye?" the man replied with great interest.

They both nodded, Alex with excitement. The old man looked over Alex's shoulder to greet his daughter who had just arrived. Alex and Val turned to see who he was looking at and saw a beautiful woman with long brown hair carrying food containers.

She smiled and continued to join her father behind the counter where he kissed her on the cheek. "Thank you, Lucy, it smells delicious." The man turned back to face Val. "You truly are returning home, and the mountain knows."

Alex's eyes were huge as he tried to understand what was happening. Val felt her heart pound in her chest and a lump form in her throat. The man showed her Star Junction on the map. They had just entered it.

He spoke with intention as he tried to help Val remember. "When your party is complete, you will join us again." He put his left hand on Lucy's shoulder and playfully presented Val with his right, "My daughter, Lucy, me, and Grandmother Flor.

A flash of recognition came to Val. A remembrance from so many years ago. "Grandmother Flor?" Her mind raced to catch up to what her heart already knew. "Oh... Mr. Edward!" she said with a mix of surprise and relief.

"Yes, and you are William's and Grace's daughter, Valerie."

"Yes. Val."

"We are glad to have you home again. Is this your son?"

"No, Cade's son, Alex."

"Alex, we are very glad to meet you. I have a gift for you."

"Really?"

Edward came out from behind the counter and placed a stone into Alex's hand—a shiny, black and green malachite, carved into a wolf. Alex couldn't help it. He wrapped his arms around Edward "Thank you! It's amazing!"

Edward returned his gaze to Val. "Val, do you remember Lucy?" He gestured to his daughter who smiled warmly.

"Hi, Val, welcome home." Lucy said.

"Wow! Of course! Forgive me. I didn't know if anyone would still be here after so many years." Val struggled to find words. With all the memories coming back to her, she hadn't thought to consider whether the beloved fixtures she had called family as a child would still be there or remember her thirty years later.

Edward laughed and said with a wink, "Where else would we be?" He always had a way of lightening her mood. Suddenly, Val had so many questions to ask.

"Mr. Edward, did you know that Sissy moved back here?"

"Yes. We were saddened by her passing."

"And that her son Jake is in foster care?" She didn't give him time to answer. "I didn't know. Not until yesterday." She looked at them and Alex.

"Valerie, you have returned home for a purpose, perhaps beyond what is known in this moment. We have looked forward to your return and trusted it would be in perfect timing. It will be for young Jake and the whole family. Trust that all is well." Edward's tone had shifted from playful to serious. He highlighted the map to show her the motel and the location of children's services in Exton for the morning.

"I hope you are right, Mr. Edward. Thank you."

"What about the eye?" Alex was still anxious for an answer.

"Ahh, there will be plenty of time for that, young Alex. In the right time, I will tell you about the Eye you saw and many other mysteries if you'd like."

Alex's eyes widened in excitement. "I'd like that a lot!"

Lucy stepped forward to add, "You are probably tired and hungry. My restaurant is on the way to your motel. You can order takeout, if you'd like." She pointed it out on the map.

"Thank you, Lucy. I appreciate it."

"I promise it's good!" Lucy said with a smile.

When Val first walked into the gas station mini-mart, she hadn't recognized Mr. Edward—her Mr. Edward, her father's dear friend—not until his words led her to his memory. He was a bit of a magician that way. Her father William had been the same. She was stunned to realize that the woman was Lucy—the little girl she had once known, and that Grandmother Flor was still alive.

When Val left Star Junction Lucy was eleven or twelve—still a little girl to a sixteen-year-old Val who'd been forced to grow up so quickly. Val had been gone for so many years, living in a big city. She had lost touch with this way of being. Of listening deeply. Speaking mindfully. Instead, she had learned to plow through life and get things done. She had been very successful at it.

She'd started with art that transitioned into a business that grew, and sold, and grew more. Two successful businesses. A few failed relationships. She had become adept at detachment. Of just getting it done, being decisive, and not listening to the other whispers—the ones her father had taught her how to hear. She had forgotten all about those until the dreams started up again after so long.

They were subtle at first, and she didn't pay much attention, writing them off as stress or weird or nothing. Until they got stronger. More vivid. Then a hawk nested in a tree in her fancy, underused backyard. Hummingbirds began to feed on the hanging flowers the gardener had planted. Suddenly she would catch herself singing her dad's songs in her mind and smiling at a whispering wind. Perhaps not as suddenly, but more surprisingly to her, she began to truly feel the emptiness of her home and her life. She hadn't been enjoying work in "forever." It was just what she did.

One day, after one of those whispers—a hummingbird buzzing by her ear—she had the inkling to paint. She hadn't done it since the beginning of her first business twenty-plus years before. She bought a canvas and new paints, got out her brushes, set up the easel—and stared at it.

She checked email, looked through files, dealt with employee questions and client questions. It didn't matter that it was Sunday. The canvas sat quietly, waiting. Beckoning. She finally dipped a brush into some orange paint and drew a giant question mark in the middle of the canvas. This made her laugh and just surrender to having fun with it.

She painted words, symbols, and random shapes, putting her hands on it to feel the paint on the canvas. Blue, yellow, orange, purple, green, and black paint oozed from her fingers. She thought it would just be an abstract mess for the trash until she saw something in the chaos—a bit like the edge of a cliff, a little jagged and uneven, but steep. She played with it. And then a shadow from the lamp. Then she wondered what it would look like if she just added a little blue over to the right. By the time she was done, she discovered that by losing herself in the process, she had found her joy in it.

Without being planned, the finished painting was of a house—a home, really, with kids and trees and life and a mountain in the background. The mountain reminded her of Star Junction. That night, the dreams became clearer, and she could make out some of the people. Her father, mother, elders she hadn't seen in decades, and the kids she didn't know.

For the first time in longer than she could remember, her heart asked, *Papa, what is the meaning of the dream? Why does it keep repeating?* The answer that came was that she was being called. She just didn't know for what until the morning Cade called.

Star Junction was meant to be a place of connection, wisdom, and community. The name came from ancient myths of being guided by the stars. It was said that all over the world were junctions, places where the stars meet and open portals for communication, connection, magic, and teleportation. It was said that this was how people first came to this planet. By the junction of seven stars.

As they drove through the small town, it felt a bit like a ghost town. Val noticed empty buildings and few people. The surrounding towns had become industrial wastelands. People had moved to them because it was "easier" to be closer to work and others. Val knew that Star Junction had once been a community of friends, and she hoped it still was.

She was relieved the drive was done and that she and Alex could relax that night. Seeing Edward and Lucy had lifted the weight of not knowing whether she would be returning to the place and people she had treasured or whether it would be different now, and the people departed.

The motel room was small and dimly lit. When she was a child, the motel was used mostly by the mill workers and others passing through for temporary work. Things had been busier then. Alex sat in the corner huddled over his sketchpad under the lamp. He worked fervently, never taking his focus away from his drawing. Val smiled as she watched him instead of replying to emails. Her intention was to catch up on work, but she found watching him much more appealing.

"What are you working on over there?"

Alex didn't look up. "The Eye." He closed his eyes briefly, looking inside his mind for details as he saw them, and opened them back to the page and the motion of his pencil recreating what he saw. Val's email chimed.

Boss, it's only been a day. The ship is fine. Despite their tone, nothing is truly urgent in those emails. (I know you will go through them all tonight anyway, but you can't say I didn't warn you.) Take care of you and the kid and get rest. You know, it's that thing that other people do! ;-) Humbly, Elliot.

Val knew he was right, but the distraction was too alluring. Keeping her mind focused on work had made her very successful. Right now, all she needed it to do was keep her busy until she could sleep.

THREE

Val woke to the daylight peeking through the curtains and muffled sounds of life outside as people walked past, talking in the distance. A subtle relief washed over her with the discovery that there were still people in Star Junction. Last night must have been unusual. Val was less relieved to realize that she had slept until 7:00 a.m. despite an alarm she thought she set for six. She quickly looked over to Alex's bed to discover him sitting at the table instead, drawing.

"Good morning, Alex. Have you been up long?"

"Hi, Aunt Val. I don't know. Awhile, I guess."

"Did you sleep okay?"

"Yeah! I had lots of dreams. I'm just trying to draw some of it now. Can we get breakfast?"

"Yes, absolutely. Give me fifteen minutes."

Val took a very quick shower and tried to remember the last time she had slept through the night. The water felt especially good as it washed away the long drive and the thought loops from the day before. *Thank you, water. Mother Earth. Thank you for this cleansing and restoration.*

They were in the car and on their way to Exton by 8:30 a.m. It was later than Val had planned, but she was learning that time felt a little different with kids. They would still make it to the 10:00 a.m. appointment with a few minutes to spare.

"Aunt Val, what's going to happen?"

"What do you mean?"

"I guess I mean, what is he like? Is Jake going to like me?" Val put her hand on his shoulder in reassurance.

"Well, I like you."

Alex still looked uncertain.

"The truth is, I haven't seen him since you were a toddler. I only know that we are all meant to come together now. You've both had a tough time the last year or two. It may be a little slow for you to get to know each other. So be patient, okay?" He searched her face for any signs of doubt. She smiled and repeated, "Okay?"

He nodded. "Okay."

The lobby walls were dingy, the dim fluorescent lights flickering and dreary. Alex stayed uncharacteristically close to Aunt Val. Ms. Ramirez was polite without warmth. Her suit, professional and a little too tight, was well-used.

The walk to her office was quiet as Val somehow knew not to speak yet. Once seated, Ms. Ramirez looked closely at Val as if doing some complex equations to solve great mysteries. Val felt the inquiry deeply and took a deep, patient breath. Alex squirmed.

"Are you sure? Really sure?" Ms. Ramirez held her cases close to her heart and held a skepticism about long-lost relatives.

"Yes, I am sure. I would have been here a year ago if I had known. In fact, I am not clear as to why we weren't notified. Jake has family. We are his family."

Ms. Ramirez pushed the file she'd been holding toward Val with care. "Your attorney sent the paperwork yesterday with proof of relationship. I still need to verify your ID and you need to sign the forms on top."

Val took the file with a polite smile and handed Ms. Ramirez her ID. The overworked social worker began to soften. "Then we can go get him. There will still be formalities and a court date."

"Thank you, Ms. Ramirez. I am grateful for your help." Val made intentional eye contact when she said it, allowing her sincerity and gratitude to show through to give Ms. Ramirez hope and a reminder of why she became a social worker—deep-rooted desire to help born from her own rocky beginnings. Hope. She now had hope for Jake and would let that feed the hope she held for all of the kids.

"Please meet me at the address on the file at noon. I will have him ready for you." Ms. Ramirez smiled at Val and Alex for the first time.

In the car Alex looked at the picture of Jake attached to the file, "Aunt Val?"

"What's up?"

"I've seen him before."

"Really? Where?"

"In my dreams. Just like I saw you. I just didn't know who you were. I didn't know who he was." His voice was quiet and unsure.

Val smiled to reassure him. "You're having those dreams, too, huh?"

He nodded. "The dreams are good. They can tell us stories and maybe give us messages. Do they frighten you?"

"Um, sometimes. I don't know what they mean. Kinda confusing. Sometimes they scare me." Alex shifted in his seat and tightened his grip on his sketchbook. His gaze moved from the windshield down to what he held but really to nothing at all. Val stayed in his silence with him for a moment, her face soft with kindness and under-standing.

"You know, I used to have a lot of dreams like that when I was younger. I learned how to look at them so they weren't as scary. My dad helped. Maybe I can be there for you in the same way. If you have dreams or something you aren't sure of, you can talk to me. I will do my best to listen. I may not be perfect. Right? But I will do my best. And, if I am not listening or not hearing you, tell me."

"How do I tell you if you are not listening?"

Val laughed. "Hmm, good point!" She smiled and kept it light. "I don't know. Let's see, maybe you could call a timeout. Do you know how to do that?"

He made a T with his hands to practice. "Yep, that's it. But please only use the timeout when it is important. Okay?"

"Okay, deal."

"So you ready to meet your cousin?"

"Yeah. Maybe he will want to find the Eye with me!"

Val smiled again to reassure him and herself. She took a breath in and shook her head while making an exaggerated face with eyes wide open and a closed-mouth smile. She was being playful to shake off her own nerves and release the tension she felt.

Alex watched with his eyebrows raised in wonder.

"You try," she encouraged. He repeated her motions and funny faces, and they laughed together. Val realized it was a strategy her father often used with her. He taught her to shift her energy and mood with playfulness and laughter. *Thank you, Papa.*

When they pulled up to Harmony House, Ms. Ramirez was standing at the door of the haggard two-story home. Jake sat on the porch steps, his shoulders strong and squared, armored with silent rage and mistrust. His head was angled slightly to the side with his headphones on. Val noted the broken sign declaring Harmony, and the faded, peeling paint, cracked window, broken porch railings, and dead plants. Guilt surged through Val as she approached, Alex just behind her.

"Jake?" Jake looked up for just a moment and then looked away. Ms. Ramirez started to move closer and speak, but Val waved her off and walked closer to Jake. When she was directly in front of him, he looked up again, noticed Alex peeking around her, and locked eyes with Val.

"What took you so long?" His look pierced through her well-meaning-ness.

She slowed her breath and looked past the shield of anger. She saw the heart of the boy inside him, shattered by broken promises and adults who failed to help him feel safe. Jake's heart had no reason to trust but so desperately wanted to know faith again, all encased in the bravado of rage, fierceness, and the defiant challenge of "get close if you dare."

"I didn't know, about your mom, about you being here. Jake. I'm so sorry." Val spoke softly, her eyes meeting Jake's. "But I'm here now."

Jake held her gaze and sized her up, not knowing what to think for long enough that Ms. Ramirez considered encouraging him along. When he was ready, Jake let out a breath and stood up, grabbing his hefty bag and backpack all at once.

"Are we going?" he spoke as he headed toward the car. Harmony House was ironically named, and Jake had been praying for a way out since arriving. He had been praying that one of his aunts or his uncle or someone, maybe even his father, would come for him. He had no idea that none of them knew to come.

"Yes." Val and Alex headed for the car with him. "Jake, this is your cousin Alex—Cade's son."

She let the boys head back to the car before turning back to Ms. Ramirez and mouthing, "Thank you."

The boys agreed they were hungry and Val decided lunch would help to break the tension and hopefully open up communication. Lucy's restaurant was quiet except for the remaining dishes from the lunch rush being bussed and banged. There hadn't been a lot of talk so far, despite a few attempts by Val and Alex. Finally, his food half eaten, Alex asked the winning question.

"How long did you live there?"

"I don't know—seven months? I was with a foster family before that. I guess this was better," Jake responded without interest.

"Were you scared?" Alex asked with the innocence of being ten.

Jake listened with jaded ears and shot Alex a hard look.

"Scared?"

"Yeah, I'd be scared. I think." Alex was so open that Jake softened a little despite rolling his eyes.

"Sure, maybe at first." He shrugged and adjusted in his seat. "But you get used to things, I guess."

Val watched and took it all in. Alex wanted so badly to connect. Jake was guarded and strong, but he had this touch of soft-heartedness. She wanted to thank him for the bit of kindness he just showed Alex and to ask him so many things about what happened with his mom and how they got here. She was just finding what to say when Jake spoke again.

"So when are we getting Lilah?"

Both Val and Alex must have had the same look on their faces— some combination of shock and putting a name to the girl in the dreams. Jake looked at them, waiting for an answer.

"My sister. Half-sister. They took her and put her with a family somewhere else. Not sure where. We have to get her too. I won't go anywhere without her."

"Oh my god—when—how old is she?" Val tried to put together pieces of the story. How could she not know? When did Sissy have another child?

"She's five."

Val was processing her shock. "Why didn't Ms. Ramirez tell me?"

Jake just shrugged. How would he know why an adult wasn't honest and forthcoming?

"But she knows. Right?"

"Yeah, of course she knows." He stopped eating and met her eyes with his. His answer was matter of fact and openly indignant. He no longer expected better from most adults. He wasn't sure about Val yet, so he searched her eyes for some evidence that she could be trusted. And Alex—was he that naïve?

Val found her reserves. That voice that had been leading all of this. That voice that knew the dreams were a call to action and how to do it. It was the voice that spoke now.

"Okay, we'll find her." Her eyes stayed with Jake's. He didn't look convinced of her intentions and so she addressed his reservations. "Jake, I can't pretend to know what you've gone through. I don't know how or why I didn't know what was happening. I spoke to Sissy." Val called the memory back to her, trying to figure out when they spoke, and the realization hit. "It must have been just before she died."

Tears clung to the corners of her eyes and her breath stuttered as she continued, trying to summon her CEO-self to take over. "She didn't tell me about Lilah. She didn't tell me she was sick. I didn't know until two days ago that she was gone. The only promise I can make you is that I will do my best with all of this and all of you, and to find your sister—and any other pieces that are missing. For you, for Alex and Lilah and Sissy. I will do my best for all of us."

Jake worked to fight the tears that began to well up in his steel eyes as he swallowed and looked away. "Yeah, okay."

"I believe her, Jake," Alex said quietly.

"I said okay." He rolled his eyes and adjusted in his seat, fighting to find words instead of the emotion looking for a way out. "So what are we going to do?"

Val thought for a moment before answering. "I don't know, yet." She watched Lucy enter and speak to one of her staff. "I do know it will include a call to Ms. Ramirez and one to my attorneys. But it is too late to go back to Exton today. I think we should start with the people who know this area best. They may be able to guide us."

When they walked through the door of the mini-mart, Edward was busy with other customers. He smiled a greeting to them and directed Val to the office. For Val, the office was a time capsule, the walls covered with photos spanning decades. Many contained

William, Grace, and Val as a child. A couple even had Cade as a baby. She hadn't been aware of so many photographs existing of that time. One, in particular, called her attention. It included William, Grace holding baby Cade, Val, Edward, and Grandmother Flor. They stood before the fire of the Fire Festival with musicians in the background. William looked so alive and vibrant in that picture; it reminded her of how much he loved life and her. She wondered if he knew then that he was already sick. Alex saved her from diving further into that wondering.

"Who is that, Aunt Val?" Alex was ever curious. She pointed to William.

"This is your Grandfather William. Your Grandma Grace is next to him, holding your dad. That's me. And that is Mr. Edward and Grandmother Flor."

"Is Mr. Edward your uncle?"

Edward walked in. "We are all family. It does not matter the blood, only the heart." Alex liked the idea that they were family, even though they just met. It felt exciting—like he was a part of something much bigger. Like he used to feel at home until everything changed. Edward put his hand on Alex's head as if he understood his thoughts. "We are all connected, young wolf—always."

Jake let out a scoff of internal doubt. "If we are so connected, why didn't anyone come for me?"

Edward gazed upon him with kind eyes. "You've returned with young Jacob. This is good." Only Edward called him Jacob, like his Grandma Grace had when he was little. But Jake barely remembered her and only knew Edward for a short time. They felt more like people he had heard about or seen in a movie than ones he had known. "Welcome home, Jacob."

"This isn't my home."

"Isn't it?" Edward's voice remained kind.

Alex fingered the photo Val described for him, looking as closely as he could to William's image. He searched the other photographs as well.

"So that's my grandpa?"

"Yes, you look a lot alike. Don't you think?" Edward replied.

"Mr. Edward," Val interjected. "We could use your help. Jake just told us that he has a sister that children's services neglected to inform me about."

Edward sat down next to her. "Yes, young Lilah. I'm sorry. You did not know?" he asked with some surprise in his voice.

Val shook her head with exasperation.

"I am sorry. I did not realize you didn't know. I am sad they didn't tell you." He looked at each of them with compassion. "Please, do not worry," he said looking at Jake. "It is late in the day, and now the weekend. Monday you will go to children's services again, but tonight it is important that you all laugh together. Worry will not help, but being together will. There will be music tonight at the Star Pavilion. You remember, yes? The Gathering Place."

"Don't worry?" Jake seethed. "How can you say not to worry when you knew she was taken somewhere else?"

"Young Jacob, I say do not worry because worry will help nothing. It only feeds that which you wish to change." He stood up and began toward the office door. "See Lilah with you as you sing and laugh. Trust my message. It is the energy we are healing. You must fix the bridge."

Jake rolled his eyes and shook his head. *I didn't break the bridge,* he thought.

Though Val didn't feel much like being around a large gathering, she heeded Edward's words and took the boys to the town center. The Star Pavilion doubled as a beautiful park in the center of town. It was the gathering place of generations, where the community came together every week to remember themselves and celebrate life. Memories of music and dancing around the fire filled Val's attention.

Jake was secretly glad they came, despite the outward resistance and anger brewing. He had loved coming here with his mom and sister before Sissy died. They always left feeling like life would all be just fine—as if the world couldn't reach them. The music would play in his mind for days.

To Val's perception, he came reluctantly, keeping his headphones on and talking as little as possible. Alex, on the other hand, was full of curiosity and questions. He asked them so fast she didn't always have time to respond.

"Aunt Val, what is the pavilion?"

"Aunt Val, do they do this every week?"

"Why?"

"Did you and Dad come here as kids?"

"Did he like it?"

"Do you think I look like Grandpa?" That one pulled her back. She looked at him and smiled.

"You know, I think you do. And yes, we came to the dances when we were kids. I got to come to more of them than your dad since he was so much younger. I am not sure he would remember," Val said.

"Why do they do this?" Alex continued.

"Well, partly because it is a tradition. But my feeling is that they discovered that it is a really good way to help people remember."

"Remember what?" Jake masked his interest with an indignant tone. Val acknowledged him with a look and continued.

"Remember that they are all neighbors, that no matter how hard your week might have been, you can let it all go and dance instead of letting it weigh you down. Remember how it feels."

"Very wise, Picaflor," Edward said. He and Lucy had found them in the crowd. "The music and the dance help us to remember the truest essence of our being." Edward paused, looking directly at the boys. "Sounds so mysterious. Doesn't it?" He laughed with joy.

Lucy smiled at Val and gave her a hug. "This must bring back many memories."

Val couldn't even begin to count them. The pavilion was lit with multicolored lights in mesmerizing patterns, a new touch since Val had last attended. A fire was going, but this was not the big Fire Dance Festival. That would come closer to fall before school began again when people were ready for cooling temps and reaping harvests.

"Is Grandmother Flor here? I was hoping to see her." Val was surprised not to see her at the fire.

"Mother is with the mountain tonight, but I am sure you will see her soon," Edward answered.

Val looked toward the mountain top, taking in his meaning, but the crackle of the fire called for her attention.

"Aunt Val, did you and my dad like coming here to the fire when you were kids?"

Val smiled but kept her eyes on the fire and the memory it was showing her. "Yes, Alex...I loved coming here when I was a kid."

Thirty-Nine Years Ago—Star Junction

Seven-year-old Val danced in the circle around the roaring fire, lost in the beating drums and the voices singing. She danced until she heard her father's voice whispering through the drums. She stopped and found her way out of the crowd, beyond the pavilion, following the whispers riding on the wind. There he was on the porch, waiting for her patiently as he whittled.

He started singing, *"Dear Picaflor, this is my prayer. Listen now, to the drum. Dance with the fire of life, drink in the joy, and plant it like the stars in the sky. Joy is the nectar, playfulness delight, elixir from the wisdom of all time. My little hummingbird flies with speed and light, no limitations, no need of might. Dear Picaflor, dance with the world. Spread your joy and love, fly with Spirit, and delight the stars above. My dear Picaflor, please find your way home tonight."*

Before looking up he was aware of her presence. "Thank you for coming, Valerie. You listened well." He looked up at her beaming with joy.

She beamed back, feeling so much joy when her father was happy. It felt like they shared the same emotions.

"Papa, did you see me dancing?" She climbed up on his lap and he welcomed her with the love of the universe.

"Even better. I felt you dancing. You danced with your whole heart, and that is a gift of joy for all." She rested her head on his shoulder like the moment would never end until she remembered that her father had called her.

"Papa, why did you call me to you?" She lifted her head, and he gestured for her to sit on the seat facing him.

"I was testing to see if you were ready. To see if you could hear me with your heart. My heart called to you, not my voice."

"Is that why it was a whisper? And I could hear it through the drums?"

"Yes, young Picaflor. You listened well."

"I like that my heart can hear you. It will always listen for you, Papa."

"I am glad, Valerie. Your heart knows how to listen to many things, but your mind can get distracted. You must remember when you get distracted by things, when you feel confused or unsure, make sure you are using your heart to listen instead of your ears." He gently tapped her head, heart, and ears as he spoke of them.

"Okay, Papa." She looked away and shifted in her seat, her feet beginning a steady wiggle as if tapping out the letters of an unknown language. "But I feel weird. Is something wrong? Did I do something wrong?"

"No, sweet child. You have not done wrong. But it is important for me to teach you now that you are ready. Teach you better how to live with your whole heart. Many people forget how to do that. They go through their whole lives never knowing how to listen with their hearts. Now you know what listening with your heart feels like."

She tried to absorb everything he was saying. She couldn't help having an uneasy feeling.

William continued, "You have many gifts, Picaflor. Gifts from the stars. If you remember that, you will have a better life. Your gifts are of listening, of vision, and of strength. You are a part of the earth and the sky. Hummingbird plays in your heart, and hawk guides your sight. When you use all of your gifts, when you keep them all in balance, you thrive."

Her eyes were huge by this point, trying to imagine this wonderful world of animals and elements. She was so happy her papa wanted to share it with her. This was when the lessons began —always loving and occasionally sterner than she was used to.

CHAPTER

FOUR

Val was catching up on emails as the dawn began to break through the curtain edges. She worked quietly, and the boys slept. *This could be the closest thing I have to alone time for awhile...* she thought and smiled.

Alex began to stir, while Jake still appeared in deep sleep. What was she going to do with two young boys all weekend? How long would it take to find Lilah? And then what? She closed her work email. Nobody would be checking until Monday anyway. Except, perhaps, Elliot. Even the attorneys would be on hold for the weekend.

Val perused the map that Edward had highlighted for her and let her mind wander. She didn't think she had ever seen a map of—or an aerial view of—Star Junction. The shapes, patterns, had an intentional feel. She reached for a pencil to trace what she saw.

"*No!*" Jake bolted upright in bed. His heart raced as he looked around the room and caught his breath.

"You, okay?" Val asked with concern. Jake realized where he was and composed himself.

"Uh, yeah. Fine." He let his eyes meet Val's and Alex's and then gripped his short, curly hair with both hands as if to pull himself back from the dream. "Can I take a shower?"

"Of course. Alex, why don't you take one when Jake is done." She looked at him to confirm he heard her. Alex nodded his response. "When we are all ready, we will head over to Lucy's restaurant. She and Mr. Edward have invited us for breakfast."

When they arrived at Lucy's, they found Edward waiting at a large table tucked away in a back corner. It was slightly removed from the rest of the dining area and obscured from view by an attractive partition. His smile brightened when he saw them approach.

"Good morning, a beautiful sight you are."

They all responded in unison, "Good morning, Mr. Edward!"

Val continued, "How are you this morning?"

"How could I be anything but wonderful?" Val smiled in response. "Please, sit," he said as he pointed to the waiting chairs. On cue, Lucy appeared from the kitchen. Rather than interrupt, she smiled her greeting and sat next to her father. Beaming, Edward lifted a large tote bag off the floor and placed it in front of Val.

"What is this?" She was surprised.

"Grandmother Flor and I thought this could help you to remember, and all of you to learn about our home and each other."

"I don't understand." Val was hesitant to accept anything she thought might be a gift.

"What is it, Aunt Val?" Alex asked as Jake stayed quiet and watched.

"It is yours, Valerie. Your family's. Before you all moved away, when Sissy and Melanie had barely begun to toddle, Grace had a vision and foresight. More and more of her life before Emmet was being removed from the house. She thought if she gave some of the photos and memories to us to protect, that she would be able to share them with her children someday."

"Pictures? Wow, that's why we didn't have any pictures, because of Emmet."

"It is a time capsule for you. A portal for initiation," he whispered to her as the boys tried to hear. "Miss Valerie, do you remember when you started calling me 'Mister'?" Val got lost in his eyes for a moment; his question circled in her thoughts.

"Can we see the pictures, Aunt Val?" Alex had a way of calling her back from her thoughts.

"It is a wonderful way for you and the boys to get to know each other and this magical place...and for you to begin to remember."

"Okay, here we go." Val looked in the bag and pulled out one of the two albums. She also noted a large shoe box but could only take in one bombshell at a time. This album looked preserved. She searched the cobwebs of memory to find what might be in it, and prepared herself before opening the cover.

This is ridiculous, Val...pull it together. Let it be fun, she told herself.

Edward broke her tension with, "Don't worry. It won't bite." He laughed jovially as he looked at the boys. Lucy nudged Val with a reassuring nod, and Val let out a breath, cracking a smile as the album crackled when she opened the cover.

"Wow, they look so young..." Val swallowed and took in a slow breath as she saw her mother and father, Grace and William looking back at her, happy.

"Yes. We were still in school there. I think William was seventeen, Grace sixteen. If I remember correctly," Edward offered.

Alex came around to look over Val's shoulder not wanting to miss anything. Jake remained in his seat, watching but not engaging. Val noticed and decided to skip ahead to find more recent pictures. At least more recent than fifty years ago.

"Let's see what's in the box!" She opened the lid and saw herself, Cade, and Sissy with baby Melanie. "Jackpot" she thought aloud. "Jake, this one has your mom. All of us. Sissy was probably about one then."

She reached to hand the picture across the table to Jake who received it carefully, self-conscious that people were watching. Val started with the next photograph and diverted attention from Jake.

Lucy noted the sound of a chime from the kitchen and excused herself. "Alex, can you help me?" Alex followed her to the kitchen. When they returned, Alex was carrying a large fruit plate filled with cantaloupe, watermelon, pineapple, and loads of fresh berries. Lucy brought a frittata in one hand and fresh baked spice muffins in the other. "You will have lots of time to look through this treasure. But first, let's enjoy breakfast."

"Oh, my goodness, Lucy. This all looks and smells amazing! Thank you." The boys nodded with Val's statement.

"Mr. Edward, how long did you know our grandfather and grandmother?" Before Edward could answer Alex's question, Jake interjected.

"He wasn't *my* grandfather."

"I'm sorry. I forgot... but we have the same grandmother. Right?"

Jake shrugged agreement. He didn't know why he felt different from them, but he knew he didn't like it.

Edward answered, "William came to us when he was, hmmm, about ten. I think. His mother and father and he moved here from the East Coast, where his grandmother had moved as a teenager."

"Wait, what?" Val was hearing new information. "Do you mean that his grandmother was from Star Junction?"

"Yes, his grandmother, Maren, was a child of Star Junction. She dreamed of returning one day but was not able. She was a friend of mother's, Grandmother Flor that is. Though older. Maren's daughter Sofia grew up hearing stories and felt it was a better place for William."

"I had no idea..."

"No, you were quite young when your father left this plane. He did not have time to share all of the stories with you." Edward paused, letting the words settle. "But Grace, your grandmother," he said as he looked at the boys, "she moved here when she was fourteen. Her father traveled often for work. When he came to Star Junction in those travels, he decided to move his family here, her mother already deceased. Of course, we are inclined to believe that Star Junction called to them. It was a good place for Grace, her brother Ray and the family to be. They were protected here and guided."

"Oh, I think I remember Uncle Ray...was he at Grandma's funeral?" Jake asked looking at Val.

"Yes, Jake. You remember that?"

"Yeah, kind of. He made me laugh a lot. I liked him."

"Yep, that's Ray. He always makes me laugh, too," Val agreed.

"Is Uncle Ray still alive?"

"Yep! He lives in California with his wife, Beth.

"Indeed, Ray was born with the special gift of levity," Edward mused. "Grace and Ray became a welcome addition to our extended family. William, of course, won Grace's heart." With those words he stood up to excuse himself. "You have many treasures to uncover here, and I have a gas station to open. Take your time and savor the journey."

He patted Alex's head affectionately before turning to Val. "Don't forget to reintroduce yourself to our beautiful community, and the mountains, and trees. We are not the only ones who have missed you."

Val stood up to hug Edward. "Thank you for the time capsule." He was about to respond but she anticipated and added, "And for taking such good care of it."

Edward smiled at her and patted her shoulder affectionately.

"It was our pleasure." With that, Edward winked and exited.

Val looked at the pile of pictures, clippings, and other papers and knew she needed a better plan of action.

"You know what, boys? It is a beautiful day outside and Mr. Edward had a great idea about seeing it. Let's spend a few more minutes sifting through the photos. Find a few that jump out for you, ones that you want to know more about. Then we'll wrap up the rest and go for a walk to explore the town. I'll do my best to tell you everything you want to know. When we are ready, we'll look at the next batch."

"Cool!" Alex had enough enthusiasm for both of the boys.

The weather was kind and the morning temperatures mild for the summer day. A refreshing breeze played along with the sun, and the trio's walk through Star Junction memories and legends was pleasant. Val decided that the pavilion was a good place to start.

"Okay, who wants to go first?" She knew Alex was chomping at the bit, but she wanted Jake's engagement. "Jake? What did you find?"

"Let Alex start. I'm not sure what I want to ask yet." Jake gripped the photos in both hands.

"Okay, Alex. What did you find?"

"I think it is you and Grandpa, but it has a sketch with it and says 'Picaflor's successful climb.'" He held out a page filled with sketches showing a mountain, trails, and a large circle with directions and a spiral. The photo attached showed eight-year-old Valerie and her pleased papa William.

"Wow…" was all she could muster as she took the page in her hands and searched the drawings.

"What is it from? What climb?" Alex persisted.

"Clarity Mountain."

"What's Clarity Mountain?" both boys asked in unison. Val turned toward the mountains to the north of town center and pointed to the tallest peak overlooking the town.

"That's Clarity Mountain."

"So what's the big deal about climbing it?" Jake pushed.

"Well, it isn't a typical mountain, exactly. Reaching the top requires focus and openness. This one may take a little more time here in Star Junction to answer."

"Did Grandpa draw this? What's the circle?"

"Yes, your grandpa drew it. That's the Circle of Perspective. Climbing the mountain and using the circle are both ways of approaching a problem and releasing the obstacles to find resolutions you might not have come to by just thinking."

Jake scoffed and rolled his eyes. "Seems weird."

"So you climbed it? By yourself, Aunt Val?" Alex's curiosity was both sincere and endless.

"Yes and no. This photo was from the first time I climbed it, with your grandpa. It was my eighth birthday present. I did climb it a few times on my own after your grandpa died."

"Is the Eye on Clarity Mountain?"

"That is harder to say. The Eye...well, the path to the Eye is a different one. Wow, I haven't thought about all this in ages."

"Did Dad ever climb it?"

"Yes—just before we moved away to Phoenix, Cade climbed with me."

"What about my mom? Did she ever climb?"

"No, Jake, I don't think so. She was very young when we left here. I wasn't allowed to take Sissy or Melanie hiking. Emmet didn't care much for nature."

Thirty-Eight Years Ago, Star Junction

Little Valerie was an excellent hiker. William taught her how to let the land help her to walk and climb, taught her how to conserve and restore her own energy as she hiked—not that she had any shortage of energy—and how to pay attention to the messages meant to guide her.

"There are helpers for those who know to listen with an open heart. The plants will move or whisper like the wind. Birds may call from above and show you the way." William's words were filled with magic for little Valerie. She listened and watched carefully, not to miss a thing. Little Valerie loved hiking with her father so much that he gifted her a special hike on her eighth birthday.

"Picaflor, my little hummingbird, eight is a great number; let's celebrate with a special hike. You are ready. Today I will introduce you to Clarity Mountain."

Grace sometimes joined on the hikes, but this one was different. Grace stayed home with baby Cade and prepared Valerie's favorite dinner including a birthday cake. Grace made the best cakes filled with love and deliciousness.

"Always pay attention, Picaflor. It is important to remember to walk with an open heart and gratitude. And to play. Talk to the plants and the sky. Talk to the animals and rocks like they are your friends. And thank them when they help you." He had been teaching her since she was able to walk. He had only added more words now, to plant seeds of memory. Every word was a prayer from him that she would remember this magic. Valerie walked with bright eyes and light feet, listening to his words and his whistling song.

"If you are ever frightened, ask for protection and help. Say thank you. They will take care of you."

It felt like he was talking about a different world. She tried hard to listen and looked around at everything. Just when she started to think it was all too unreal, she heard his voice in her heart. "Picaflor, listen with your heart and speak with your heart. There you will understand the magic."

They had hiked many trails together, often repeating favorites to visit the plants, boulders, and animals they knew as friends. This was the first time they climbed Clarity Mountain. It probably had another name, but the locals knew its purpose. Making it to the top required openness. If you were not paying attention to the signs, you would hike in circles. If you were focused only on conquering it, you would not.

One could only reach the top with an open heart and pure intentions. If you were conflicted about something, climbing to the top would help bring clarity. When Valerie was older, she heard Grandmother Flor explain that many people used structures, labyrinths, medicine wheels, and other forms as tools for prayer and meditation. Walking through a problem, allowing different points of view and perspective, clearing one's path by clearing the mind of obstacles to come to understanding. William took Valerie for her eighth birthday because he wasn't certain how many more birthdays he would be there for. He was determined to create this gift for her before he was gone, hoping it would serve her well.

While climbing with her, reminding her gently of her lessons, he quietly let her lead. It had to be her climb. At one point, Valerie realized he wasn't leading. She looked back at him repeatedly.

"Papa, why are you back there? You need to show me where to go."

He did not answer out loud. Instead, she heard in her heart, "Your heart knows the way. I have already shown you." She looked at him again and took a deep breath. He smiled at her.

"Don't forget to have fun, Picaflor. You are the bringer of joy!" he said playfully.

"Oh, Papa." She paused to take in all her options. She looked all around and smiled. She imagined asking all that she saw, "Which way?" And followed up with, "Thank you. I love you." She felt the breeze flow past and make the leaves dance on the tree to the right. She flashed an excited look at her dad and started walking in the direction of the tree. William followed, humming and whistling her song all the way to the top.

Clarity Mountain offered a 360-degree perspective. "Papa, we can see e-v-e-r-y-t-h-i-n-g!" Val went closer to the edge and looked down toward the town. Then she moved along the edge as if memorizing every detail she could. She noticed a circle about twenty feet in diameter with four markers and a smaller circle in the center with lines to the markers and a star-like pattern.

"Picaflor, do you remember what Grandmother Flor taught you?" Valerie looked at her father, at the circle and back at her father. Grandmother Flor played many games with Valerie, though she hadn't realized they were lessons.

"The directions?"

"Yes, Valerie. This is a place to practice. This is our Circle of

Perspective. Use it like a compass to your heart's wisdom. Call upon the directions, which hold powerful help for you. Call upon your soul. Call upon Source to help you remember and listen."

"And offer my gratitude," she added, excited that she remembered.

"Yes! You remember well, Picaflor!" William was thrilled and relieved that his daughter had been ready for this test. He hoped it would be enough to help her when life changed.

Present Day, Saturday—Star Junction

"Can we climb Clarity Mountain?" Alex was excited. Val pondered his question but enjoyed the enthusiasm.

"Perhaps someday. First, we should start with some of the easier hikes and learn the terrain."

"But you already know the terrain. Right?"

"Thirty years ago! I'm not so sure that memory can come back!" She joked with them but felt the words like rocks in her gut.

Jake looked at one of the pictures before holding it up for Val to see. Grace was holding Sissy and Melanie as toddlers while Cade stood with a gap to her left and Val next to him. Emmet stood behind and just slightly left of Grace, his hands on her shoulders and his body edging between Grace and Cade. Nobody smiled.

"Do you think Grandma was ever happy? I mean with Emmet or maybe after?"

"Yeah, I do. I know in the last years of her life she was very happy. She found her spark again, even with Emmet. I'm not going to sugar coat it. Emmet was difficult. Life with him was difficult. Alcoholism. Abuse. But she wouldn't have let him in if she hadn't seen something to love there. And because of him, she had two more daughters she couldn't have loved more. When we were kids, we were all very close."

"If you were so close, what happened?" Jake looked her in the eyes when he asked. He wanted to see her answer.

Val paused, her eyes tearing up. His inquisition struck deep.

"That is a good question, Jake, with a complex answer. I'm not sure I know how to answer it in this moment. So I'm passing for now. But we can come back to it, okay?"

Jake shrugged and nodded.

"Okay, show me the rest of what you both chose and let's see if we can make this more interactive." The boys showed her the pictures: William, Grace, little Valerie, and Edward at a creek; all of the siblings in front of the school sign; cinnamon rolls; and a roaring fire at the pavilion with Grandmother Flor and little Valerie. And one that Val wasn't ready for—a picture of all of them in front of the packed car on the day they left Star Junction.

"Ah, Moon Creek, that sounds like a great place to introduce ourselves!" She tapped the picture of them at the creek and started walking. The boys shrugged at each other before catching up.

Moon Creek ran mostly north-south through town, just west of center—a small branch off of the Sky River, which flowed through the mountain and fed many smaller creeks and streams. A walking path had run along the creek for many generations. It was typically peaceful and well-shaded, enjoyed by people and animals alike. It was also somewhat hidden by trees and brush that had been allowed to create a protective barrier and keep the creek side an oasis of sorts. Val slowed as she approached the trees, silently asking permission to enter. Asking to be shown the opening that she once knew without looking.

"Where are we going?" Alex asked, confused by the wall of shrubbery.

Just then Val lit up.

"Ah! There you are." She slipped through the opening. "Come on, boys!" They walked through a narrow path that angled through the thicket. Just as the boys began to think Val had lost it, they came to the other side, the creek side. The sunlight filtered through the trees, creating flickering shafts of light as Val took a deep breath. It looked just like she remembered.

"Wow, this is pretty cool." Jake approved.

"Is this the place in the picture?" Alex asked. Val looked at the picture again and pointed downstream toward a large stump and good sitting rocks. The creek widened for about twenty feet, forming a gentle, round pool.

"Over there." She pointed and headed that way. "It's also a good place to sit."

They found a shady spot and Alex took his sketchpad out of his pack. Jake watched him.

"Do you take that everywhere?" he asked Alex.

Alex paused and looked up at Jake. "Um, yeah...pretty much. I like to draw things. It helps me remember. What do you do to remember new places?"

"I don't know. Nothing I guess." Jake shrugged, but he did know. He just didn't know how to explain it.

Val sat in silence, listening to the boys and the water ripple gently through, watching the light dancing with the ripples in flickers and flashes.

"Aunt Val, did you come here a lot as a kid?"

She looked at Alex and smiled. "I did. I came here a lot with my parents. And when I was a little older and needed a break from stuff, this was my secret place. I'm guessing your grandmother might have known where to find me, but Emmet never did."

"Why is it called Moon Creek?"

"That's a good question. I don't know for sure, but I do remember a story. The water from this creek comes from and returns to the Sky River—the big river in the mountains. The river has many branches, but this branch is the moon's reflecting pool."

"Its what?"

"The story is that no matter the time of year, you will always be able to see the moon's reflection in this creek at night. Right here, in the round. The story goes that the creek widened here so the moon could see all of itself when it is full. The other narrower sections could only show slivers of light."

"That's crazy." Jake shook his head in disbelief.

"Maybe, maybe not, but that's the story." Val winked when she said it. She wasn't sure where the sense of playfulness was coming from, but she liked it. "You don't have to believe it. But another reason that people come here, other than for a little peace and moon reflections, is the water itself. Water can be very healing when we ask nicely and have respect."

Val got up and went to the water's edge. She kneeled and closed her eyes. "Thank you for having us here and allowing us to enjoy this beauty and peace. Thank you for allowing us to quench our thirst." Val cupped her hands in the water, drew them to her lips, and drank. "Mmm, it is also very cool and refreshing to drink."

"I want to try!" Alex jumped up and joined her at the water's edge. He looked at her. Val gave him a reassuring nod. He let his hands enter the water and felt it flow through his fingers. "Thank you... for the water," he said almost as a question and then let his hands fill with water and drank. "It is really good. You do it, Jake."

"Nah, that's okay. I'm good."

Val pulled out some snacks that Lucy had sent with them, and they huddled around the photos while they nibbled at the deliciousness.

"Okay, what's next?" Val asked.

"Wait, why does this one say 'Uncle Edward' on the back? Why do you call him 'Mister'?"

Val took the photo from Alex and read the writing *Spending the day with Uncle Edward.*

"Wow, I'm not sure...but that explains his question to me this morning." She traced the words and turned the photo over, touching the faces with her fingers and pulling the memory back to her. "I did call him uncle. But I don't quite remember when it changed."

They let the rest of the afternoon be an easy one. The boys explored the rock formations, eddies, and critters of Moon Creek until Val suggested they finish the day at the motel pool and have pizza for dinner. They would have more time for pictures and questions. She was feeling drained, and she knew Alex wanted to talk to Cade. Maybe at the motel, some of the memories would slow down, and she could catch her emotional breath.

FIVE

Thirty-Six Years Ago—Star Junction
"From what direction does the sun rise?"
Valerie looked around and pointed to a vague east.
William smiled. "And what direction is that?"

Val smiled as another memory of her father flowed through as if it were happening in this moment. She watched herself as a child—playful, eager, and overflowing with joy. For all the joy she saw in these memories of her father's lessons, she could see the anger and refusal of joy in the memories of her stepfather, Emmet.

One thing Val knew for sure about herself was she could hold a stance. She used to envision herself like the trunk of a tree when she needed to be strong—sturdy, powerful, immobile. Then she learned about the walking palm trees that use their roots to reposition themselves and realized that immobility was not the same as strength. Not everything was as it seemed.

"East?" Val scrunched her brow and shrugged the answer. William smiled again. "Yes, Picaflor. East is the direction where the sun rises and the day begins. We have the energy of renewal. New starts. Beginning. Opportunity.

"It's a whole new day!"

William laughed. "Yes, Picaflor. From the east we are given new beginnings. And in what direction does the sun say goodnight?"

She scrunched her face again and pointed—her hand still close to her body—toward the west. He waited for her to say it.

"West?"

"That's right. The sun says goodnight to the day in the west. The west reminds us to release the happenings of the day, the thoughts that don't serve us, and other things it is best to let go of."

"But if the east is for beginnings and the west is for endings, what about the north and the south?"

"Excellent question, Valerie! Let us look at each direction as if they are good friends who help us on our journey. East reminds us that we can always start over, begin again. Each day is new, each day its own. West reminds us not to end, but to let go of all but the learnings and the love. If every word we say were a rock, and everything that happened in a day a stone that we had to carry, we would have a very heavy load and would not be able to move forward. The West reminds us to let the stones go because they are not ours to carry always—just ours to have known. The north is like our guiding light reminding us to stay connected to our earth and listen to the wisdom within. Like a grandmother. The south reminds us to play, to live each day with passion and courage and faithfulness."

Young Valerie sat with this for a moment, recording every word of her father's meaning. "Daddy?"

"Yes, Picaflor?"

"We are very lucky to have so many good friends in nature. Aren't we?"

"Yes, you are very wise to recognize that!" And he laughed with approval and agreement.

———

When her family was moved south by Emmet, Valerie forgot to look to her friends for help. Forgot to trust in the east for new beginnings. Forgot to let her troubles go down with the sun. The truth was that by the time they had moved, Picaflor had become Val, and sixteen-year-old Val had lost her joy.

William fit as many lessons as he could into the time they had. The lessons often came on hikes, working with nature, the earth, and all that could be learned from her. Valerie loved every minute. Sometimes lessons were in the kitchen or on the front porch, just like the night she listened with her heart and came home from the fire. William cherished his family, and Picaflor felt like an expression of his own heart. He had one more devastating lesson to teach.

Valerie had noticed that her papa had lost weight, but she didn't know why. She didn't think to ask. Nobody else talked about it. She didn't know that this was one of those secrets that adults sometimes kept. He felt so strong and dependable to her she couldn't imagine him being any other way—despite her dreams of not being able to find him and despite the one where he disappeared in front of her.

One day after school Uncle Edward picked her up. His voice was softer than usual. "Miss Valerie, please come with me."

She was confused by what she was feeling. She was not afraid, just unsure.

"Uncle, where are we going? Where is Papa?"

He put his hand on her head gently. "I am taking you to him." She knew from his look that something was wrong, so she did what her papa taught her. She closed her eyes, put her hand on her heart, and listened.

"Picaflor, my little warrioress... My Val-or-is ... you are strong. You will always be able to hear me if you listen with your heart."

She looked up at Edward hoping he would understand all the questions and fear that just came to her heart.

"He is talking to you in your heart. It is important for you to listen. And he is waiting to see you."

Little Valerie ran into the hospital room. "Papa! Papa, what happened?"

William sat up as best he could in the bed. He held his arms out to her, and she planted her face in his chest, her ear to his heart. Now she could hear it, faintly.

"Valerie, I am glad you are here. I have been waiting for you, sweet child."

"Papa, what is happening?"

He caressed her head for a while, allowing the words to form themselves as she opened to hearing them. "I taught you before that we can always hear each other. Yes? You can talk to all of your ancestors, all of your loved ones, whether living here or in the heavens. Picaflor, this is a hard lesson. Not everyone we love gets to stay with us physically."

Val began to sob quietly with occasional heaving as the meaning of his words became clear. Suddenly she could think of every conversation of the last year—all of the lessons. At age nine, she understood that he had been preparing her, and it really made her angry.

"Why, Papa? I don't want you to go! Why didn't you tell me? You can't leave me!" Her sobs got louder, and her heaves released the weight of all the emotions that were knotted up in that moment. He held her quietly, meeting her exactly where she was. When she had begun to calm, he started to speak again.

"Picaflor, you are a child created in love and always surrounded by love. You will never be alone unless you choose to believe it is true. Your mother loves you and aches for you. Your young brother smiles when you are near. Your Uncle Edward and Grandmother Flor are your family, too. You do not have to understand everything now. But you do have to trust that love is always with you. Your life will take you many places, and it will return you home. I love you with all of my heart, completely. My body cannot continue, but our love will always be here, in you." He continued to hold her until she stirred. "There is nothing to fear unless you choose it. Remember what you've learned Picaflor. Remember to talk to me and listen with your heart."

"I love you forever, Papa." Somehow, she felt calm or maybe numb. But they were pulling her away from him and she wanted to see her mother. Edward took her home.

As they were driving, Edward began to speak to her. "Miss Valerie—" But he stopped and let her be. He sent the words with his heart instead. *Let your mother be there for you. You have felt what it is like to listen with your heart—always remember. We are family, here to love each other through.*

By now it was getting dark. The sun setting behind the mountain, casting a hazy orange-gray look to the dawn of night. Val sat in the car for what seemed like ages. She just couldn't seem to make her hand pull the handle to open the car door. Edward sat in silence with her until he saw Grace open the door of the house. He looked at Valerie with love and kindness and his own broken heart, and she looked to him and took in a breath big enough to help her float away. Edward got out of the car and walked around to her door and opened it. "You are never alone. Our love is always with you."

Little Valerie didn't feel so little anymore. She walked up the path to her mother feeling old and heavy. She resisted this connection with her mother until she reached Grace's side. Then she lost control, and Grace wrapped her arms around Valerie and let her sob.

Valerie felt cold and couldn't find the sun. After the service, Grace, Val, and baby Cade joined Edward and others in the courtyard behind Grandmother Flor's home. Val loved it here with no shortage of wonders to explore and discoveries to make. But today, she couldn't find the sun. It felt like the day hadn't really come at all, and they were all just waiting and wondering if it ever would. Cade chose Grace's lap over toddling. Efforts to tempt him away with toys or play were met with crying. Val just stared into the distance.

Edward approached them, his eyes freshly kissed with tears. He and Grace met eyes and shared understanding. He quietly sat beside her. She inhaled the deepest breath she could to hold back tears. "Knowing doesn't make it easier." They had prepared as best they could.

"Knowing that something is coming doesn't stop emotions. Feel, dear Grace. Let yourself feel it. Let your children feel it. We can't outthink emotion by being prepared. I feel the loss of my brother, though I know he is always with me. I feel his loss when I gaze upon you and these beautiful children. I feel his loss when I wish to have his company. I feel his loss when I notice the absence of his hearty laugh and gentle voice."

He touched her gently on her back between her shoulder blades. "You are safe to feel it all, Grace." After a few moments, he held his arms to Cade who climbed in, and held his hand down for Valerie. She didn't want to go anywhere. "Picaflor, will you join me for a time?" Little Valerie looked at her mother who nodded. She took Edward's hand and walked with him to the fountain, leaving Grace in a moment to herself, to breathe, to feel, to let go.

Valerie wasn't talking yet. This was a new side to her. Words and expression usually came in a generous flow, but she just didn't know how to start and feared that she would never be able to stop. Edward sat with her and Cade, slowly enticing Cade to play with the fountain and let the water do as water does. Valerie continued to stare into the distance.

If the sun would come and the haze would lift, she would be looking upon the Eye. The Watcher in the mountain. William had told her stories. Grandmother Flor had told stories. Edward told the stories. William was supposed to take her there, to find the Eye that watches over Star Junction as a guardian. Val's nine-year-old mind couldn't understand how a loving guardian would not protect her father from dying or protect her from losing him. What kind of guardian was that?

Eventually, Edward spoke to her thoughts. "The guardian cannot protect against the happenings of life; it can only warn us of things or changes that come toward us. It is up to us to prepare and decide how to engage or react to those things." Val scrunched her brows and let out a quick, frustrated breath.

"It didn't warn me!"

"No, but William did his best to prepare you, to teach you, and to love you completely."

She dropped her head. "But I am not prepared. I didn't know. I don't want him gone; I want him here!"

"Yes."

She looked up at him and couldn't hold the tears any longer. Her sun could not rise. She leaned into her uncle and sobbed while Cade played with the water from the fountain, wetting his hands in the sparkly water and then bringing them to Val's head, and then to Edward's head. Somehow, both felt lighter with the gesture as the water trickled down their foreheads and led them to smile at Cade's play.

"Can I go there?"

"To the Eye?"

"Yes. Papa was supposed to take me."

Edward closed his eyes for a moment to feel his answer.

"Yes, I will take you to the way when it is time." He paused to look in her eyes with reassurance. "Soon."

A few weeks after William's service, Grace made pancakes with little Valerie. It was one of her magical powers—turning something simple into an adventure. Turning heaviness into light. Little Valerie shifted right into playful helper. Not with the usual enthusiasm, but with just enough light seeping through to lift the cloud over the household. Cade watched their show of adding ingredients, mixing with dramatic flair, and making designs onto the griddle. It was enough that Valerie forgot herself for a bit and enjoyed the pancakes.

As Grace began to clean up, she saw Edward sitting outside waiting. He had told her that he would come when the time was right for Picaflor to climb to the Eye. She nodded to him, pleased that the time had come. "Picaflor, when you are done, your Uncle Edward is waiting for you."

Val's eyes lit up. She hadn't let anyone call her Picaflor since William died, but this time it didn't faze her. She took her plate to the sink, ran to her room to get the bag she had prepared days before, hugged Grace, and kissed Cade on the head.

"Thank you, Mama. I love you."

"I love you, Valerie, completely and full of mush."

Val rolled her eyes and smiled as she went through the door. She stopped at the top of the steps, clutching her bag to her chest.

Edward stood. "Good morning, young Valerie."

"Good morning," she said sheepishly. She had never hiked without William.

Edward looked to the sky and spread out his arms. "It is a beautiful day for a hike." He smiled, and she felt herself breathe and return his smile. "Shall we go?"

She nodded and put on her backpack.

Edward whistled as they walked through town. It was a lovely tone designed to relieve any pressure the child may have felt to speak. He knew when she had something to say, she would. Val walked quietly alongside him feeling that she had known the tune as she had known the town they walked through. But it all felt so different.

"Mr. Edward?" This was the first time she called him Mister instead of Uncle. A child's confusion believing that if her father died, the one he called his brother could no longer be her uncle.

"Yes?" Edward responded despite the change.

"He shouldn't have had to die. Nothing feels the same anymore."

"Hmmm. Maybe it is you that doesn't feel the same."

She scrunched her lips into her cheek and crinkled her forehead trying to figure out what made more sense. All she knew was that it felt like her entire world changed.

"Look at the buildings," he spoke slowly with a beautiful nurturing tone and paused between sentences. "Have they changed? Are they bigger? Smaller? Has the pavilion moved? Young Valerie, it is your lens that has changed. We all have limited time in this world. Your father used his time wisely. We all must choose to love freely, even with the knowing that our time here is precious and short. It will take time for you to adjust and feel like you again."

"Do you feel like you?" She looked up into his eyes.

"Not all of me." He patted her on the head gently. "My closest friend, my brother, can no longer walk beside me, and I feel great sorrow. Yet I also feel joy for my brother who no longer walks in pain. As my sorrow lifts, I can feel him and know he is near. This will be true for you as well."

They walked again in silence as Valerie wrestled the thoughts and feelings and just how much she didn't like it. "It doesn't feel fair. I feel like everything is wrong and I don't know what to do."

Edward stopped at the giant boulder. Val knew the marker well when hiking with William to Clarity Mountain. She stood in front of him, shifting her weight from side to side, uncertain about why he stopped.

Hoping to speed things up she offered, "I know this boulder; we go left here to go to Clarity Mountain."

But she had never come across the Eye on Clarity Mountain. Edward leaned against the boulder and closed his eyes. Val realized this was an intentional pause and sat down on a smooth rock to wait.

After fidgeting and playing with the dirt, she settled in and caught sight of something out of the corner of her eye. She stood up and looked over toward the right, beyond the trees and up the mountain. It was the Eye, watching.

"Mr. Edward!"

"Ahh, now you are ready." They continued on a path to the right that she had never noticed before. The climb was steady and filled with plants, trees, and other remarkable things. Val had found the playful part of herself and couldn't help but tell Edward every fantastical discovery she made on the path. The ground squirrels watching them. The woodpecker working away on the Ponderosa Pine. The hummingbird that buzzed around her head. Edward listened but did not respond. The path changed directions as they found their way through trees, boulders, and grass. They reached a plateau where the path seemed to end into an open area with boulders and trees around the edges. She wasn't sure where they were or why they were stopping. The Eye was not here.

"Young Valerie, I will wait here for you."

"But why? I don't know where to go. You can come too."

"You know how to find the way. You have been leading all this time." He winked at her. "This is *your* visit with the Watcher—not mine. I will be here waiting. And I will be there to help if you should need it."

Valerie knew he wouldn't change his mind. She looked all around, studied her options then closed her eyes. "Papa, which way do I go?"

She heard his answer in her heart, "Don't forget to play, Picaflor; listen to your helpers." The gentle breeze tickled at her ear, and she heard birds singing. She opened her eyes and moved forward.

Valerie stopped and stood motionless for some time. She had been letting herself have so much fun to reach the Eye that when it was suddenly before her, she froze. All of the emotions, the things she wanted to say, ask, scream all caught in her throat and constricted in her chest and nothing came out. The enormity of the formation so close was astonishing. She could see the reddish and sandy-colored layers of time as well as the smoothed, grooved outline clearly defined.

Something seen only from afar could not be gauged by nine-year-old eyes. Finally, she gave up on words and moved closer to the Eye, her hands lightly tracing the parts she could reach. The arc rose much higher than her arms. Her forehead leaned into the wall and rested there.

After many breaths in stillness one word found its way out from her lips as a faint whisper, "Why?" The weight of her body felt too much, and she shrank along the wall of the Eye to curl up at its base and sobbed tears that spoke for her.

Why did he die? Why did he leave us? Why hasn't everything stopped? Why didn't he teach me how to be without him? Why do I have to feel all of these things?

The tears etched the dirt beneath her until her attention was shifted to them and the spot to her left at the corner of the Eye. Water seeped from the stone and trickled down to form a small stream that joined with hers. She hadn't noticed it before. She stood up facing the Eye. "Why are you crying?"

"We never weep alone," the deep soft voice answered quietly.

"But you are, um, a mountain."

"My heart is as yours."

"I didn't mean to make you cry." She touched her hand to the wall.

"Dear one, it is compassion. Expression. What you feel, I feel. What you release, I too cleanse and release. You do not weep your loss alone. In time you will understand better. Let your tears fall to the earth and from them, flowers will bloom. There is always heal-ing." She put her cheek to the mountain, and together they remained until the tears stopped.

She kissed the Eye, whispering, *"Thank you,"* as she left to return to Edward.

Edward was exactly where she had left him. She ran up and wrapped her arms around him, and he held her. The sorrow, no longer as heavy, now called for touch. Each held the other that they might feel William's love through them.

SIX

Val and the boys were eating breakfast at Lucy's restaurant. Monday had finally come, and Val was preparing to go to Ms. Ramirez's office with Lucy as support. Val thought that having Lucy with her would help show her connection to the community as well as keep Val grounded. Lucy offered, and Val accepted readily.

"I'm going with you," Jake announced. He suspected his aunt would want to see Ms. Ramirez without him, but he couldn't let that happen.

Val understood why he wanted to go. She would have wanted the same.

"Jake, it is not a good idea this time."

"I don't care. I want to go. I have a right to be there. She is *my* sister!"

"You are angry and want to express it. And I understand."

"But?" Jake snapped as he glared at her.

"But part of my job is to protect and advocate for both of you. And that means asking you to stay with Mr. Edward and Alex at the shop while Lucy and I go."

Jake shoved his chair away from the table and dropped his fork on the plate. "Right. Cause you know so much." He put his headphones on and stormed out. Alex wanted to follow, but Val went instead. She found Jake just outside the door leaning his back against the building. She did the same.

"Jake, I'm sorry. I need to address Ms. Ramirez in an adult conversation."

"I'm not a child. I'm not Alex. Lilah is *my* sister. I *am* responsible. I am the one she was taken from!" he shouted.

"No, you're not a child anymore. Not like Alex is. But you're not an adult either. The reality is that Ms. Ramirez may not talk as openly in front of you. And we need answers. It isn't fair and probably doesn't make sense, but that's how government agencies are. I want you to understand, but even if you don't, it is the way it needs to be today. If it doesn't work, we will try other approaches."

"That's what adults always say, you know? They need to have an 'adult' conversation. And nothing ever changes." He turned to face her again and commanded, "Find my sister."

With the boys helping Mr. Edward at the gas station, Val and Lucy arrived at Ms. Ramirez's office. Ms. Ramirez was expecting her. "Please, have a seat."

Val stood. "Where is she?"

"I understand that you are upset. It is complicated."

"No, it isn't. I was here, in this office on Friday to pick up Jake. Why wouldn't you tell me about Lilah, knowing I would want her too?"

"Please. I assumed you would know you had a niece. When Lilah wasn't mentioned by you or in the paperwork your attorneys sent... Well, I wasn't sure why."

"It doesn't matter why. I live in California. Sissy lived in Arizona. Life often separates family. The only mystery is why none of Sissy's family was notified when she died. Not me, not her brother Cade, not her other sister Melanie. None of us knew. For a year. How is that possible?

"I-I don't know." Ms. Ramirez was tired. She took a breath and sat down at her desk. "I didn't know you weren't notified. We thought they didn't have any family. I do apologize for not letting you know about Lilah on Friday. I was following orders but expected you to return. Lilah is okay. It is just, well, it will take time." Val watched Ms. Ramirez shift her gaze from Val to Lucy to papers on her desk, and the lamp.

"Time?" Val's eyes were fixed on Ms. Ramirez. "I don't understand. Who would give an order that would keep a young girl separated from her only brother?"

Ms. Ramirez couldn't answer. She met Val's eyes and held her gaze.

Val took a deep breath and scratched her head. "So you were instructed to withhold information. You are still withholding information. And for as long as you do, those two kids who lost their mother are being kept apart."

"Again, I am sorry. I have been working on it. Ms. Ramirez straightened out the stacks of files on her desk while calming her own nerves. "There are processes in place."

"Processes?" Val shot back with exasperation. Val caught herself elevating and summoned her cool. Not because she conceded but because it wasn't working. They weren't getting anywhere. Val pulled the chair closer to Ms. Ramirez's desk and sat.

"Ms. Ramirez, where is Lilah?" The pause was too long. So Val found other ways to ask. "Do you know where she is? Has she gone missing? Who is she with? Are they being uncooperative? Wanting to adopt her? Do they know she has a brother? If they truly care for this child, they would want her to be with her family, especially her brother, who we both know is very attached to her, and she to him. Keeping them apart makes no sense at all."

"As I said, there are processes in place and information that I am not able to divulge."

"What can you divulge? Let's start there."

"With all due respect, I don't have to divulge anything further at this time."

"Yet. That's what you mean. You don't have to divulge anything further yet, because you do not have a court order in front of you. Which my attorneys could easily get. It took them a day, maybe less, to get you paperwork for Jake. Is that what I need to do?" Val paused and took in the room, the stack of files on Ms. Ramirez's desk, the stressed expression on her face.

She felt Jake's expectations and desperation with her in the room. She also felt a nudge from the inside. Something calling her to shift her approach. Railing against and threatening Ms. Ramirez was pointless. If she was truly following orders—which she likely was—she wasn't the one to go after.

"But I don't really want to do it that way, Ms. Ramirez. I think you care too much about these kids not to help. You are clearly passionate about your job. You feel responsible. Maybe you are a procedure person, or maybe you are just backed against a wall. I don't know. I don't know how this all comes together. But I do know that I made a promise to Jake to find his sister and a commitment to this family that we would come together. You can help us to do that. And I hope you choose to because it seems to me that these kids truly need to see adults working together for their well-being."

Ms. Ramirez looked down at her desk and tapped her file. "I agree." She paused as she met Val's eyes. "I need to share something with you. We believe that Lilah has special needs. She doesn't talk, at least not to us. She is very withdrawn and sensitive. On a personal note, I fear that another disappointment could break this child."

"Then let's not disappoint her. Reunite her with her brother with whom she is deeply connected, and with the family she has waiting."

Val easily shifted into her CEO tone. It was not a request. She was not asking or pleading.

Ms. Ramirez felt the tone but did not respond. There was more she wasn't sharing, and Val would get to it.

"For the sake of the children, let's figure it out quickly. And, please, keep me informed. That will be very helpful as I field Jake's questions about when Lilah will be back with us."

Ms. Ramirez held her lips tightly together. Val embraced the pause and smiled as she stood up. "It looks like you and I will be getting to know each other quite well, Ms. Ramirez." Her smile was sincere but her tone all business. "Because I will not let Jake down."

Lucy waited until they were back in the car. She put her hand on Val's and felt it shaking. "Val, it will work out. You are meant to be here. You can do this."

Val looked at her with the hope that her words were true. "How do you know? I've never had kids. I left here so long ago. Where do I even start?"

"You already started. You are here. The boys are here and together. Lilah will be here too. And in case you forgot, you helped raise your brother and sisters."

"If this were business, I would know what to do. I would know the right words, moves, steps, and strategy. I am way out of my element here." Val paused to find her words. "I really didn't expect the emotions."

Lucy smiled. "Val, emotions are what make you alive. You left Star Junction, but it did not leave you. All that you were taught still lives inside you. It is what called you home."

"You sound like your father."

"And like yours."

With that reminder, Val's tears released and carried with them the heartbreak of so many years. Val fought to compose herself as Lucy held her hand in silence.

"Thank you, Lucy. I appreciate your encouragement and kindness. I have spent decades learning different ways. This all feels more like a dream than a memory."

Alex sat with his sketchpad in Mr. Edward's office. He studied the photographs, sometimes tracing the faces with his fingertip, absorbing every bit of their meaning and life and stories. He wanted to know them completely. Edward came in to check on the boys as Alex began drawing.

Jake leaned back in a chair with his headphones on. He watched Edward enter the room but didn't show any acknowledgment. *Where was he? Why hadn't he come—at least to visit?* Sissy had told Jake that Mr. Edward had been like family when she was little, so why didn't he come to help Jake and Lilah?

Edward felt the boy's questions. He glanced at Alex's sketchpad and the detailed drawing taking shape. He slowly drew in a long, deep breath, nodded to himself, and sat next to Jake. He tapped Jake's feet which were up on the desk. Jake lowered them with dramatic thuds and looked at Edward with skeptical eyes.

"I hear you clearly," said Edward.

Jake skewed his eyebrows in a quizzical look as Edward continued.

"You want to know why I didn't come. Why you were alone all this time."

Jake's look shifted from defiant to pained, but he bit his lips to keep them closed as his eyes became glossy.

"I would have the same questions. In the eyes of the universe, we are family. In the eyes of government agencies—counties, children's services—we have no legal relationship. That shouldn't matter, and doesn't to your ears. It took much time for us to find out about your mother, to confirm what we felt. When we did, our requests to see you were denied, and we were not told where you were."

He took a long pause as he considered his next words, and Jake wrestled with truth and anger, fear and heartache without taking his eyes off of Edward. "I am going to tell you something that will be hard for you to understand today. I believe you will understand it better in the weeks to come. We have known your family as ours. And have known that they would all be called to return home. We were called to trust the vision that your aunt would come, and your uncle, and others. We had to trust but that meant not intervening. We also trust that we all walk the paths we came to walk."

Jake lowered his eyes from Edward's for the first time. He had heard Sissy talking about paths before. And Lilah, too. "You're right. I don't understand." Jake paused. "But I think I believe you." He hesitated with a swallow; his voice quiet. "I really needed someone to show up." Edward put his hand on Jake's shoulder carefully. Jake looked up at him, "And I really need Lilah back."

Val dropped Lucy off at the restaurant. "Will you let your father know it will be a little longer? I think I need a walk."

Lucy nodded with a reassuring smile.

"Of course. Take the time you need. The boys are fine where they are."

Val wandered through the town square, stirring memories with every shop door she passed—Oaks Market and the ice cream shop, Bishop's Music and the library. She found herself at the Star Pavilion. Historically it was a ceremonial space, an outdoor church. They had plenty of indoor sacred spaces as well, but this was where they came together in celebration of life, of each other, of seasons and harvest and sowing seeds. This is where she danced by the fire as a child to the music that played in her heart. The place where the whole of the town became one.

But today she lay on a bench and drifted into memories.

Thirty-Eight Years Ago—Star Junction

William and Grace watched as Valerie picked at her pancakes instead of inhaling them.

"Picaflor, what is on your mind?" Little Valerie hadn't realized that she was not eating. In some ways, she was still dreaming. Her father's question startled her awake. She looked at her food and at her parents.

"Sorry... I don't know why."

Grace came over to her and kissed her head. "Did you sleep okay, sweetie? You seem tired."

"Mama, I don't think so. I think there were too many stories in my head."

"Ahh," said William, "you were having lots of dreams?" Valerie nodded as she poked her pancakes with her fork.

"Do you not dream every night?"

"Yes. I dream every night, but sometimes they feel different."

"What felt different this time?"

She wasn't sure how to answer. She stopped poking her food and scrunched her lips in thought. "It was too much. There were so many people, and it kept changing, and some were mean, and you went away. I couldn't find you." Grace and William exchanged a look of understanding.

"And it upset you."

"Why couldn't I find you?"

William scooted his chair back and held out his arms for her. She quickly moved into his lap with her head on his shoulder and arms wrapped around his neck. They had talked about dreams before, about the different types. Sometimes they just helped the mind process the day, and sometimes they had messages and messengers and information from our soul. Our loved ones could come in our dreams to guide us. Dreams did not need to be feared, just paid attention to. William understood that Picaflor was afraid of the dreams, upset by the message she wasn't ready to understand.

"Picaflor, I am here, loving you completely. Your mom, too."

Present Day, Monday—Star Junction

"You are deep in memory, my child." The voice pulled her back to the present. Val looked up from the pavilion bench to see Grandmother Flor watching her.

"Grandmother Flor! It is so good to see you!" Suddenly Val was sixteen again and elated at the presence of one who understood.

Grandmother Flor smiled in return. "We are happy you have returned. You were missed here. Picaflor was missed."

"I haven't been called that in a long time." Val heard the words as if an explanation of an adult growing out of childish nicknames. Grandmother Flor knew better.

"Yes, she has been missing for a long time." Grandmother's eyes were knowing with the ability to pierce the heaviest armor. Val found herself looking away. *Why did I do that?* She wondered if Grandmother Flor had gotten old, though she looked exactly the same.

Grandmother Flor was the matriarch, the elder and spiritual leader of this village. She had no title but grandmother and was called that by all who knew her. She spoke the wisdom of the ages and the messages of the ancient ones. She was a healer and a leader. Her understanding of the medicinal qualities of plants was extraordinary.

She emanated love freely and had no tolerance for fools or narcissists, which is not to say she would not help them. She simply would not waste time or energy on empty acts. If someone was not ready for her work, they would not stay.

She commanded respect by her presence alone, and that respect was shown by a person's presence—a reciprocal exchange of energy. Some were fearful as they were attached to their illusions and did not wish to let them go—not even for the freedom they longed for.

Her eyes alone could cause one to feel dizzy. She called them memory portals, for truly gazing into them could help one's willing soul to awaken and remember who they were.

"When you are done remembering, collect the boys and move into our home. No more hotel. We have room for you. You are welcome, and it will give you time to discover what must be done. Be there by 4:30. You will help with dinner."

"Grandmother, thank you. That is very generous, but—" Grandmother Flor was gone. Val smiled and laughed to herself. There would be no denying Grandmother Flor. "Okay, we'll be there," she said to the air.

But Val wasn't done remembering. She sat back down entranced. "How did it all go so wrong? Papa, Emmet was no replacement for you."

Thirty-eight Years Ago—Star Junction

Star Junction was small then. Not too many options of mates for a woman with two kids who felt she needed one. Emmet wasn't from there. He had taken a job at the mill with a plan to be just passing through. He saw Grace at the market one day, her long hair partially fallen from its tie and caressing her face. He waited as she ordered meat from the butcher and watched the ease of her conversation and the warmth of her smile.

The butcher handed her the order and said, "Thank you, Grace."

Emmet felt as if the words came from him.

She turned to continue her shopping in the market and said, "Oh, please excuse me," as she hadn't seen him or realized he was standing that close.

"No, ma'am, excuse me. I was surely distracted." He didn't include the "by you" part. She smiled politely as she went by, and Emmet was smitten. Every day he went to the market at that time and then multiple times a day, hoping to see her again. Grace didn't have Valerie or Cade with her the day they met. When he found out about the kids, he told her it didn't matter. A part of him wanted it to be true, but before long he became bitter at having to support another man's "brats."

All of his love was for Grace until she gave him daughters and not a son. He tried to love them—tried to know how. But love wasn't his first language and came with rules he didn't know or understand. All he knew was his woman had given another man a son and an uppity daughter who stopped listening to Emmet early on, and then she'd given him two more girls. What was he supposed to do with them? He hadn't meant to have a family, but if he had to, it should have been a son that didn't look like another man. And his wife should put him first. Sometimes, he just needed a couple of drinks before going home so he could tolerate the little brats. And then maybe a couple more when he got there if things were too much.

In his saner and sober moments, he longed to feel connected to them all. To feel something other than resentful or terrified. At times he would feel guilty. Sometimes Grace would say something to inspire him or convince him momentarily to try harder. She'd make him think he really did want to love them, that he cared.

He would feel bolstered up and issue an invitation to bond like it was a command. "Everybody, come now, we're going to do this together!" When the kids would react with confusion and uncertainty, he would shut it all down, yell at those nearest, and storm out.

Any good intentions early on were replaced with: "I agreed to raise them, not to love them." He couldn't help feeling tricked somehow, as if Grace's beauty had cast a spell upon him, and now he was being punished. Val received the bulk of his wrath, as she saw through to the closed heart of the man.

William had taught her that hating someone was a misunderstanding. "Do you hate your teacher because they teach you math? Or because they tell you when your answer is incorrect? People are put in our lives for many reasons. They are not always pleasant experiences. Sometimes people will play roles in our life that cause hurt or pain, but it is important to remember that they are always there to be teachers. Pain and difficulties are temporary."

Valerie tried hard to love Emmet at first. Then she tried not to hate him. But truthfully, she hated everything about him and what he had done to their lives. She hated how her mother had changed and become quiet and withdrawn. She hated how guilty she felt when she could feel the hate so fully that she tasted it. Her heart would beg, "I'm sorry, Papa. I know I'm not supposed to hate him."

SEVEN

Val and the boys retrieved their belongings from the motel. Val didn't think any of them would miss the dark dingy room, but she noticed she felt a bit nervous. Some of it felt like excitement to see and be around this long-lost family, Grandmother Flor and Mr. Edward, but she also felt fear. She just wasn't the girl they had known so many years ago.

They arrived at Grandmother's compound, which was the only way Val knew to describe it. The whole family lived there together in separate but connected dwellings. They shared a beautiful enclosed patio, opened to the skies in the front, and a large courtyard that accommodated Grandmother's food and medicinal gardens as well as plenty of space for the kids and dogs to play in the back. In fact, the yard didn't end; it just opened to the hills above them. Lucy was raising her children there as she had been raised.

It had always been a mystical space for Val. Mysteriously peaceful and vibrant. Rich with activity yet void of chaos. As a child she had gotten lost in her explorations, letting her imagination go without filter or limits. As she walked through the front patio, she knew it hadn't changed a bit. She could smell the herbs and plants standing guard at the gates. Rosemary, rue, oregano, thyme, epazote, sage, juniper, and lavender, all there awakening her senses and stirring memories once thought lost.

Lucy met them in the entry. "Welcome!" Val couldn't imagine Lucy ever not being welcoming. She met Lucy's warmth with her own as they hugged and smiled.

Lucy continued, "Boys, I'll show you where to put your stuff. Then you can join the others in the courtyard. I think they're playing some not so serious soccer. Val, you have been requested to help in the kitchen." Lucy gestured for them all to follow. Val dropped her bags in her room and looked to Lucy.

"Should I be prepared?"

Lucy smiled. "Always—and you will be fine." Lucy and the boys continued to the courtyard. "Okay, boys, please make yourselves at home. Feel free to join the game." She pointed toward her kids playing soccer and introduced them, "Vivian, Malia, and Eli-Koa."

Val had fond memories of Grandmother Flor from her early childhood. She had never known more than a day without Edward or Grandmother Flor before Emmet became her stepfather when she was ten. Edward was her uncle in all respects but blood. They were the family she knew along with Grace and William. She relied on their existence, on knowing they were always there and a part of her life.

Emmet's need to control his family and his discomfort with what he considered competition and threats to his authority caused him to limit their contact with these loved ones. It started off slowly, but by the time she was a young teen, she wasn't allowed to see them at all. He only tolerated brief encounters thought to be accidental path crossings—at the market or in the square.

In Grandmother's world, nothing was by accident. Brief encounters to plant and water seeds of connection, to whisper to her soul, were always orchestrated and intentional. But planned visits were out of the question. This only sealed Val's hatred of Emmet and the disappearance of Picaflor. It was hard to be the cultivator of joy when she was casting hate upon another. They could not occupy the same space in her heart.

Grandmother Flor was Edward's mother. The town called her grandmother as a title of respect, reverence, and affection. But for Val and her family, Flor was the only Grandmother they had known. She had taken William in as a boy and taught him alongside Edward. They were schoolmates to the world but brothers in spirit. William and Edward learned well from Flor about the truth of our essence and the world around us, the assistance and medicine that plants can give us, the allies that remain invisible to most but are powerful nonetheless, and the way to listen. They were good students.

William's mother Sofia died when William was ten, soon after arriving in Star Junction. His father Sully did his best to provide shelter and food, as any "good" man would do. Conversation with his son however, was not a strength. Perhaps mostly because he didn't want to risk the rage coming out in such a way that it may never stop. Instead, it burned him up from the inside with the help of cheap whiskey. He joined his wife when William was just twelve, and Flor took over.

This was a time when people took care of each other without interference or even notice from official agencies—another benefit of a small town bearing an unofficial name. Val hadn't understood the details or depth of this as a child. All she knew then was they were the family that she knew. She had never even asked questions. But now she would learn more, for "as we heal ourselves and our family, we heal our ancestors."

Young Valerie had often helped Grandmother Flor in the kitchen. It always felt like play as Grandmother would tell stories of generations, of how Star Junction came to be, of things so fantastical that little Valerie's eyes would be opened wide so she wouldn't risk missing any of the details.

She didn't know the stories were true, yet she never thought to suspect that they weren't. She had put the stories in a box at the back of her mind. Her adult-self suspected that Grandmother had reasons for her presence beyond "helping" in the kitchen, but she found herself excited about being with her again. Like a piece of her past was awakened and reunited, and they hadn't even started yet.

The kitchen was ideal for cooking for a large family, both rustic and efficient with plenty of workspaces. Val surveyed what she had to work with and quickly knew that nothing had changed in the decades that had passed. Val had become accustomed to instant pots and espresso machines, gadgets that made things faster. There were no shiny gadgets here. There was cast iron and a sink that outlasted every fruit, vegetable, herb, and dish washed there. The cooktop was ahead of its time with an indoor grill. The counter combined a butcher block wood with natural stone. The handmade wood table had stools to match. She took it all in and smiled realizing she had lost touch with the food itself, with the very source of the point, and with the joy of the work. They would be doing this all the "old fashioned" way. Intentional. Connected. Feeling every ingredient.

Flor was waiting for her with the same gleam in her eyes. Val wasn't sure she had aged at all. To Val's childhood eyes, she had always seemed old in a grandmotherly way. But she hadn't changed. This was the image that came in Val's dreams. Grandmother opened her arms. Val smiled and went in tentatively for the hug. Grandmother held her with such certainty and warmth that Val melted.

"You have always been right here, child." Tears began to flow from unexpected depths. Val felt nine years old again, being held in a love she had been afraid to feel for decades. Grandmother Flor was once again real, once again an adored and trusted family member, once again her grandmother—the only one she had ever known.

Words slipped from Val's lips. "I missed you so much."

Grandmother held her just another minute and then gently pushed her to arm's length, put her right hand on the center of Val's chest and looked her in the eyes. "I am always right here."

Val nodded, understanding the words and hoping for their manifestation.

It was time to get to work. Grandmother pointed at the pile of potatoes, corn, onions, herbs, peppers, and greens. Val smiled and rolled up her sleeves. Flor watched carefully and Val caught her look as well as the memory that came. "First, we praise the bounty with joy, appreciation, and gratitude for the abundance. Then we clean and prep the vegetables," she heard it clearly in her mind in Grandmother's voice.

"What a beautiful assortment of plants. We are fortunate to have such abundance. Thank you. It is a joy to prepare this meal of good fortune to share with so many," Val announced. This was the game they played when she was a child, and only now did Val realize the power of the words. "I am truly grateful and honored." She looked into Grandmother Flor's eyes as they gleamed approval.

"You see, you *do* remember," Flor challenged Val's story of forgetting.

Val stayed quiet and heard the words in her heart again. "You do remember." It felt like an incantation, summoning ancient memories and magical secrets long buried. She hoped it worked. Peace washed over her, only to be replaced suddenly by a bolt of fear and doubt and the edge she knew well.

"Why are you so quick to reject the peace that came?" Flor asked gently.

Val wasn't sure what she meant.

Grandmother Flor cleaned and cut the potatoes. She had a way with them that was both gentle and effective, her movements graceful, her knife cuts rhythmic.

"Did I ever tell you about the warrior who couldn't find his courage?" Val shook her head, though she wasn't sure as Grandmother used to tell many stories.

Grandmother spoke as she chopped, "He was very distraught. In truth, he was angry because without his courage, he knew his fear. He began to fear that he wasn't a warrior anymore.

"He looked everywhere, in all the cupboards and under the sink. He suspected others. His neighbors. Even his friends. One day he was so angered by not being able to find it that he slammed the door, causing a mirror to fall off the wall. He looked down at the broken mirror and saw his reflections looking back at him. Pieces of him. All gave him an image but none that was whole. He searched the reflections and then gathered the pieces carefully until he had them all. He tried to piece them back together, but then the reflection became worse, fractured and distorted. He wrapped the pieces and shards in a cloth and carried them to the home of the healer who lived through the woods and by the lake.

"The healer didn't answer the knock. The warrior heard something by the lake. He went to look but saw nothing. He heard it again. This time it was a loud shriek. He dropped the cloth of mirror pieces. When he bent down to pick them up, he saw his reflection in the water. His image shifted—strong, confident, clear but then blurry, smaller, afraid, and back again. He recognized the strong image as himself. As he did, a bear emerged in the image behind him. He held his gaze and did not turn around. The image of the bear dissolved and the healer stood behind him.

"The healer said, 'You did not lose anything. You just forgot where to look. The truth is always inside of you.'

"The warrior turned to face the healer and asked, 'But why did I feel I lost it?'

"The healer answered, 'Looking elsewhere will always create confusion. Nothing of you can be outside of yourself. You cannot put together broken pieces of a mirror and expect to see something whole. Pieces only show pieces. Your courage was never the absence of fear. Only fear could tell you otherwise. Were you afraid when the bear appeared?' The warrior nodded. 'Why didn't you run? Because courage is a part of you that can never be separate. Courage rises because fear calls it.'"

Val listened while she chopped the onions and vegetables for the salad. She tried to remember if she had heard that story before. If felt so familiar. "Courage rises because fear calls it." Grandmother Flor put the potatoes in the pot to boil and started to hum while she made the dough for flatbreads. Her hands knobbed with strength and age, her voice elixir to memories. "Hmm-hmmm-mmm, hmmmm, hmmm-hmm-mm, hmmmmmm…" Every so often, Val would notice Grandmother Flor watching her as she hummed.

When Val was fifteen and Emmet was out of town for a few days, Valerie went into town to run errands for her mother. Grandmother Flor found Valerie at the market and had Val "help" to carry her bags home. Val knew her mom wouldn't mind since Emmet was gone. Her heart raced at seeing Grandmother Flor again. Since Emmet had moved them to the edge of town and had been around more to control her, she didn't get to spend much time with the matriarch. As they walked to Grandmother's house, Flor told a story about a young warrioress who had to travel far from home.

"The young warrioress was forced to leave her family to protect them. At first, the warrioress was sad and angry because it didn't feel fair. She wandered and tried to understand if she could have done anything differently. She hated the chief who had caused her to leave. While she was gone, she learned many things. She learned that she could be strong in ways she hadn't dreamed of. She learned she could inspire others and lead them well. She learned her value to others and many of her gifts.

"As time went on, she became numb and closed off. Despite all that she had learned, she was disconnected from her family, all the ones she truly loved. She tried to reach them and send them messages, but felt they had moved on without her. She felt separate and rejected and alone. She became busier in her new life and stopped trying to reach her family until she had herself convinced that her past was little more than a fairytale. One day her mind wouldn't focus on work, only on the hummingbird dancing around the flowers. This was when the memories began to whisper. She began to dream again, big dreams she didn't understand with people she might have known.

"She received a message from her family and learned that they had been waiting so long they weren't sure for what. She returned to answer the call and found her old self there to greet her, so glad for all that she had gone out to learn. She would need those skills now."

Val lost herself in the memory of that story as she realized for the first time that it had been a foretelling. On the verge of tears, she stopped chopping and looked up at Grandmother. "How?"

"My dear child, our paths are chosen before we come. There was never a time when you were not walking."

Val felt like she was spinning. Thoughts of the past circled in her mind. Her father's lessons. Her mother's choice of Emmet as a replacement husband. Emmet's meanness and dictatorial ways. The other kids. Having to leave home at seventeen. She never felt like she was walking. It was either running with terror or standing still, immovable. Val's thoughts were interrupted by Grandmother Flor, "Tell me, why do you think you left Star Junction?"

"Because Emmet didn't want us here. He was an abusive control freak and a drunk who ruled over his family with meanness and fear. Because he didn't want to compete with my father's memory."

Flor continued, gently, "Then, when you left the family a year later, why didn't you come here?" It felt like an invitation as she looked into Val's eyes.

Val was confused by the question. "Well, because—I don't know. Mom arranged for me to go to California with Uncle Ray. She made the plans. It didn't seem like an option. Maybe she thought Emmet would find me here."

"No, child. You did not return because you were not meant to at that time. You were meant to go to California, to study, to learn, to build a life. You were meant to do everything you did there."

"But why? Why couldn't I have created a life here?"

"Because that was not your path. And because you would not have been equipped to do all that you have now come back to do. Your experience trained you and prepared you to be here now. To unite this family. To shepherd Jacob, Alex, Cade, Lilah, and Melanie too, when she is ready. This is the time to utilize all that you have learned and created—for you, for your family, for Star Junction."

"But I have no idea what I am doing." Val felt overwhelmed.

Grandmother smiled and responded, "Your mind doesn't know, but your heart does. This is why you are being helped to remember." They worked silently for a bit as Val let things soak in.

The aromas of the meal signaled Lucy to come and help carry the food to the outdoor table. Grandmother Flor put her hand on Val's arm and stopped her from following.

"Before you moved away, you climbed the mountain and buried something."

Val nodded.

"Soon, you will climb again to reclaim it. It will help you." Val swallowed as she nodded. She knew she wasn't ready for Clarity Mountain. She also knew that if Grandmother Flor spoke it, she would be facing the challenge soon.

***

Thirty Years Ago—Clarity Mountain

There it was. The hawk had shown her the quick route. Val took her shoes off and walked the perimeter of the circle of perspective with Cade following her footsteps. She entered from the east and went to the center. Val kneeled and opened her backpack. She pulled out an apple and half of the crackers and placed them in the center. Cade had heard about this but hadn't seen it before. He watched quietly but wanted so much to know what she was doing.

"You know they call this Clarity Mountain. Now you've seen part of why. There is no single path to the top. It always changes. The top gifts us with the Circle of Perspective. To see from all directions and to have vision and understanding. Reaching the center requires letting go of the thoughts and emotions that cloud our vision. When we release those, we can see the path. It is good to leave an offering of gratitude. Gratitude itself is enough." Cade knelt down and closed his eyes. Val looked around for the spot in her dreams—a small nook between boulders and trees. Not really big enough for resting but perfect to hold and protect a treasure. When Cade stood up, they headed to it, and she pulled a spade out of her backpack. "Cade, find some flat rocks that are not stacked."

"What are those?" He pointed at the stacked rocks that were marking different places on the plateau.

"They are called apachetas. People leave them to always remember a spot and have the spot always remember them."

"Can I do one, too?"

"We will join them together." She dug a hole deep enough for her bundle and then kept going. She felt the deeper, the better for its protection, but in truth, that was her own anxiety. She knew the mountain would protect it for her. She held her bundle to her chest and then her forehead, kissed it and placed it in the hole. She began to fill in the dirt.

"Wait!" Cade ran over and pulled the totem that William had carved for him when he was born from his pocket. It was a beautiful wolf. William was a master carver.

"Cade, are you sure?"

"Yes." Val backed away and gave him space. He did what he saw her do and then placed his wolf on top of her bundle. Together they filled in the dirt and packed it so that no one could tell it had ever been disturbed. They stacked their apachetas together just outside the nook, and said a prayer of protection and remembrance.

"Make sure you remember this spot. Pay attention to which side we are on and what is around it. Some of it will change before we can return, so this is for us to remember and so it remembers us."

Present Day—Dinner in the Courtyard

Edward, Lucy, and Lucy's kids were already at the patio table when Val and Grandmother joined them. Alex and Jake were just taking their seats.

Val introduced them, "Jake, I think you already know each other. Alex, this is Grandmother Flor, Mr. Edward's mother."

Alex froze when he saw her. He tried to nod but couldn't.

"Alex, thank you for coming all this way. It is an honor to have you with us." Grandmother noticed his reaction to her and hoped to break the trance with kind diversion. "I can see your grandfather in you. Yes, and Cade."

Alex perked up a bit, smiling that he might look like his grandfather and father.

"Thank you." His voice was quieter than usual, but the words came out. "It's nice to meet you."

Flor smiled. "Now that we are all seated, let us give thanks for this bountiful meal and cherished family. Please enjoy." She gestured with her hands that they should begin eating.

Edward led the way.

After the meal, Val sat on the patio and watched the kids resume their game as she soaked in the peace. Her mind continued to tell her that she had work to catch up on, but she couldn't seem to compel herself to move. Edward sat next to her, and they watched for a while in silence.

"I remember I called you Uncle." She startled herself by speaking. "You were, I guess are, my beloved uncle." He gently placed his hand on hers. "I'm really not sure why I stopped, but I think it was when Papa died."

"Yes, that is what I remember."

"I was confused about what his death meant. I'm so sorry. Why didn't anyone correct me?"

"There was no need to correct you. You were navigating new waters and defining new boundaries for yourself that felt safe."

"But I was never not safe with you," she declared.

"Feeling close to someone, being attached and losing them does not feel safe to a young child. You had just lost your father. Your fear guided you to create distance between you and others—for what was to come."

"You've never stopped being my beloved uncle, in my heart or memory."

"True, I have never stopped. You are family and can have it no other way." He smiled and winked.

EIGHT

Val woke up with a start. She looked around the room trying to orient herself. Not home. Not the motel. She closed her eyes and took a slow breath to find herself in it. The memories flooded back as if they were all happening again, all at the same time, washing over her and thrashing about.

For the first time in years, she put her hand on her heart and started speaking to her father, "Papa, I hear you. Please forgive me for forgetting, for not listening. Are you still there?" She listened.

"Picaflor, enjoy the nectar that you are cultivating. You are fierce and wise. Let yourself guide the wolf and the eagle. The little hummingbird is coming soon. Let the eagle sing with the drum while you dance with the sun."

Val wasn't sure what it all meant, but she somehow trusted that she would. She closed her eyes and smiled, feeling into the message. *"Dance with the sun? Father, you always liked your riddles."*

Alex was up with the sun and ready to go. He had a hard time waiting for others to wake up, so the sketchpad had become a morning necessity. Val encouraged Alex to sketch his dreams and whatever else came to him while waiting for others to get up. She hoped it would help him to understand his dreams better and not be afraid of them. He quietly picked up his sketchpad and pencils and found a place to be. This morning's choice was the kitchen table, and the drawings were fast and furious. Val found him busily drawing and realized she may need to invest in a bulk pack of sketchpads.

She sat next to him and motioned to ask if she could see what he was working on. He held up his hand as if to say, "Wait—not done."

She felt he was such an amazing kid. She didn't know the whole story with her brother, his deceased wife, or the new ex-girlfriend. She just knew her brother asked for help and this kid was special—though she may need to start drinking more coffee to keep up with him.

It took a few moments for her eyes to adjust to the drawing. It was a detailed dimensional drawing that required focus. "Alex, this is amazing. Tell me about it."

He looked at her for a moment as if deciding and then pointed to different elements on the page. "The mountain is pulsing. I don't know if that is the right word. But it's like, alive. There is an eagle here, flying above. I'm not sure what this is. It wasn't clear, but I think it's an animal." He was pointing to a fuzzy object near the mountain.

Val pointed to another small spot, and he answered, "This part feels like an opening. That is the joy coming, but I don't know what that means. They are all coming for the mountain, helping. And that's you." He pointed to what looked like a vortex point or tornado.

"That?" she asked, bemused.

"Yes, that's you." Her lines extended through the page. She would have to sit with that one.

"Thank you for sharing this, Alex. I love how you see things."

Thirty Years Ago—Star Junction

"But it is so far away." Grace's voice was pleading. Val came home from school to find Grace and Emmet talking in the kitchen. Emmet usually worked until after five o'clock, so Val was cautious and stayed out of view.

"Doesn't matter," said Emmet. "I am the man of this family. I provide. I decide."

Val's heart sank as panic coursed through her. What were they talking about? She only knew it wasn't good. Emmet stormed out of the kitchen door, likely to the bar. When he was gone, Val quietly entered the kitchen where her mother was crying.

"Mama?" Grace stopped crying immediately and tried to act as if everything was okay.

"Val, I didn't hear you come in." She stood up and moved about the kitchen as if in a hurry to cook dinner for imaginary guests.

Val moved closer and hugged her from behind.

"He is moving us away to Phoenix. We have two weeks." They stood there quietly, Val holding Grace, her head resting gently on Grace's shoulder. Grace always hid her tears and was grateful that Val did not force her to turn around.

"It will be okay," she whispered to Grace without certainty. She wanted to say, "Let him leave without us." She wanted to say, "We don't need him; we are better without him." She wanted to yell it and scream and beg, but she knew Grace would not leave him. Val truly didn't understand why.

Present Day—Star Junction

Val and Jake took a walk around Star Junction while Alex helped Mr. Edward with a project, hoping, of course, to learn more about the eye and the mysterious things in the shop. Val wanted time for her and Jake to get to know each other. The walk was quiet—excruciatingly so—until Val caught Jake looking into Bishop's Music shop as they walked past.

"Do you want to go in?"

He shrugged, not wanting to let on that he thought about this store all the time and that all he wanted to do was play music. She led the way. Jake looked at the guitars, letting his fingers glide over the curves of the body and frets up the neck. The shop owner, Daniel, saw him and came over.

"Jake, good to see you again buddy! How do you like your guitar?" Jake's face dropped.

"Uh, I don't have it anymore, but it was real nice."

"Oh, that's too bad. Well, let me know when you are ready for a new one. It'd be a shame for you not to play."

Jake smiled slightly.

Daniel handed him a guitar to try out. Val stepped away to give Jake a little room to breathe and be himself. She looked around the shop and found the old photos on the wall. This was the music shop William had brought her to as a child. Jake sat down on the stool and started strumming. It was pretty and reminded her of a song her papa used to play. Jake just hummed lightly, no words.

Daniel approached Val. "Are you William's daughter?"

Val hadn't been asked that since she was a child. "Yes, I'm Val. Jake's aunt."

"Yeah, I thought so. I'm Daniel. You probably don't remember me. This was my grandfather's shop. I was just a kid when your family left town. But, well, Edward tells good stories."

Val smiled. "That he does." They both laughed while Jake played. "I used to come here with my father all the time. And Mr. Edward."

She looked around with nostalgia. "It brings back so many memories. And I do remember you!" She held out her hand to indicate how tall she remembered him being.

"Yeah, my grandfather had a way of bringing people in. I think all the musicians used to rehearse here."

"Yes! They did." She turned to him with pause. "They don't now?"

"Not so much. Things have changed a bit."

Jake's playing got a little louder and more confident and Val's attention went there. "Where did he learn to play?"

"He's really good, right?" Daniel answered. "He's a natural. I gave him a few lessons when they first moved here. He picked it up so fast—like he was born knowing how to play. Sissy bought him a used guitar. Said it was a special gift. I'm really surprised he doesn't still have it. He carried it with him everywhere. It was a really nice one."

"He's had a rough year. Daniel, after we leave, please pick out a guitar for him—one that matches his talent. I'll be back to get it."

Eighteen Months Ago

"This is Val," she answered the phone without looking.

"Hi. It's Sissy."

"Oh, Sissy, sorry. I guess I am in work mode! How are you?" Val was genuinely glad to hear from her. She had tried to call so many times, but Sissy was always "busy," so they rarely talked. Val had stopped trying.

"I'm good. I didn't mean to bother you. I guess you're busy," Sissy replied.

"No, it's fine. Talk to me. I miss you."

Sissy didn't know how to find the words she wanted, so she found different ones. "I miss you too. Everything is fine. We're doing good, you know."

Val could hear the tone in Sissy's voice—the bits of hesitation and inflections that Sissy had had since childhood and always said so much more than her words. "Sis, are you okay?"

"Of course! Just a little tired, I guess. It's nothing. How are you? How is California?" Sissy just couldn't voice the truth of why she had called. Her resolve shut down as soon as Val answered, and she didn't know how to start it up again.

"Well, I'm okay. I just keep busy with work. It is beautiful here. Do you want to come visit? See the ocean? Jake would probably love it. Sis, I would love to see you."

Sissy's mind had wandered. She wondered how Val would react when she showed up with an extra child. Why hadn't she told her? "Oh, Val, that sounds nice. We'll see how it goes. Anyway, I should go."

"Sissy, are you sure you are okay? You sound a little off."

"You don't know everything, big sis. I'm fine. We're fine. We'll talk again later."

***

Present Day—Star Junction

"You play great." Val was hoping to get Jake talking, but he just shrugged. "Did you used to play for your mom?"

He looked at Val and then looked away. "Yeah, we would sing together. You know, sometimes. Lilah, too." He wasn't ready. He looked through the window of the ice cream shop.

"Chocolate or vanilla?"

"What?"

"What's your flavor? Are you a chocolate guy? A vanilla guy? Or maybe, something a little more exciting?" Val prodded playfully.

He rewarded her with a grin. "Coffee mocha chip and peanut butter chocolate swirl." He opened the door.

Now walking with ice cream cones in hand, his a double-scoop, they continued. This time, he started.

"Where do you live?"

"Near Los Angeles in California."

"So you're planning to move us there?" He was still feeling her out, still deciding if she could be trusted, if she can be cared about.

"Honestly, I don't know what we will do. I don't know yet what will be best."

"But don't you have a job?"

"Yes, I own two companies. You've seen me on my laptop. Fortunately, I can work from anywhere, most of the time. Even here."

"Wow. So are you rich?"

"I guess it depends on who you ask. I work extremely hard and am constantly busy and very fortunate. My companies are successful." Val didn't mind answering his questions; at least it was engagement.

"Is that why you stayed away?" He tried to be neutral, but the edge in his tone commanded Val's attention.

"What do you mean?"

"You stayed away from here, from us. Mom said you were always busy, and a few other things." He baited her.

"Hmmm. Well, our family moved away from Star Junction to Phoenix when I was sixteen and your mom was seven. When I was seventeen, I had to leave home and my family because things were not good for me with your grandfather Emmet. It wasn't safe for me to stay. Your grandma, Grace, sent me to live with Uncle Ray and Aunt Beth. It was the hardest thing I ever did. I tried to stay in touch. I wasn't much older than you are now. The longer I was away, the harder it was to talk and connect. I guess I became better at working than at family-ing. I started to feel like a bit of an outsider, you know? Because I was missing everything." As she spoke, she tried to be thoughtful and intentional. She hadn't told the story in years, so she chose words slowly and carefully, pulling each word like a treasure from a haystack of emotions.

"Is that what happened? I mean, is that when you stopped being close?"

Val paused before answering. The move to Phoenix changed the family in ways they struggled to understand. Despite Grace's and Val's efforts, something shifted between them all. They no longer fit. Cade got moodier and more distracted. Sissy withdrew into herself more and Melanie got louder. Val stopped pretending with Emmet. She openly ignored him, stepped in often to defy him and protect the others, and wore her contempt in full view. Grace just wasn't the same. Instead of Emmet being happier and more secure, he had become more demanding and harder to please. Apparently, Star Junction had had a calming effect on him.

"Yes, everything changed when we moved to Phoenix. It's hard to describe, but it felt a bit like the heart was taken out of us. Even Emmet got worse and harder to deal with. It's just my view, but I think it's true. Your grandfather used to drive wedges between us. He would treat your mom and Melanie differently and encourage them to feel different and more entitled. Your mom was the sweetest kid. I think she had started to see through her dad's lies and behavior, but Melanie soaked it up—maybe needed to feel special. Anyway, after a year there, it was too much. Emmet was threatening me daily. Your grandmother and I agreed that I should go. I didn't know that she had already made plans for me to stay with Uncle Ray and Aunt Beth in California. It was a gift, truly, but at seventeen, absolutely heartbreaking to lose my family." She stopped talking. She really didn't want to continue down this road.

"Mom was seventeen, too. When she moved out. That's what she told me."

"I had forgotten that. I think you're right, though. It didn't end up being easier for her, unfortunately. At least she stayed close with the rest of the family."

"Mom thought you didn't accept her, you know."

"What do you mean?"

"I mean, I heard her tell Aunt Melanie not to tell you about my dad because she didn't want to 'hear it from you.' Like you would judge her and wouldn't understand."

Val's eyes closed; she took a deep breath to collect herself and sat on the nearest bench. "Wow, that makes me sad. Your mom was so beautiful. She loved deeply and with fierceness. She poured so much of herself into others that she didn't have much left. That is what I tried to tell her—to take care of herself, too. To put herself and you before any others. The last time we spoke, I felt like she was trying to tell me something, but she couldn't. Instead, she told me how great everything was. Maybe she was trying to prove me wrong. I probably said the wrong thing way too often. She was angry with me when I told her I didn't think she should take your father back. Maybe she never forgave me."

Val was ignoring her ice cream as it dripped down her fingers. She couldn't find the "right" words. They sat in silence until the words found Jake.

"You were right," he said, pausing to look at her. "About my dad." Despite his anger and lack of trust in adults, Jake was inherently honest and saw with precision. "It didn't last long. One day I saw him drive by from the playground. I knew something was wrong. I ran as fast as I could. By the time I got home, I found him attacking her."

He slowed his words, and looked away from Val. "She was on the floor, bleeding, broken eggs all over that she dropped when he pushed her. He was so drunk—if she had seen him coming, she could have gotten away." Jake took a beat to calm himself. "We kicked him out and moved across town for a couple of years. Then moved again, to this place." They walked together in silence. "I think he would have killed her if we hadn't moved." They both held those words in a hard pause. "It seemed like everything was better up here, but then she got sick."

"I'm sorry, Jake. I wish..." her voice paused and cracked a little. "I wish we had never gotten so disconnected. If I had known your mom was sick—" she cut herself off again and changed course. "She deserved better." Val needed to lift the mood. "When your mom was a kid, she had the funniest laugh. It would start as this little snickering sound that would end in a snort, which she would find hilarious and would burst into uncontrollable giggles. When she laughed, we all laughed until we cried."

Jake lit up. "It sounded like a sheep motor!" They both laughed. "She could always make me laugh," he added.

"It was one of her superpowers," Val concluded.

Jake liked that idea and nodded. They walked over to the fountain and rinsed their hands from the ice cream drips. "Mom told me once that you used to sing to her when she was little. That's why she sang to me. When she couldn't sleep or was scared, you would sneak in and sing to her because somehow you just knew. I guess we all sing that way." She smiled warmly at the thought.

They headed back to the gas station to collect Alex from Edward. It had been a full conversation, and Val thought it was a miracle that Jake was finally talking—even though she wasn't always sure how to respond. On the way, Jake stopped walking and paused.

"They took it from me. The first foster family when Mom died. They took my guitar, and then the man from children's services took Lilah. And I hate them for that."

Val bit her tongue and just listened. The ways she learned as a child were coming back to her, little bits at a time. She listened and waited.

"I hated everybody, including you. But maybe you're not who I thought I hated." He looked her in the eye when he said it, and Val felt so grateful for his words but uncertain she deserved his forgiveness. As they walked Val remembered the day her siblings found out they were moving away from Star Junction.

Thirty Years Ago—Star Junction

After school, Cade, Sissy, and Melanie sat at the kitchen table to do their homework. This always came in the hour before dinner, giving Grace time with them before Emmet came home. As she prepared dinner, the kids did their homework. Val sometimes sat at the table but often helped with the dinner and helped the others with their assignments. Sissy would worry about not being able to write neatly enough or draw a good enough picture. Melanie would roll her eyes and scribble away at her work. Cade would ache to be outside playing and spent the time doodling the activities he wished to be doing like climbing trees, skateboarding, and playing basketball.

"Okay, it's time," was Grace's big announcement. It was time for each of them to share the favorite part of their day. "Whose turn is it to go first?"

It was Sissy's turn, but she didn't jump in. Grace and Val exchanged glances as they waited. Sissy was usually ready with a handful of favorites and always wanted to go first. She squirmed and stared at her unfinished homework.

"Sis? You, okay?" Val inquired, but Sissy just shrugged and kept looking down. Melanie rolled her eyes and jumped in.

"She's just sad because kids were making fun of, um, were being mean." Sissy glared at her. "Can I go instead?"

"You have to wait your turn," Grace replied.

"But Sissy doesn't want hers!" Melanie persisted.

"Melanie, I am looking forward to your turn, but first we are sitting with Sissy and giving her a chance to share."

When Grace spoke this way, the kids knew to stop pushing. It wasn't that she would get angry or punish them. It was that she wouldn't budge. She was simply stating how things would go, and further argument would be futile. Grace nodded to Val to sit with Sissy. Val pulled up the chair next to her and nudged Sissy playfully with her shoulder.

"Hey!" she whispered loudly. "Spill the beans." She'd bounce her shoulder into Sissy's, or say, "I'm going to make you laugh!" Sissy tilted her head to the side and let out a sigh and a slight giggle. "That's better. What's got you down?"

"I don't like my teachers anymore. And my classmates are mean." Grace and Val exchanged glances.

"Okay. Tell us more."

"Miss Riley was talking with other teachers outside the classroom." They waited through each long pause after every sentence.

"We all heard them. They were talking about us, about Daddy, about *'alcolic'* or something like that. And they said it was just as well that we were moving away." Sissy's face had never looked so dark and serious. "Then some kids started saying mean things, calling me names. Why? I didn't do anything to them!" And the tears flooded out.

Val hugged her tightly. Grace washed her hands and went over to Sissy, leaned down, and kissed her on the head.

"Sweet Sissy, please let those words fall away from you now. The teachers made a mistake."

"But are we moving?" All of the kids looked at Grace.

"I am sorry to say, yes. Your father got a new job."

Val had known the news, yet bristled when Grace said *your father.* She let the words go by her and rallied for her sister. "Sissy Sunshine, the keyword is 'we.' *We* will still be together."

Sissy looked up at Val and Grace. "I guess this is my favorite part of the day." And she squeezed Val back. She didn't feel much better, but she didn't want to talk about it anymore. Val whispered, "*We,*" into her ear again and Sissy smiled.

"Can I go now?" Melanie didn't waste a second.

Present Day—Star Junction

Alex had asked if he could help Edward at the mini-mart in exchange for more information about the Eye of the Mountain and to learn anything else he could. Mr. Edward showed Alex the backroom and suggested it would be helpful if Alex opened some of the boxes that had arrived in the days before.

"It would be very helpful, young Alex, to know what is in these boxes and have them properly addressed." Edward was playful as ever. "Otherwise, the backroom may never be clean again." He winked and left Alex to it.

Alex dove into the task, convinced that treasures were waiting. The first few boxes were a little disappointing. They had keychains, postcards, and travel-sized sundries. He quickly found places for them on the shelves and kept going. The fourth box made up for all of that. As Alex dug through the layers of the box, he found a huge crystal cluster.

"*Wow!*" It was bigger than his head, had three larger crystal points pointing up but slightly angled, and a couple dozen smaller crystal points of varying sizes all clustered around as if forming a base for the larger ones. It was mostly clear except one of the crystals seemed to have purple and gold floating through it. It was heavy! He discovered more crystals in that box and the others. Alex peeked out onto the sales floor.

"Mr. Edward?" Edward looked over from the front counter. "Um, I'm not sure what to do with a couple of things. Can you help?"

"Of course, thank you for asking."

Edward walked to the back, saw Alex's work so far, and smiled. "You've been working hard."

"Yeah." Alex smiled and shrugged. "It's kinda fun. I found these giant crystals, but I'm not sure where to put them. Unless I move the books over to that shelf." He pointed.

"That would be a fine idea, but the crystals are meant for the sales floor. We will find space together. They should be in a location where the sunlight comes in to find them."

"We could put them on the shelf where the maps are. They'll get lots of sun there."

"Agreed. Where should we put the maps?" asked Edward.

"Umm, near the magazines?"

"Yes!" Edward showed more enthusiasm than usual. Alex wasn't sure if he was serious or just playing with him. "Shall we get started?"

"Okay." Alex followed Edward to the maps, and they filled a cardboard bin with them. They walked over to the magazines and books and started moving them to make space. Edward hummed as he worked. Alex began placing the stacked maps onto the shelf. As he lifted a stack, a couple fell out. He reached down to get them and noticed they were different. *Maps to the Watcher*, *The Secret of Star Junction* and *Guide to the Stars*. "Where do these go?" Edward just watched him as his eyes grew and his imagination sparked.

"I will tell you when we are finished. Just set them aside. First, we must bring out the crystals. Take the rag and clean off that shelf, and I will carry them."

Alex hopped to. He couldn't wait to see the crystals in the sunlight. Edward returned with the largest of the crystals. As he carefully removed it from the box, he closed his eyes briefly. "Great Spirit, thank you for this blessed crystal stargate. May it guide us all well." His hand went north, east, south, and west and then spiraled his blessing over the top.

He nodded at Alex to help him lift and place it carefully in the center of the highest shelf. Edward then turned it slightly to adjust the direction of the large points. Alex watched in awe. Edward nodded and smiled with satisfaction. "Let's get the others."

They worked in silence, placing all the crystal points. Alex carefully unwrapped each one and handed them to Edward, who, in turn, found the perfect placement for each. They were on the last shelf when Edward spoke again. "Crystals are beautiful reminders of light and powerful conductors. The maps you found are for you. They will help you understand where you are."

Alex's excitement quickly transformed into perplexity. "What do you mean where I am?"

"Our town is not just named Star Junction, young wolf. It *is* a star junction—a place where stars come together for us. There is much to learn from the wisdom in the skies."

Alex waited for him to continue, but Edward finished placing the crystals in silence. When he was done, Edward spoke again.

"Close your eyes."

"Why?"

"Because you wish to understand more."

Alex obeyed and squeezed his eyes shut.

Edward laughed. "Not so tightly! Just as if you wish to feel something without your eyes."

Alex's eyes softened.

Edward lifted Alex's hand. "Relax."

And his arm softened too.

Edward slowly guided his hand over the crystals, starting with the smaller ones on the lower shelves.

Alex's eyes were darting under his eyelids. His breathing became deeper.

"Feel." Edward moved his hand to the next shelf and then to the top. Alex started to pull his hand back, so Edward waited for Alex to soften again. "Do not be afraid of what you feel. There is no danger here."

"It's... What is it?"

"Energy. Light energy. You feel the energy's vibration."

"Wow, cool. What does it mean?"

Edward was amused by the question. He paused briefly and then quipped, "It means you are alive."

Later that evening Jake was in the courtyard petting Blu, the cattle dog. Edward was watering plants and saw him.

"Would you like to play it?" Jake had been eyeing Edward's guitar in the courtyard for days. He looked up when Edward asked.

"Can I?" Edward smiled and nodded.

"Of course. I would like to hear you play if that is okay with you."

Jake shrugged. The desire to play was greater than the discomfort of someone else listening. Besides, he was starting to like Edward. Jake jumped up, went to the guitar, and gently picked it up like it was a delicate, long-lost treasure, meant to be treated gently and with reverence. That was music for him—something that transformed and transcended, not that he would use those words.

Some might say that Jake would quickly lose himself in the sounds as he is transported into a different space and time. Edward would say that he would find himself in it. Jake ran his hand along the length of the instrument, his soul asking permission with his careful beginning. The purity of his intentions was made clear with each moment of communion. Then he sat with the guitar and began to play each string, checking the sound and feeling the vibration it created in the body.

Edward continued with his work in the courtyard while he listened to what moved through Jake. After a while, he felt Jake's attention return to him. Jake was, in fact, watching Edward. "How did you know my mom?"

Edward stopped what he was doing and sat across from Jake. "I knew your mom, and your aunts and uncle when they were children. I knew your Aunt Val best, I suppose. She is the oldest, and I played the role of uncle to her then."

"But then my grandfather made them move away?"

"Yes. Emmet did not understand life here nor the connection we all had to each other. I think your mom was probably a little older than Lilah is now when they left here."

"But if they left, why did you still care? I mean, people forget and move on."

"I suppose some people do. Could you? When you were in the foster house, did you think about leaving? Running away?"

"Yeah, I wanted to."

"But you didn't. Why?"

"Lilah. I couldn't leave without Lilah."

"Then you understand. You are not strangers to me, or to any of us here. You are family. When your mother's family moved away, we felt the loss and hoped for the time in which they would return. We don't forget because we are still connected in spirit. Our souls know each other. Something in your mom's soul brought her back here, and even though you had never been here before, something in your soul was a part of that decision. The part of you that feels at ease, as if you can breathe without being on guard all the time, the part that finds himself in the music you play is the part that knows it is home."

Jake gave a little smile as he realized it was true. "Yeah, I guess I do. It feels kind of crazy, though."

Edward let out a generous laugh and stood up. "Ha! What is wrong with a little crazy?" He winked as he left the courtyard. "Home is home. There are no rules about sane, serious, or even normal."

Jake scoffed a little with a smile. He hoped it was true, hoped he could trust the feelings of home, hoped Aunt Val would let them stay, and hoped more than anything that Lilah would walk into the court-yard right now, so then, maybe, he could trust that they were home.

CHAPTER
NINE

Thirty-Eight Years Ago—Star Junction

"*Take off your shoes.*"

Valerie had become cranky and tired. She started complaining in a whiny voice that William had not heard often. Even at eight years old, she rarely whined. She was in love with life and the world. Her curiosity never stopped, and her discovery of little miracles in nature never ceased. The father and daughter were on one of their hikes. Instead of her steady flow of questions and joyful discoveries, Valerie's head was low. Her shoulders drooped, and her arms hung and swung in a dramatic fashion.

They had been hiking every weekend now and sometimes after school. Valerie loved the hikes but felt something was wrong that her parents weren't telling her. Last night she dreamed that she was hiking without her father; she desperately tried to find him, but he was nowhere to be found. It left her troubled and feeling vulnerable and unsure. William watched as his daughter worked her way into a meltdown. She let out a big, dramatic sigh and grunt, stomped a little, walked into branches, and tripped. "Stupid tree!"

William stopped walking; he just watched her with love, always with love. Valerie went into a full pout. He tried speaking to her heart, but she couldn't hear him. So he spoke aloud. "Picaflor, take off your shoes." She looked at him like he was crazy.

"I don't want to take off my shoes."

He stood quietly and waited for her to comply. She squirmed, pouted, sighed while sneaking looks at him to see if he was watching. He was. He watched her closely with patience and perhaps the slightest amusement. William had never seen his daughter in such a state. It was good for her to experience. Valerie found herself leaning against a boulder. William sat on the boulder across the path. He removed his eyes from her and took in the view.

"It is a beautiful day, Picaflor. You are missing it."

The pressure was too much. She slid down the rock to the earth and cried. She didn't know why, which made it feel worse. William hummed her song. She cried into her knees until she wasn't crying anymore. She took in a huge breath that shook as it came in as if sucking oxygen from the earth herself. She found the courage to look up at her father. She had never felt she needed courage for that before, but somehow shame had found a way in. William gave her a kind smile, reassuring her that she would be okay. She saw that he had taken his shoes off. She took another deep breath, this one easier, and slipped her shoes off her feet. She stuffed her socks inside her shoes and wiggled her toes in the dirt like her father was doing. She couldn't help but giggle as the soft dirt fell between her toes and tickled.

"I'm sorry, Daddy."

"Why are you sorry, Valerie?"

She looked down at the earth. "That I was unhappy and crying."

"Sweet girl, don't apologize for having feelings. Our feelings are information for us to pay attention to. Crying is cleansing." He let her ponder this as her feet played with the dirt. "Do you know why you were upset?"

"I dreamed that I couldn't find you again. I was hiking alone in the mountains and I called you and called you but you weren't there."

William waited for her to find all of the words.

She furrowed her brow and squirmed a bit on the ground before quietly confessing, "I couldn't hear you. In my heart, I couldn't hear you today. I'm sorry, Papa."

Listen again, Picaflor. She looked up at him with eyes open wide. "You couldn't hear me because of all the thoughts and fear in your head. They are like heavy armor, and the more you listen to them, the heavier they become. When they become too heavy, they muffle our heart and distract us so much we think we can't hear."

She nodded.

"So what do we do when that happens? How do we cleanse those thoughts and connect to our heart again?"

Val's attention went to her feet playing in the dirt, making angel wings. She began to smile. "We take off our shoes," she said as her smile grew.

"And?"

"Feel?"

"Yes, Picaflor. You were not yourself this morning. Whenever you feel that you are not yourself, you can reconnect by connecting to the earth, she is our mother and energy. Ask Spirit and Mother Earth for help. Call to your soul. Call her back to you. And give thanks. And when you forget and it builds so much, let yourself cry and release it that way. God gave us so many tools to help us."

"Papa, are you going away?" William opened his arms to her. She got up and went to him, taking her place on his lap and in his reassuring arms.

"Picaflor, many things will change in this life. And there will be a time when I cannot be with you physically. My body will be gone, but I will always be in your heart. I will always be with you whenever you call to me. When you are yourself, you will be able to hear me."

Valerie was mostly satisfied with his answer but hoped he was talking about a time far, far in the future. She turned in his lap and hugged him fiercely.

"Shall we continue?" William asked.

Valerie got up and went to put her shoes on, but William shook his head. She smiled and put her shoes in his pack. Before they started on their way, she went over to the tree that she had called stupid. "I am sorry I said that. You are not a stupid tree. You are beautiful!" She hugged the tree as the needles rustled.

***

Present Day—Grandmother's Compound, Star Junction

Another week went by without answers about Lilah despite Val's daily calls to Ms. Ramirez. Val was distracted by her work and appeasing a major client with video meetings and personal calls. Alex was spending a lot of time with Edward at the gas station, hoping to learn everything he could about the Eye and the stars.

Jake was bouncing off the walls. He listened to music and got to know the dogs. Blu was a blue healer cattle dog. Foxy and Flex were siblings, a bit smaller than Blu, with too many breeds to count. Leelo was the little one with a sparky personality. Jake seemed to prefer their company but mostly because he was avoiding people.

The more time passed, the more agitated he became. Every day started with him reminding Val that she promised to find Lilah. And every day Val responded with, "I am doing what I can." But Jake couldn't see what she was doing. He didn't know about the phone calls and emails to attorneys and Ms. Ramirez. He only knew that Lilah still wasn't with him. To his view, all Val did was work.

Jake tried to talk to Val twice as she was on her client calls. She waved him off and hoped he understood. After the second time, he watched her through the window like a predator studied its prey. When he saw her finish the call, he pounced. Jake was so focused on Val he didn't notice Alex coming home.

"When are you going to call her?" he demanded.

"Jake, do you really think it would help to call her every hour? It won't. I am doing everything I know to do."

"Then where is Lilah? I thought you were supposed to be some important successful business person. Why can't you get them to give her back? Or maybe you just lied about all that, too."

"That's enough. I know you are frustrated. I am too. But I am doing what I can. I have other responsibilities, too."

"Bull. You're just like the others. You just keep saying stuff you don't mean or don't know. You don't care."

"Jake, I do care. I'm here. I wouldn't be here if I didn't care."

"I don't believe you! You all lie!"

Jake couldn't contain his rage anymore. It just burned through every part of him. Every cell. Every membrane. Every breath. He slammed the door behind him. It didn't matter if Val was telling the truth. It didn't matter if she was doing her best to find Lilah and help. It just didn't. Not in this moment. Not for this release. Sometimes a volcano must erupt. It was the only way for the new terrain to form.

Creation was expression in all of its forms, and it was no different for humans. Nothing new could begin without the flow of expression, whether lava or words, ash or emotions. And people tightened their valves from fear of the very expression that set them free. Containers of pain walked around hoping someone could magically release the pressure inside without setting off the explosion.

Val closed her eyes in that moment and breathed slowly as if understanding despite her own fear, sadness, and heartache. Regrets flowed through the energy currents, pulsing, buzzing. *"What are the energies? Who is speaking?"* Her father's voice came to her.

"Picaflor, who is speaking that thought in your head?" Whenever she was angry or doubting herself, critical or short-tempered, she learned to ask the question, "Who is speaking?"

At seven years old, discovering that the critical voice wasn't *her* voice had made her giggle. It was the most freeing thing. Of course, it was a little confusing at first.

"Picaflor, you must learn to recognize the speaker. If the voice causes you pain, you must identify the source and release it. Anger has a voice. Disappointment has a voice. Fear has a voice. Insecurity has a voice. When you can recognize the source, you can heal and use your true voice or the voice of Source."

Anger was speaking for Jake. Val understood his rage, fear, and longing. Alex wanted to go after him, but Val stopped him.

"Alex, let's give him some time to breathe. He will come back." She realized she knew so little of Jake's story, but she remembered being fifteen.

Alex complied but still wanted to follow. "But what if he doesn't come back? You have to care!" he shouted.

Val held out her arms to Alex. He was still learning to trust and feeling very attached to her and Jake and this new family. Alex missed his dad terribly and his mom more, and he felt so vulnerable to loss and people coming in and out of his life. He accepted her genuine hug allowing the calm that came through to help him.

"Hey, take a breath, okay? Slow, deep, easy. Alex, we will find him."

Val remembered her rage. The rage she tried not to have after William died. The rage that burned with defiance when Emmet entered their lives. It was slow at first, but something in her kept her from ever trusting Emmet. Something warned her to be careful and on guard. It was not her, not fear, nor the rage. It was clear, calm, and reassuring. Something spoke through her heart and she heard it clearly at first. *Be careful.*

But the rage heard it too and fed itself with its warning. She would not be open with this man. She would not give him a chance. She would protect herself, her mother, her brother, and when they came, her half-sisters. By the time she left, she could not see the man nor the soul within. She could only see the entity that she had been fighting off all this time. The man who lied. The man who tricked.

The man with fiery breath who taunted, teased, forced, berated, battered, and dictated.

Thirty Years Ago—Star Junction

Valerie defied Emmet's orders to stay home and any authority he fought to exert. Pretending her compliance was only out of respect for her mother. They all pretended a lot with Emmet, to avoid the anger, threats, and drunken tirades. But sometimes Val could not help herself. She would dig her heels in and stare him down.

She had lost any true willingness to offer kindness or compassion to this man. He had taken away every bit of connection to her father, to her extended family, to the ways her father had taught her, and to the community. Forbidding her to go to the Fire Dance was a straw she wasn't willing to sacrifice. As he left the house after dinner to go drink, he said, "You better be home when I get back."

Grace saw the look in her daughter's eyes. "Valerie, please. Just stay home this time."

At sixteen, Val's will was unflappable.

"Mama, there won't be another one for us. Why aren't you coming? Why have you let him take everything we loved away?"

"We love each other, Valerie. We will always have that."

"I have to go. I'm sorry, Mama." She didn't wait long enough for another word. She didn't know Emmet would get kicked out of the bar that night and would come home to find her gone.

Present Day

After an hour Jake still hadn't returned. Val noticed Alex hovering anxiously. "Okay, Alex, we'll go find him."

They walked through town and around the back of the compound and then to Lucy's restaurant, hoping he might have gone there. Val had kept herself and Alex calm, but that calm was disappearing the longer it took to find him.

"We can't find Jake!" Alex exclaimed to Lucy when they entered the cafe. He couldn't hold it in or be calm. Lucy could feel the anxiety coming from the two.

"I know where he might go," she said as she came around the counter and led the way.

Val knew the house immediately. She knew the front porch with the hand-carved railings and door frame. She knew the tree that greeted them on the path and the bench on the front porch. She knew that the inside had the same attention to detail.

She knew because it had been hers for the first ten years of her life. The beautiful little house had been home for William, Grace, little Valerie and baby Cade. They only moved when Emmet came along.

Val looked at Lucy in disbelief. "This is the house that Sissy owned? This was *our* house!" She couldn't help but believe that Sissy had been guided there. There was no other way. Sissy wouldn't have known the house.

As they walked up the front porch steps, Val could feel William there, sitting in his chair, whistling and whittling. The house had been battered over the years but still stood. It seemed that nobody noticed its abandonment, like a bubble of protection had been put around it. The yard had managed to do for itself. Overgrown had a different look in the high desert. Val asked Alex and Lucy to wait with a gesture and opened the door. It was like walking into a time warp. She saw Sissy's furniture and pictures and stuff overlaid by her memory, her parents at the table, music in the background, the smell of Grace's cookies somehow delicately mixed with freshly smudged sage. She closed her eyes and called herself back. "Hampui Valerie, come back, come back."

The air was stale with the remnants of old food and work unfinished. She walked through to the bedrooms and found Jake in what must have been Sissy's bed, holding her picture. He looked up at Val, his eyes swollen and red, his rage mixed with deep sorrow and softened by exposure to air. Val quietly walked over to him and waited for his nonverbal permission to sit.

She joined him and they sat quietly in this stillness. He noticed the tears that flowed down her cheeks and he softened a little more. They both grieved—him for his mother and sister and the life that Sissy tried so hard to give him, her for her sister, and father, and the life she tried so hard to hold on to. She opened her hand.

He looked her in the eyes in the way kids aren't supposed to with adults. "Promise me that you will find Lilah."

She held his gaze. "I promise I will not stop until we have her back." He took her hand and held it until he heard the others coming down the hall. He gently pulled his hand back, and she gave him a loving smile and nod.

"Jake! Are you okay?" Alex's concern was sincere and not what Jake was used to, though it reminded him a bit of Lilah.

Jake was amused by his cousin. "Man, you can be so dramatic! Geez," he replied.

Alex rolled his eyes. "Did Aunt Val tell you? This was her house when she was little!"

Jake looked at her quizzically. She just nodded and shrugged.

Val looked around for the first time, noticing the Sissy touches and pictures. There was one of Sissy, Jake, and a beautiful young girl with flowing golden hair. The girl in the dreams. Lilah.

Val walked over to the desk with papers on it. There was a stack of letters ready to be sent, paid bills, and paperwork. Val, Cade, Melanie, Jake, and Grandmother Flor each had a letter addressed to them and stamped. Two letters just had names: "To Z" and "Max."

"Jake, do you know why these didn't get sent? These are the papers that were needed."

"No. Mom had an appointment in Exton. We stopped at the store to pick up snacks." He paused, visibly uncomfortable, biting his lips.

He looked at her with a pained look. "She collapsed at the store. They hospitalized her there and didn't bring us home until she, um. Then they brought us to pick up clothes and my guitar. They said they would send someone else to collect the papers and contact people."

Alex couldn't help himself. He hugged Jake tightly, which Jake appeared to only tolerate but secretly appreciated except that he wasn't sure he could stop from crying. Lucy put her hand on Val's shoulder.

"I'm so sorry, Jake. I know this is painful. Do you know if your mom had an attorney?" Val asked.

"I don't know for sure. She had one before we moved here, in Phoenix, when she divorced my dad. I wanted to come back here when I was at the foster home, but it was too far to get to before they caught me. This is the first time I made it here."

Val once again had tears forming and flowing. She wiped them quietly, sucking in as much air and composure as could fit through her nostrils.

"I guess that explains why we didn't know. The people meant to notify us hadn't been notified. Jake, I'm so sorry." *Why didn't I think to find Sissy's house before now?*

Alex saw her tears and went to hug her. She accepted. Neither boy was used to seeing adults express this kind of emotion. Crying. Vulnerability. Something happened for each of them at that moment.

Jake softened even more with the realization that maybe, just maybe, not all adults were out to betray him. Alex saw the release and flow of energy around his aunt. He wanted to hug her, not just for her sadness but because it felt like something beautiful that he didn't know the words for. The four of them stayed in that for moments or maybe hours—a snapshot moment not for a sight seen but for a moment in time that transcended understanding and the mind's need for categorization.

CHAPTER

TEN

Val opened the letter addressed to her.

Dear Val, big sister Val,

It is too late to tell you now. Too late to find all the words to fit into a phone call. I guess I've never been very good at the phone. I hear your voice and am transported back in time. Suddenly I am eight years old, reading the note you left for me, not understanding. I tried to; I really did. I tried to understand and fill your shoes as Mom's helper and our protector. I never realized how big a role that was. I loved my dad so much. I didn't want to see him the way you did. I truly didn't. I think I got angry when you left. Not right away, but over time. I don't know why I am writing all this now—too late to do anything about it. Too late to say I'm sorry or to tell you why I pushed you away.

I understand now. Why you left, what you saw that I didn't want to or couldn't. Maybe you were right about Daddy, and Mom, and me. And you were right about Max. By the time I admitted it, I had already lost myself. I put poor Jake through that and Lilah. I haven't even told you about Lilah.

First, I'm writing this because when I called, I couldn't find the words. But I need to get it out and maybe you even need to know. I was angry with you for always thinking you could help like nobody could live without you.

But that wasn't the truth. The truth is I was angry at myself for not being stronger. I forgive you for leaving. I forgive myself for all the mistakes, and for letting myself believe for a minute that I wasn't strong. And I celebrate myself for these beautiful kids. Val—the kids are magic in my life. Remember how you used to try to teach me how to listen with my heart? How to quiet myself and connect to the earth with bare feet? I finally understand this better. And my kids—they are my center. I can hear them in my heart. I can hear their cries and their laughter. It is the most amazing thing!

I reached my last straw with Max when Jake had to step in to protect me. How could I have not seen that coming? But that was it. I called Cade, and he came to help me pack. We moved across town, but it didn't feel far enough. I don't know exactly why, but the only place I could think to come to was Star Junction. I barely remembered it, yet it was like a beacon for home! I sold the house and brought the kids with clothes and not much else to this little house that I just love. I have never felt more at home.

The kids took to it immediately, especially Lilah, and we met some people who said they knew us (you and me and our family) before we moved away. They have been so kind. Now I know why you didn't want to leave here. And if you ever get this letter, I hope you will return. Isn't it interesting how a place that was so hard to leave became such a distant memory? Why didn't any of us come back sooner? I'm hoping Cade will bring Alex here. It would be so much better for them since Karen's passing. Alex would love it here. He reminds me so much of Cade.

I am rambling. There is just so much to tell. Lilah was not a mistake, nor was she planned. She is this beautiful gift that I kept all to myself and Jake. I'm sorry I didn't tell you. Her father came from nowhere and disappeared again. I broke my rule with him. I felt like I had known him my whole life, and he was truly kind and generous and, I don't know, magical. One night, one time, one beautiful gift to remember him by. Can you imagine? He did not disappear completely. As grateful as I was for this child, I guess I was afraid of the comments that people would make if they knew. No, I was afraid of your reaction. I don't know why, but I was. I hope you can forgive me for that.

As I am writing this, I have terminal cancer. I am doing my best to keep the kids safe and unafraid, but I am terrified. Val, will you come for them? If you are anything like my memory of you, you would be good for them, and maybe them for you. Will you take them? Jake has the biggest heart and the world on his shoulders. He sings and plays music like an angel. And Lilah—just wait until you meet her. She is like love and joy all wrapped up in a little body.

We need you now, dear Val. I am sorry I didn't tell you before. Please come.

Love, (your stubborn little sister)

Sissy (Sunshine).

Sissy's letter served both as wound-deepener and salve. Val longed to turn back time and redo the encounters that went wrong. Perhaps she could have written her goodbye note more carefully in all the wisdom of her seventeen years. She could have sent more letters. She could have moved back to Arizona. She could have listened more and fixed less. She could have.

And while part of her knew this way of thinking wouldn't help, she couldn't stop wondering if she could have salvaged Sissy's heart and the sisterhood that should have been between them. Val wanted to scream loudly enough to bring Sissy back, and her mother back and William back, scream loud enough to reach Melanie wherever she disappeared to.

Was it possible to scream so loud to undo all that went wrong? To shake the pieces back into place long enough to find the glue? The Japanese have a practice called kingsugi, or kintsukuroi that mends broken items with gold to see the beauty in both the object and the repaired brokenness. How do you repair a piece that no longer exists?

Perhaps she would find beauty in that as well, but right now the hole just felt empty and the edges sharp. A certain helplessness came with being angry about death and missed opportunities. Val knew she couldn't go back in actual time, but she could talk to her now and make damn sure those kids had a home and family.

***

Two Years Ago

Jake did his best to help his mom since moving to Star Junction. She had gotten a job at the little hospital and gotten the house done nice. But something was wrong. She said she was fine, just tired, but Jake had been a keen observer of his mother. He blamed Max. She wasn't coming back to her "self," and he didn't know what to do to help her. To fix her and everything.

Lilah could see it too. Lilah was often shy but held the mysteries of the world in her heart. Jake was her twin in spirit. She latched on to him whenever she could, and he loved it. He relished the role of big brother and protector. And more, something about her helped him believe that life would be okay again because with her things felt so much lighter. Like it was with his mom before Max came back. He took a deep internal vow that he would make sure it never changed for Lilah.

"Mom…" He hesitated, not sure how to ask just right so she would answer it honestly instead of with the things that adults say to kids to convince them not to worry. She looked up at him waiting for his question. "What is going on with you?"

"Oh, honey, I'm fine. It'll be fine."

"No, Mom, you are not fine."

Sissy took a slow breath and looked through an invisible window into the distance beyond the walls. They were quiet together until, for the first time in his life, Jake started to feel not just as if it wasn't okay right now, but that it wouldn't be fine at all. He felt himself wanting to reassure her, wanting to hold her, but was still unsure why.

"Mom?" He sat beside Sissy and wrapped his arms around her.

They weren't a little boy's arms anymore. *Fourteen going on forty,* she thought. She held his arms against her, knowing she was supposed to be holding him and letting him know he was safe and protected.

"I'm sick, Jakey—really sick."

Val was also drawn to read the open letter at the bottom of the pile.

My dearest Sissy,

You are not alone and you are so loved. Though I cannot be there physically, I am with you. I think you know that in ways other than words can express. I am glad you have freed yourself of the suffering caused by your relationship with Max. You are doing an amazing job with our daughter. Lilah is filled with the love of you and her brother. She and Jacob are very special—which you also know.

Dear one, you are facing tough decisions. Yours is a challenge that many would fail, but your heart will see you through. Forgive and reconcile. It is time to call your family together. You feel this. It is why you returned to Star Junction. Do not be afraid. Lilah will always be safe and cared for. Jacob too, though he has his path to walk. Make the calls; write the letters while you still have time.

You are Solana, that was your mother's gift to you. Your light will always shine.

Your heart,

Z.

They returned to Grandmother's compound, and Val sat with her laptop, playing at working. There was discussion about Sissy's house not being touched, about the papers that hadn't been filed or seen. She scanned them all and forwarded them to her attorneys. The letters she held for the recipients.

Alex called Cade to update him and see when he was coming. Val assured Cade that Alex was fine and he should focus on taking care of what he needed to. Everybody seemed to settle into a relaxed evening, but Val was not feeling relaxed. She wanted to decompress... and perhaps scream some. She got up to stretch and wandered to the kitchen.

Val hoped nobody noticed that she poured herself just a little bit more wine. The kids were busy listening to Edward's stories. Although she knew whose home she was in, she quietly added to her glass. She was still processing the letter and all that came with it, and that less than two weeks ago she was living a quiet life in Southern California. Quiet in the sense that she lived alone and not that she wasn't burying herself in work that could have been done by others. She hadn't been alone since she arrived at Cade's.

A part of Val's heart had woken up and had been at full attention ever since. And a part of her was gasping for air. She was under no illusions about what wine was and was not good for, but tonight she hoped that maybe, just maybe, it would grant her at least a moment of calming the chaos beneath the exterior. She chided herself as it was just a second glass, not like she was tying one on. Not that she hadn't. But it didn't work. Not the chiding or the making light of it. Not the hoping that it would fly under the radar. She was in the home of people who would notice and would care about her well-being.

"Cotton candy."

Val turned to look toward the voice, startled more by the words than by someone speaking. She saw Grandmother Flor standing in the doorway, illuminated by the moon outside.

"Grandmother... I didn't see you there."

"I've only just come."

Val looked down, her composure at risk.

Grandmother Flor moved closer. Despite the authority, she felt no menace nor condemnation. She seemed to be pure love. "Aren't you going to ask me what I mean?"

Val tried to laugh, but she was already on the edge of tears.

"Yes, of course. What do you mean?" Grandmother Flor came right before her, looked lovingly into her eyes, and held her glass.

"Wine is like cotton candy. It tastes sweet for a moment but never satisfies your hunger or thirst. It is a reservoir with no water. If you spend too much time there, you are lost. It will never irrigate your crops."

Val took in a breath deeper than she thought she could, but when she let it out, the tears came too. She tried to turn away, but Flor held her there. Held her in the tears and the love.

"This is better to irrigate your crops," she said with a smile.

Val couldn't help but laugh. And the laughter surprised her.

Grandmother Flor continued, "There are times for cotton candy, and there are times for tears. They are not the same times."

Val sucked in another breath and nodded. She hadn't allowed enough tears in the past three decades to hydrate a bean sprout and feared opening the gates. She had told herself for so long that no problem need result in tears, just creativity and strength. And she'd be damned if she'd give anyone the satisfaction of reducing her to tears. Since she'd been back in Star Junction, she had lost control of the faucet.

"Thank you, Grandmother."

"Child, this is but a moment. You are in the right place. It is time for you to remember." She smiled. "You already are remembering. Give yourself time to catch up. And don't forget to breathe."

Val shook her head with dismay. *How does that make me feel better?* she wondered. Yet it did.

Nothing was solved. Grandmother Flor knew this. What she did was release the pressure of having anything solved in this moment. For nothing was what it seemed or as heavy as it seemed unless we tried to unpack it when we were under the spell.

Grandmother Flor understood the power of stories. She used them to teach all the time. She understood how people cast spells upon themselves. Some were harmless, and some were like casts of concrete crushing people with their own imaginings. Val had been living this story long enough. Grandmother Flor was here to help her see her truth, dispel the illusion, and begin a better story.

———

Val couldn't sleep let alone focus on work. It was unfamiliar territory. Instead, she sat outside next to the angel trumpet tree and watched the stars. Her thoughts were too many to follow, but mostly about Sissy. The truth was the sisterhood was lost long ago, only now was it permanent. There was no chance of reconciliation or recovery.

As long as Sissy was alive, there had been possibility and longing, but now the permanence of loss set in. Val's gut ached. Her heart ached. Every cell in her body ached. She felt both guilty and defensive, neither for just cause. She always thought they would have more time. Always thought they would come together.

"I'm so, so sorry, Sissy. Please forgive me." She remained there, letting the tears fall silently at the base of the tree.

"Aunt Val?" Jake's voice was quiet, trying not to disturb or wake anyone.

Val wiped her tears and turned toward him. She opened her arm and gestured for him to join her.

"Jake, are you okay? What are you doing up?"

"I couldn't sleep. I just couldn't."

She nodded and put her hand on his shoulder to reassure him.

"I know the feeling."

"I keep thinking I should have made them take me to the house sooner. Or found a way there. If I had, maybe Lilah would still be with me...and you. Maybe things could have been resolved sooner."

Val looked at him with compassion, trying not to start the tears again.

"No." She shook her head. "No, there are no productive 'should haves' and 'could haves.' Even though it is hard to understand, and sometimes really damn hard to experience, life happens in its own timing. No matter how much we wish we could control it, change it, and undo it."

She paused and took a deep breath. "I've just been sitting here thinking about Sissy and bouncing back and forth between being devastated and being really pissed off that I can't turn back time. That I can't undo the misunderstandings. That I can't go back twenty years and fix the broken parts before they got worse. All I am saying to you is don't do that to yourself. You can't change it. It was meant to be now. It was meant to be with Alex and you and... now. And, Jake, nothing, not a single thing in this situation, is your fault or responsibility. It just happened. Despite how much you loved your mother and love your sister, no matter how good you were and how hard you tried to help. It just happened. Your job now is to heal and grow and trust that good things happen too."

Jake wiped his eyes and stared at the stars. "I don't know if I can, at least not until Lilah is back."

There was a time when Sissy told Val everything. Even after Val left, she would monopolize the monthly phone call and write letters. It began to shift when Sissy met Max. She became secretive, not wanting to reveal that he was an unemployed ex-con. When he disappeared after Jake was born, Sissy shut down more. She worked hard to prove herself and to silence any judgmental commentary.

Over time, the Sissy she grew up as had disappeared, the cheerfulness beaten out of her. Her bubbly loving optimism was replaced by jitters and uncertainty, now fearful of wrong steps and stray fists. She thought she had seen good in Max, tender moments and spoken words that told a story they didn't mean.

When he returned years later, she forgot how well she was doing without him. She told herself that he had matured and changed. She told herself it would be good for Jake to have a father in his life. The first seeds of doubt came in shiny packages wrapped with bows of pretty pictures and loving joy she had dreamed about and heard others knew.

The first time Sissy was slammed into the wall, Val's words echoed in her memory. "Reminds me of mom, a bit." All at once, Sissy knew her fear and was paralyzed. She had never wanted to see her father the way Val saw him. She grew up painting a picture of love and a mother who wasn't able and needed a "good man" like Emmet to take care of her.

Emmet referred to himself that way often. "You are lucky to have a good man like me in your life. You are lucky to have a good man as your father. To teach you what the world is really like, so you will be strong and not entitled." To joy. To thrive. To be safe or feel loved. She always saw the heart in him, the part that tried to love, that tried to be a good man despite not knowing what that was. And now she saw that Max was her Emmet, and maybe the heart she saw in them was her own.

Sissy found her strength again when she saw the look in Jake's eyes as he rushed in to save her from Max's drunken rage. She found the strength to stand after shaking on the ground, paralyzed with shock and fear at the beating and the rage spewing from Max. She stood and kicked him out of her house with Jake at her side. And with Cade's help, they packed up to move the next day. She could find her way to take a stand, to heal, know another love, raise two children, move to unknown parts, but not to admit it all to Val.

CHAPTER

ELEVEN

The land was a book of stories. Early morning was a wonderful time to walk in nature. Something was special in the way the light played with all it fell upon. If you were willing, you may see magic in the interactions, as light dances with leaves, flowers, and all the beings. This was Edward's favorite time to *walk well.*

Today, Alex and Jake joined him to find out what he meant by "walking well." As the boys trudged through the bushes, feet pounding on the earth, they were about to receive their first lesson. Edward stopped and stood motionless, watching them plow ahead. Twenty feet. Thirty feet. Forty feet. Fifty. Alex started to ask a question, and they realized that Edward wasn't with them.

"Why did he stop?" asked Alex.

Jake shrugged.

They stood there waiting for him, like maybe they were walking too fast and he couldn't keep up because he was old. Edward remained motionless, waiting.

"We better go back to him," said Jake. They turned around and headed toward him confused and not sure if they should be worried. Edward remained still.

"Mr. Edward, are you okay?" asked Alex. "Were we walking too fast for you?"

Edward hid his amusement and waited still to speak. The boys shifted their feet with anxiousness and impatience.

"What have you seen on your walk so far?" asked Edward.

The boys were confused. They looked at him bewildered.

"Bushes?" Alex guessed.

"Why do you walk so hurriedly?"

The boys had no answer.

"Why are we walking?" he asked.

Again, they shrugged.

He looked at each of them in their eyes. His expression was serious bordering on stern but still showed kindness. "Why do we walk?"

"Exercise?"

"No!"

The power of his response startled them.

He paused, and they were still for the first time. "Is that not a waste? A missed opportunity?"

Silence.

Edward returned to stillness between each verbal exchange, which had an unsettling effect on the boys. "Young Alex, when you get up in the morning and draw, in what way do you look upon things to draw them? Young Jacob, when you play music, what are you listening to that you then express outward?"

They weren't meant to answer the questions out loud but to shift into a different way of seeing. "Walking well is not for the sake of walking. It is not a physical act at all. Walking well is about seeing, sensing, feeling, and being one with our creator and earth mother. We don't pound the earth with our steps; we kiss her gently, with love, affection, intention, and gratitude." As he spoke, Edward acted out each action.

"We step consciously from one miracle to the next. We pay attention and walk with a willingness to see, listen, and receive. Each of you has gifts for receiving information in different ways. And it would be beneficial for you each to learn more ways of seeing and receiving. So let us walk quietly and consciously. Let Pachamama, Gaia, our earth mother, this beautiful land, know you are thankful to be here and open to see.

"Walk gently. Breathe slowly. Close your eyes and feel. Heart open with eyes to see and ears to listen and hear. This is how we *walk well*."

They began again to take their first steps of walking well. Alex thought he saw a flicker in the grasses. He bent down to look closer but saw nothing more. He shrugged and continued on and saw it again. This pattern continued until Alex lost his playfulness.

Edward watched for a while then came to him. "Young wolf, you are trying too hard. Tune to the same channel as when you draw. They can play with you there." And he was gone.

Alex furrowed his brow wanting to be frustrated but pulled out his pretend sketchbook, nonetheless. He stopped looking and started seeing. Not the type of weed or its color, but the way it danced and moved in the breeze. Alex smiled. "I saw you! That was cool."

And the stalk repeated the dance with flare. Alex looked for Edward to share but couldn't see him. He walked to another plant and watched as it shimmied and shined in the light. He couldn't help himself; he was having fun.

Jake began to hear the music in the grasses, the branches, the leaves. He wasn't expecting it. In fact, he had plopped down between some boulders to rest in boredom until Edward said it was time to go. He was feeling like this was stupid. Like Edward was a crazy old man, but he kinda liked him, anyway.

He lay back against a boulder and closed his eyes. The leaves in the trees rustled. *Shh-sh-shh-shhh-shhhhh.* Then the wind blew through the grasses. *Shwish, shhh, swishs, shh.* A bird whistled. A twig cracked. Jake's brain played the replay, leaves, grass, bird, twig, leaves, grass, bird, twig. It was a song. He started humming along, and the song got longer, more birds chimed in, Jake tapped percussion on his knees, his whole body felt alive and vibrating on that boulder.

"Ahh, nature keeps good time." Jake opened his eyes, but Edward was nowhere near. Jake looked around in disbelief. *"But he just spoke..."* He closed his eyes again and must have dozed.

"Boys, are you going to stay all day? It is time for lunch!" Edward declared with great amusement. The boys came running, surprised to realize how hungry they were and that it could be time for lunch already. "You have done well in your first lesson. Someday you may truly know how to walk well."

Val sat at the counter in Lucy's restaurant. It was a way to have a different view for a while and get some friend time while working remotely. And the boys enjoyed hanging out and playing pinball, though they weren't with her now.

A small group of people came in, and Lucy walked over to seat them. As they passed by Val, they watched her closely. She turned to them and smiled. "Hello." A couple of them nodded, and the others just shifted their eyes and walked past. Lucy returned to continue her inventory sheet. She noticed the strange look on Val's face.

"You okay?"

"It's a little unsettling."

"What is?" Lucy asked with curiosity.

"So many people seem to know me. I catch them looking at me, and then they avert their eyes as soon as they notice that I've seen them. It's odd."

"Maybe not so odd. You are from here. It is a small town."

Val scoffed. "It's not *that* small!"

Lucy was amused by Val's discomfort and apparent lack of understanding. "Perhaps they just recognize you."

"Some of them are far too young to have known me." She paused. "It just feels uncomfortable. I don't know what they want."

"They want to see the girl who danced with fire," Lucy shared matter-of-factly.

Val's expression went blank and then perplexed. She had no idea what Lucy was talking about. "Who?"

"One of the many stories of our town is about the girl who danced with fire. From the time she could walk, she could dance with the fire during our festivals. The story goes that once the music started, the girl would close her eyes and dance as if she were the music itself. At one festival in particular, the fire took a liking to the girl, having watched her for many ceremonies. And the fire began to dance with her, following her motions, lifting when her arms raised, and dipping when they came down. It swirled when she twirled and sent sparks like stars when she would leap."

Val was mesmerized by the story. "I never heard that story."

Lucy looked her in the eyes with overflowing love. "Val, that girl was you. It is the story of Picaflor."

Val shook her head in disbelief, trying to process the message she just heard. "No, I don't remember that. I danced. I loved to dance to the music, but I don't remember anything about the fire. People have made it up."

"No, you don't remember, perhaps because your eyes were closed and you thought it was just in your mind. A little girl's imagination. But Val, I used to watch you. Even as a small child I saw what was happening." She put her hand on Val's shoulder. "Some of the people remember, and others have heard the stories. They just want to see the girl who dances with fire."

"This is crazy. Even if it was true, that girl is long gone."

"But that woman just returned. And the people who see you admire that you were ever able to be so free."

Val started laughing an uncomfortable laugh. "I suppose it is easy to be that free as a child, but I am not sure it is possible for an adult. In fact, I'm not really sure what to do with the information."

Val returned to the house to finish up work and make her daily check-ins with Ms. Ramirez and the attorneys. She had not gotten far with finding Lilah and didn't understand it. Her thoughts went to Clarity Mountain and Grandmother Flor's words, *"Soon, you will climb again to reclaim it. It will help you."*

Val wasn't ready to climb Clarity Mountain. This world still felt so foreign to her yet so familiar. She wondered if she would ever be able to be that Val again, the one her father tried to form. The one who could navigate her way to the top of that mountain. All of Val's success didn't balance the disappointment she felt in herself. William encouraged the dreamer in her, but she knew herself to be a realist. Responsible. Effective. Decisive.

She never had doubt in her business dealings. She always knew the answer. Since she had arrived back in Star Junction, she questioned everything. Today's discovery of dancing with fires left her feeling bewildered, yet it had been a good day. The boys seemed energized and excited by their hike with Edward. She got some much-needed work done, though all she really wanted was news about Lilah. It was hard for a pragmatist to trust that things would just work out. She made lists and checked things off. When new things arose, she added them to her lists. Step by step. Always move forward. This waiting-in-faith thing was hard.

Get Alex, check.

Get Jake, check.

Find Lilah, no check.

Get info, sort of check.

Make progress, no check.

Know why you're here, no check.

Find Melanie? Send letter...

Get house?

Climb Clarity Mountain and remember, no check.

Remember what?

Val reviewed the list in her head and made fun of it at the same time. She had no other choice but to laugh. She looked up to see Lucy catch her eye as she was supervising the games of the kids. They both smiled and Val shrugged. She wondered if she might relax a little and enjoy the company. It had been a long time since she had enjoyed so much company.

It was a hot day, and Lucy invited Val for a walk to Sky River. Something was powerful about the flow of water, the way it bent and wound and trickled through. Nothing was in its way, only encountered on its way. As Lucy and Val got close enough to hear the water, the pace and conversation shifted.

"I had forgotten about the river. Thank you for bringing me here."

Lucy smiled and nodded. "I could tell you that I felt you could use it, but it is the river calling you."

Val nodded and laughed. Of course, it was. As a child, she would have heard those words and felt them to be absolutely true. After thirty years of forgetting, they were truths serving to dislodge the dam. Suddenly she found herself taking in a deep breath.

They climbed over branches and debris and found a place to sit on the edge. Lucy took off her shoes first, and Val quickly followed. Before going in, Val closed her eyes and said a prayer to ask permission of the water—the teachings of her father alive and well. The water was cool and welcomed her, caressing each part of her toes, feet, and calves, washing away whatever she chose to release.

Val closed her eyes again and allowed herself to feel it fully. She let the water play and paid attention in her mind, enjoying the sensations, tickles, and feel of resistance and pulling, somehow extracting the tension and fear she had. She waded deeper in—no longer aware of clothes or convention or practicality—to the deepest part and allowed herself to submerge.

Let it wash it all away, she thought, *let it set me free.* Val stayed beneath the surface until she couldn't stay any longer and then surged above the water, taking in a new breath. She looked around her at the trees, the sky, the rocks, Lucy. Beautiful Lucy, quietly held space and allowed Val to be with the river. When Val made eye contact again, Lucy smiled, which made Val smile.

Lucy teased, "That was—dramatic."

Val laughed. "Yes, yes it was." And she splashed toward Lucy.

Val found a large boulder in the sun to sit on and dry out a bit. The boulder was warm, the sun warmer. And she was transported again, back in time.

"Daddy, the sun is wrapping me up like a towel."

William smiled at his daughter. He loved the way she described things. She was his teacher.

"I thought it would be too hot, but he is so gentle."

"Did you ask the sun for help to dry off?"

She gave him a huge smile. "Yes!"

"And so, he is. Why would he not be gentle?"

The boulder conformed perfectly to the curves of Val's body. The bumps and crevices seemed placed for a resting spot just for her. She smiled at the notion. "Thank you, boulder; thank you, sun; thank you, God."

Ground squirrels broke the silence. They chattered at each other while scurrying by.

Val came back to the present. "What have I gotten myself into? I mean, what if I can't do this? I've never had kids."

Lucy just smiled and raised an eyebrow with a gentle laugh. "Val, you've been a parent since you were a kid. You helped Grace parent your siblings. You have run businesses with lots of people who need leadership and compassion. You even babysat me a few times, which surely qualifies you!" she said with a wink.

Val laughed. "Well, that last part for sure. You were such a challenge."

Lucy was a listener even then.

"I didn't realize, or maybe didn't let myself get that far ahead, that I would be. I mean, I didn't know how this was all going to go. I thought maybe I would spend a few weeks or the summer and then take Jake back to LA with me and continue life as usual."

"But?"

"But that isn't what is unfolding." She chose the words carefully, but she realized she was talking to Lucy.

"Unfolding?" Lucy looked directly at her with an inviting look to be honest with herself. Val sighed.

"I don't think that is what I want... And I am pretty certain it is not what all this was about."

"But?"

"But am I walking away from my business? Am I relocating it? Do we stay here? And what about Lilah? I haven't gotten anywhere with children's services and Ms. Ramirez. And—"

Lucy put her hand over Val's heart. "Listen. What do you feel?"

Val closed her eyes and took a deep breath. "I don't want to leave here. Even if it weren't for the kids, the thought of returning to 'usual' fills me with dread."

"That is good listening." She smiled. "Val, trust your heart. It is your wisest advisor."

Val smiled and chuckled. "I think you might be my wisest advisor. Everyone should have an advisory board like your family!" She laughed and took a breath filled with gratitude. "Thank you, my friend, my sister."

Two hummingbirds darted past, circled around them, and headed back in the direction of town after hovering, just for a moment in front of Val. They both smiled at the confirmation.

Lucy added, "The universe speaks to us in so many ways. How

beautiful is it when we choose to listen and truly welcome the messages; how rich our lives can be." She stood up.

"Almost time to go back," said Lucy as she laid out a twenty-four-inch square cloth. "We need to gather some herbs for Grandmother. Do you remember how?"

"Maybe?" They both laughed.

"Then get busy!" Lucy had no problem playfully pushing Val. She knew her returned friend well. The successful CEO was far from brittle.

They both collected from the list: wild rosemary, mountain sage, juniper, and wild currants. They talked to each plant, asking permission and offering gratitude for what it shared. When the cloth was full, with just enough room on the edges to wrap the bounty, Lucy bundled it and they began the walk back to town.

Richard Jimenez had been the postmaster for at least fifty years. Postmaster in a small town also meant mail carrier. He had a quiet, jovial way about him. He found Val at the grandmother's compound and took a moment to scan her carefully.

Val began to think perhaps he mistook her for a package that needed an X-ray. "You are the daughter of William and Grace. Yes, you were the daughter that danced."

"Yes, sir, you remember me?" Val responded, stunned.

"I do. I remember everyone. I'm the postmaster." He smiled and winked as he handed her the package. "You've been waiting for this." He turned quickly and walked away.

"Thank you, postmaster."

He waved behind him and continued on.

Val opened the package from California. She had asked Elliot to send some papers and supplies from work. But she was surprised to find added treasures.

Val, as I gathered your requested papers these jumped from the shelf. Not kidding. Landed on my foot. Seemed like they wanted to come. I hope all is going well with the boys and your search. The fort is doing fine, and the ship is still afloat. In trust, Elliot.

p.s. You were a smart kid.

Underneath the note was a six-by-eight leather journal tied with a strap. Papers, photos, and envelopes were poking out the edges between the pages. *Wow. You're right, Elliot. They did want to come.*

This was her prized journal given to her by William when she was seven—when the lessons began in earnest. She recorded his stories, notes, things that made her laugh, and much of her discoveries with William, Grandmother Flor, Grace, Cade, and Edward. It included notes about the helpful plants and their medicinal qualities, the animal spirits and their quirks, and how to hike Clarity Mountain. Although she had chosen to bury her magical objects, she had been able to keep the journal well-hidden from Emmet. He wasn't much of a reader.

She untied the strap, laid the book on its binding, and let it fall open where it would. A picture of William and Grace holding Cade fell out.

Baby Cade is here. That's what Daddy calls him. He is so small. I'm not sure that I was that small, but I guess he will grow big like Daddy. That would be good for him. Daddy says that I get to teach him lots of good stuff because I am the big sister. It takes a special person to be a big sister. I think Mama is happy too.

Things to teach Cade: How to play well, how to make Mommy and Daddy happy, how to listen with his heart, how to know joy.

Val put her hand on the page, gently feeling the words of her sweet list. *How did I know so well at eight what I struggle to know now?* Her fingers moved to the picture, outlining William's face, Grace's face, and baby Cade.

Grace was so young. She truly never felt like her mother was young. Grace always felt like the adult watching over her and William's playful ways. "I'm sorry, Mama. I bet you would have liked to play, too." Val touched each word of the list of what to teach Cade. "How could I teach him when I forgot myself?"

Thirty-Eight Years Ago

William watched Valerie study the landscape and examine the leaves and the branches. She went back and forth from boulder to bush to tree. She looked up at the sky and seemed to be in deep deliberation. He watched. And waited. A swallow swooped by and Valerie watched it intently. William was becoming amused and perhaps a bit impatient.

"Picaflor," he finally asked, "what are you doing?"

She turned to face him with all the authority of her eight-year-old self and stated, "I am studying all the signs so I know which way is the right way and don't make a mistake."

He couldn't help himself. He laughed at her seriousness. He laughed for her. In fact, he laughed with so much joy that she began to laugh even though she didn't know why he was laughing and was a little hurt. He noticed her confusion and calmed his laughter.

"Picaflor, my beautiful little hummingbird, when did you decide that you must be so serious?"

She looked at him blankly, not sure how to answer. She scrunched her brow and her mouth, sucking her bottom lip under her teeth in a slightly crooked way. William wanted to laugh more at how this beautiful child expressed everything on her face. He truly hoped she would never be a good poker player, though he suspected if she ever tried, she would be the best. But not yet. Now she was all pure, visible expression, and he was grateful. He hoped, prayed, and worked toward helping her stay true to her expression and find the balance between this fierce and serious side of her and the joy that poured from her heart.

Valerie couldn't find an answer. She let out a defeated sigh as her shoulders sank and a pout overtook her face. William didn't shift his loving gaze, still waiting for his answer. "But I'm doing everything you've told me. I'm watching the leaves and the birds and the boulders and the shadows. I'm looking at everything and nothing is talking to me!"

"Are you sure you have remembered *everything*?" He smiled at her, prodding. She was lost enough that he started to give her silly visual clues. He smiled. Made funny faces. Acted like he was dancing to music that wasn't there.

She watched him, trying with all her might not to laugh at his antics. Val had a stubborn streak that was planted in the core of the earth. Yet William just looked at her with love, patience, and absolute faith that she would find her answer.

"Is it possible..." he said with great exaggeration, "that you forgot one ingredient?" With that he took her hands and started to dance. He led her in all kinds of directions until giggles echoed on the mountain.

"Daddy?"

"Yes, Picaflor?"

"I think I forgot to play."

"Yes, Picaflor, I think you are right!"

"But why is that so important?"

"Because we are not meant to be so serious. The animals and the trees don't know how to be that serious. It is like we are speaking two different languages. If you are serious and they are not, you are on a different channel and can't hear them. And while they are communicating like they always do; they don't understand why you aren't responding. They were talking to you the whole time; you just couldn't hear them because you were on the wrong channel."

"But I didn't want to make a mistake."

"Why not? What is wrong with learning?"

Val looked perplexed. She wanted so badly to please her father. She could feel his desire for her to learn all these things.

"My amazing Picaflor, we learn by making mistakes. There is no wrong. There is no error. It is just learning what works and what doesn't. Just information. It is not a trick. Everyone wants to support you." He could feel how much she wanted to please him and wondered if he had made a mistake trying to teach her so much so quickly. "Valerie, do you know why I call you Picaflor?"

"No," she replied with a shrug and head shake.

"Picaflor means hummingbird. Hummingbirds are believed to bring joy. They teach us to embrace the sweetest nectar of life. That nectar is joy and love and play. You are so very bright and strong. From when you were a baby, I knew that if you decided something, you would do it. No question. My deepest desire is for you to decide to choose joy each and every day. That is why I teach you. That is the most important thing I want you to learn. Play. Make everything play. On that channel you will receive all your greatest messages."

"Okay, Papa, I'll remember. I like to play."

But Val did forget. Her serious side became a wall forged like steel against those she didn't trust and, eventually, those she didn't know. Emmet was the first followed by her peers, professors, and colleagues. She was never mean. Her idea of play just became the challenge of each endeavor and of winning. Getting the client.

Building the business. Going beyond the Emmets and all those who would cast her in a different role. The helpless female or the one who needed to be put in her place. The novice or the bitch. She was quite certain that she was never icy, though she may well have turned up the heat when she felt she had something to prove. And some part of her always, always did. Mostly to herself.

She encountered many in her professional life who strived for her success. Some were jealous. Some assumed or projected many things about her to discredit her work, effort, and talent. A part of her scoffed and laughed it off, and a part sought the next victory to add to her pile. Take that. She tried to live there, tried to keep the callings of her heart quiet and the lingering feeling of emptiness far out of her mind. Except it wasn't. She worked day and night to keep her mind busy and her body tired. But there was no hiding the truth. No hiding from her dreams.

CHAPTER

TWELVE

awn had not yet begun, the magic still lingering just beyond the horizon. Grandmother Flor found Val working on her laptop in the kitchen.

"You will not find the sunrise there. Nor the answers you seek."

"Grandmother, good morning."

"Yes, it is. A good morning to watch the sunrise, to listen to the birds, to connect with this place, each other, and the memories you wish to have behind you." Flor's voice was both playful and stern.

"I'm just trying to get some work done before the boys get up. Not sure what we will do today."

Grandmother Flor just looked at her and smiled. Val shifted uncomfortably before letting out a sigh. She couldn't help but smile, too, as she closed her laptop. "What do you suggest?"

"I suggest you start with the sunrise and listen to the birds. Let the memories come. Let the pictures and your journal help you. Let the boys be curious. Tell them the stories that have been missing for them. This is the work you are here to do."

"I'm not sure I can." She had avoided the photographs. The

portal to remembering, as Edward had called it, avoided any chance of the dam breaking on her.

"Nonsense, child. All it requires is for you to allow it. For you to stop 'doing' and allow. Allow the memories. Allow the emotions. Allow the healing." Grandmother cupped her face in her hands. "Go, start with the sunrise and listen to the birds."

Val obeyed. She watched the sunrise, listening to the birds as they began their first songs of the day, and once again offered her tears to the angel trumpet tree.

***

Twenty-Nine Years Ago

Barely a year after moving to Phoenix, Val left with Grace's help. They hadn't talked about it, but they both felt it coming. Grace had tried to make it better for Val, but she just couldn't. She was too afraid of life without a man she called "strong," even if strong meant impossible and mean-spirited. The night before she left, Val had a dream that woke her: Emmet setting fire to all of her things, her art, her clothes, her dreams while he stood on top of her so she couldn't get up. When she tried, he threw a fireball toward Grace and Cade. She heard a voice say, "You or them."

She packed what she could carry in a small duffel and her backpack. A few clothes, her journal, a few art supplies, and treasured pictures. It was Emmet's day to take "his girls" to school—a ritual that repeated once or twice a month and included treats like donuts, hot chocolate, and feeding the idea that they were special because they were his "real kids." His desire to create a wedge between the girls and Val worked better than he could have imagined on this day. Val was effectively prevented from talking to the girls and saying goodbye.

After breakfast she walked Cade to school and told him she had to leave. They had talked many times about her leaving, but Cade fought it.

"No! He should be the one to go. He is the problem and now you're going to leave me with him."

"No, I am leaving you with Mama. Emmet will be fine with you if I'm gone. Let him feel in charge. Let him think you're listening," she said the words she hoped were true.

"Why can't I come with you?"

"Because you have to stay with Mama. She needs you here, and I'm only seventeen...and you're ten. I have no way of taking care of us." Cade grabbed on to her and squeezed as tightly as he could for as long as he could. Val held him close. "I love you, Cade."

When Val returned to the house to get her stuff, Grace was sitting at the kitchen table holding a picture of William and praying. Val sat down quietly, reached out, and took her mother's hands in hers.

"I love you, Mama."

Grace managed a soft, sweet, but hard-fought smile. "When he died, a part of me died too. I didn't know how to keep going or how to give you what you needed. I couldn't pay the bills, but it was more than that. Emmet seemed to come at just the right time. He said he didn't mind that I had you and Cade, but I should have known then that wasn't enough. He never said he would love you. Please forgive me, child. I've been sitting here asking your father for forgiveness. He was such a wonderful father and teacher. I wish Cade had had a chance to know him as a father, truly. But you have continued shining your father's light for Cade. And the girls. I have watched you and been so grateful. But Emmet, he can't understand...or compete."

"Mama, I have to go today. I can't stay here anymore."

"I know." Wiping her eyes, Grace stood up and went to her pantry cupboard. She pulled an envelope from behind layers of canisters, cereal boxes and canned beets. "I spoke to my brother, your Uncle Ray. He and Beth are expecting you. You can stay with them until you find your way. And it is near a college. I know you will get in. But please, Picaflor, do not lose touch. Not with your brother, not with me, and not with *you*." She handed Val the envelope. Val opened it and found $732, a bus ticket, photos, and two letters.

"Mama, this is too much. How did you?"

"I was hoping we could postpone this day much longer to give you so much more. But if my dream is right, we have no more time."

Val hugged her mother longer than the night William died. And though they would talk monthly, it was one of the last times she would see her mother alive.

Present Day

When Val came back into the kitchen, she came with her journal and the tote of photographs, which she placed on the table where the boys were eating breakfast. Grandmother Flor offered her a plate without speaking. Val wasn't feeling hungry but accepted a small portion and some fruit. And when she sat, Grandmother came behind Val and placed her hands on Val's shoulders.

Grandmother led, "Today is a good day for stories, and your aunt has many about your family. Stories to release and heal."

Val stayed quiet, letting the warmth from Grandmother's hands flow through her.

"So you're not going to work today?" Alex asked with enthusiasm.

Val cleared her throat. "Nope, today is for us—the three of us. Besides, it's Saturday."

"That doesn't usually stop you from working," Jake poked.

"True, but I'm learning."

"So what are we going to do?" Jake asked.

Val opened the journal to the various loose papers and cards that were held within and smiled as she picked out one of the folded papers, clearly well-used and stained. "We're going to make cinnamon rolls."

"Grandma's magic cinnamon rolls?" Jake asked.

"You remember them, Jake?"

"Yeah, I do. I remember that they were awesome...and Mom always called them magic."

"I don't remember them. Why are they magic?"

Val smiled at Alex.

"Well, they are magic because they are filled with magic and love. And because when your dad and I were kids...and your Aunt Sissy and Melanie, sometimes we would have them for dinner. Just your grandma and us. Emmet would be out of town or out drinking. It was our secret, and something about that always made us feel good. No matter what was going on or how hard things felt—our secret, magic cinnamon rolls always managed to bring us joy."

"Cool, I want to try them!"

"Good, because we are going to make them today. I am going to teach you both the secret recipe."

"Is it true what you said at Grandma's funeral?" Val looked at Jake perplexed.

"What did I say?"

"That Emmet had taken all the food money and Grandma couldn't buy groceries."

Val paused before answering. She had forgotten the conversation. Uncle Ray wanted the others to know the truth and understand better.

***

Seven Years Ago—After Grace's Funeral

Uncle Ray led them. Rallied them to have some food, to sit because the cleanup could wait. "Just be together. That is the point," he said it with a true mix of authority and love. Something about that cracked the veil of grief and seriousness.

"You sound like Mom," Melanie offered.

They all laughed with recognition of that truth, and it was their turn for stories—the stories that only they could share about their childhood, their mother, their Grace. They drank wine and nibbled at casseroles they couldn't quite describe while taking their turns like they did when the homework was done and Grace kept them busy while she cooked.

Uncle Ray got teary. "You don't realize how much of a compliment that is. Your mother raised me when she was still a child herself. It was only because of her that I had the life I did because she knew." He looked at Val. "Like she knew for you."

"She did." Val nodded.

"What do you mean?" Cade asked the question that Sissy and Melanie had on their lips.

"Yeah, what do you mean?" Sissy repeated.

Val knew they didn't know. They thought Val just left. Uncle Ray had said it on purpose. The relationship between Val and the others suffered from distance, time, and misunderstanding. He could feel it in the room and see it in the interactions.

Val shrugged slightly at him as if to say, "It's okay. Don't worry about it." But the door was open.

"He means Mama arranged for me to go live with Uncle Ray and Aunt Beth."

"No way. She was devastated when you left. You broke her heart!" Melanie and the wine spoke in unison. She was the youngest and angriest.

Uncle Ray wouldn't stand for that. "No, Grace arranged it with me—that Val would come and live with us when she was ready. She hoped it wouldn't be necessary but feared it would happen. Beth and I were prepared two months before Val came."

"But she was devastated," Sissy objected.

"Yes, of course she was. You were all devastated. Val, too. You all had each other but Val was on her own. She had your aunt and me but not you or her mother. Occasional phone calls and a letter or two."

"Ray, it's okay. Mom knew I needed to go, and she sent me to you. And I am so grateful. I am still so sorry that you were all young enough that you couldn't fully understand. Hell, I didn't fully understand. I still don't. But I knew it was the best thing."

The tears built up but she wouldn't release them. "I hate that you blame *me*, are angry at me. I was seventeen years old and shouldn't have had to be in a situation that required me to separate from my family."

"Right, you still want to blame everything on Daddy."

"Have some more wine, Melanie," Cade snapped.

Melanie felt the compulsion to protect her father, but even Sissy had let go of the idea that Emmet was a loving father. For her, that process began before they left Star Junction.

"Do you remember the first time we had our super-secret cinnamon rolls?" Sissy had always been a peacemaker. Contention became smiles with the thought of those delicious, top-secret rolls.

"I remember. Mom and Val made them. Best dinners ever!" Cade meant that. Laughter entered the evening with the thought of cinnamon rolls.

"Why did she say she was making them again?" asked Sissy.

"Because we were so good," Cade said with a smile.

Val found herself retreating from the fond memory. So many special moments were born from something else. Cade saw the look Val had and nudged her. She looked up and took in a breath, diluting the words being formed.

"She said we all deserved a special treat once in a while. The first time was the day after Emmet pushed Mom and me over and left with the grocery money for five days. There wasn't money for dinner food."

She looked carefully at Melanie before continuing, "But we had flour and sugar and everything to make cinnamon rolls. So Mom did what she did so well. She made it magical."

Ray gave her a reassuring nod. She bristled a little at her own edits, trying hard not to ruffle Melanie more than she had. "She made a lot of meals with her magic that week and the community vegetable share that Star Junction had."

An awkward silence followed as the others worked to process the information. Sissy broke the silence. "They are still the best cinnamon rolls I think I've ever had. Aren't they, Jakey? Mom made them for us when we came for her birthday."

Jake nodded enthusiastically.

Present Day—Flor's Kitchen

"Yes, Jake. It is true. But I'm kind of sorry you heard it when you were so young."

"It's okay. I mean, I've heard a lot of worse things."

"Are we really going to make them now?"

"Yep, we are going to make them to have for dessert tonight. And I will do my best to share our family's stories. At least the ones I remember and know."

Val got up to take her plate and realized that Grandmother Flor had already set out the ingredients on the counter. *How does she always know?*

They took a break while the dough proofed, the ingredients for the next step prepped and waiting. Alex and Jake kicked the ball around until it felt too hot, so they sat in the shade of the awning with the dogs. Alex was drawing, Jake playing Edward's guitar.

"Jake?" Alex waited for Jake to look up. "What was Grandma like?"

"Um, she…" He stumbled over his words, realizing the Alex was too young to remember her. "She was beautiful, soft and warm when you hugged her. She was the only one then who called me Jacob. I wouldn't have liked it if anyone else had called me that, but it felt like her special name for me. The one only she was allowed. I don't know if that makes sense. And she always could make you feel like you had her undivided attention, that she was listening to every word of your story. Even if you were not making sense, she seemed to follow. I don't know…I still miss her. Even though it seems so long ago. I loved her hugs."

Alex didn't respond or look up from his sketchpad.

Jake added, "I'm sorry you didn't have a chance to get to know her. You would have loved her."

"Thanks, Jake, for sharing her with me." He stopped sketching and smiled at what he'd drawn—Jake, himself, and Grace standing between them with her arms around them both. Jake looked at it stunned.

"Whoa, how did you do that?"

Alex shrugged.

Val sat in the kitchen, thumbing through her journal and assorted pictures. Feeling them more than looking or reading. Tucked tightly between two empty pages of the journal she found a note she wrote but never sent. "Mama, Uncle Ray just told me about your father and how he was. It helped me understand better why you put up with Emmet…but I still wish you wouldn't. I'm sorry I didn't before. I love you." It just about took her breath away.

Did I ever tell her? Val wondered.

That night they enjoyed the magic cinnamon rolls for dessert while they sat around the fire pit with Grandmother Flor, Edward, Lucy, and her kids who had just returned from visiting their other grandparents. Her kids had overheard people talk about ethnicity, ancestry, and evolution, which made all the kids wonder.

After some discussion Alex asked, "What are we? Where are we from?" Grandmother Flor smiled and took in one of her signature breaths, long, slow, and deep enough it seemed to fill the lungs of the earth. This was the cue to all of the others that she would be the one to answer.

"Picaflor, thank you and the boys, for these truly magical cinnamon rolls. It is no surprise to me that your mother had magic. Tonight, it shines once again to give us opportunity to both enjoy every delicious bite and open this conversation to learn. This talk of differences, of countries, ethnicities—it is a lie. There are no differences, only stories. Illusions for our mind. Wanderings of time and space. The names of countries, states, and cities are only names. Places are only locations. They did not have names until we named them. Nor did the people. We gave them names to create clarity for navigation. But people forgot. We forgot. How could a people belong to a location on a map? As if it were their source of identity. It could be funny, if not for the confusion it creates." She paused and took in another deep breath. "We are all of the same source."

"But we don't look the same." It was a question—the one Grandmother Flor waited for and Alex delivered.

"Are you sure?" She smiled. Alex, Jake, and the other kids shifted in their seats, anticipating more mysterious words. The tone of Grandmother's voice signaled the importance of her words, but they were hard to wait for and follow. "Those two trees in the courtyard. One of them is tall and has grown in two directions, the trunk having split into branches to capture more sun. The other is shorter and has many branches closer together. Are they not both trees? Do they both not look like trees? Do all birds not look like birds? Dogs like dogs? Mountains like mountains?

"Take a moment to look at each other. You see what you see on the outside. Hair, skin, shades of colors, and the kisses of the sun. Tall like a tree. Short and scruffy. Do you see differences? What does it matter? Or perhaps, what does it mean? Does how we look serve a purpose? Or maybe, it expresses something more. How do you feel when you look at each other? How does that person feel to you? You are all smiling. Is that a smile of joy or discomfort?

"You can feel the difference. If someone is smiling from joy and love of life, pure presence, or if their smile is a mask put on so you won't notice their pain, so you won't look too closely or know too much. Maybe because they don't trust you, or maybe because they simply don't trust themselves and the emotions to pass through safely. They fear the pain will never stop and that you may see them as weak for feeling it."

Her words found their way skillfully to the hearts of each one there.

"Now gaze deeply into each other's eyes. Don't look away. Relax, and hold the gaze. Our eyes are our gateway—a portal to our very essence. Be brave. How does it feel to be seen? How does it feel to see? You are safe. What do you see when you truly let yourself see?" She hummed gently as she watched them closely, as the kids shifted, stopped squirming, and softened. When she knew they had each seen, she continued. "Children, what did you see in each other?"

"Myself," said Jake.

"Stars," said Alex.

"Wolf."

"Eagle."

"Universe."

"Fire."

"Love."

Flor smiled. "You all saw well. How can we be different if we are all one? We do not come from countries. We come from the stars, all to be unique expressions of the same source."

The kids were thoroughly mesmerized, and more questions were forming than they could verbalize. Edward began playing softly on the guitar, and Lucy played her flute. Grandmother Flor continued with a story.

"When the Ancients arrived, there was much to do to learn to live here as humans. They chose to come with many faces and many looks because they could. It was like play. The one we call God, the creator, Great Spirit, Inti (Cosmic Father), Great Father, Source made this beautiful home for us, his 'Intiq Churinkuna' (children of the sun) with Mother Earth, Pachamama, Gaia. So many names, all so beautiful but none right or wrong. Creator ensured that we have all we need, that we are always safe and protected, and that we always have access to help through the tools he/she provided. We have angels and divine beings and guardian spirits that live as mountains, oceans, trees, animals, and elements. Air, fire, water, earth. There is wisdom for us in every direction through the compass of our hearts. The Source is in all things. There is no separation. But as time went on, people started to forget. They started to believe in the names created simply as reference tools and started using them as identities. As if it made a difference.

"There are many Star Junctions, not just this one. We didn't come to different places. We just came to different locations of the same place. But we all came. Chose to come. Then forgot that we came and began to believe that these labels own us. Should we divide people by eye color? By the straightness of our hair? By dimples? Ha! None of this is real. Look at me now. What do you see?"

In that moment, Grandmother Flor transformed into Alex, Jake, Val, Lucy, William, Grace, and Sissy. She was an eagle and a dove, a flower, and a tree. And she was herself as a child and aged to how they know her now, Grandmother Flor. Val felt waves of emotions. Had they all seen that, or was it just her? The boys seemed mesmerized but not startled. What did they see?

"Hi, Dad!" Alex had a thousand things to share with Cade. He wanted to tell him everything, but mostly he wanted to know when Cade would join them and to tell him how much he wanted to stay in Star Junction.

"Hey, bud, how's it going there? Are you having a good time with your Aunt Val?"

"It's awesome. Aunt Val, Mr. Edward, Lucy, Grandmother Flor, the mountain and Jake and everything. We made cinnamon rolls today! Dad, when are you coming here? I think we should live here."

"I'm glad you are having fun." He had forgotten their names. They were more like memories out of a story book. Listening to the excitement in his son's voice reminded him of how he felt things as a child. With love and openness and curiosity.

"Dad, are you okay? I miss you." Alex worried about his father. He didn't want to sound like he was having too much fun without him. Kids have a natural intuitiveness and he was no different.

Cade was still figuring things out. Deciding the future wasn't as easy as he thought. He was doing community service and outpatient treatment for grief and alcohol as a sentence for his accident. With no injuries but his own, minor damage overall, and a clean record before, he finished in a month. Of course, without Alex there or his girlfriend, he made his community service work a second full-time job. He was in a hurry. He wanted his son with him. But he still wasn't sure what that looked like.

His grief counselor encouraged him to visualize where home was and what it contained. To go through the items in the house and purge what didn't belong in the new life. In their sessions, he mentioned Star Junction often, to which the counselor asked, "Is Star Junction home?"

Cade didn't know the answer. A part of him certainly said yes. But how? He was successful at work, had a network and client base. How could he just move to some small town? How would he support Alex? How would Alex respond to moving away from his friends and the life he had known? If Cade had been paying attention the past couple of years, he would know that Alex didn't really have friends anymore.

"You know I miss you too, bud. I bet those cinnamon rolls were good. I'm good. I promise. Just sorting things out here."

They had agreed to find a new house, which made it easy in some ways to purge as he packed for them. Some of the purging was easy, things that he and Alex just didn't use or notice. Karen had her touches, which he loved when she was still alive, and if he were forced to be honest, he'd avoided since she died. Three years of averting his eyes. Three years of sleep-walking through days because he was afraid to wake up without her. Three years of Alex feeling that he had lost both of his parents. Of retreating deeper into his dreams and drawing.

There, in the midst of the dreams, in the center of uncertainty, fear, doubt and questioning of it all, this boy talked to his mother, and whispered to his father's soul, "Wake up, Daddy. I'm still here. See me." And he was the strong one, the one with patience and faith because there was no other way for him to be, despite the circumstances. Because his mother's spirit whispered to him, *"You are not alone. Keep trying. I love you."* And so, he continued to draw, hoping Cade would see what the drawings were, would recognize the essence calling to him. *"Come back, Cade, come back."*

In the Andes, the Quechua word Hampui was used to call your soul back to you. To call the help of the Apus, the Ñustas, the angels, and beings. In truth, we lose bits of ourselves, bits of our soul during traumatic events, life changes, hardships. Sometimes our soul retreats. The bit of our soul of that moment leaves and our bodies shut the door. We bury it, hide it, disguise it and do whatever we can to move past the unpleasant emotions of life.

Yet when we do that, we block the passage for that bit of the soul to return. We lock in the pain and energy of that emotion instead of expressing it. We lock out the healing of our soul instead of allowing it in. Cade's journey of sleep walking lost him in the despair and took him to an abusive relationship. And Alex with him.

And although Cade wasn't with Alex in Star Junction now, Alex could feel his father better than he had in three years. "Dad, when are you coming?"

"I'm not sure yet, but it will be as soon as I can. I love you, Alex."

"I know, Dad. I love you too."

THIRTEEN

The sun was just beginning to stream into the patio garden, its light filtering through the branches and bouncing off the leaves. Alex was mesmerized by the way the light played with all it touched. He had awoken from a dream and couldn't sleep, so he went out to the patio with his sketchbook and pencils to watch as dark became light. He started by drawing the dream, but as the light began its morning dance, Alex began a new page to capture what he saw. He didn't see like other people, but he didn't know it yet. Alex thought he was alone. Mr. Edward said his morning prayers and gratitude as he watched Alex quietly, recognizing that this was Alex's way of doing the same, though Alex didn't know that yet either.

By the time the patio was in full light, and all the plants and beings now fully awake, Edward spoke. "Ah, daybreak is my favorite time as well. So much magic in this time."

Alex was slightly startled by the sound of Edward's voice, but he was too intoxicated by what he drew to react. He looked up at Edward who was now just a few feet away and smiled.

"Hi, Mr. Edward! It really is."

Edward smiled with the boy. "May I see what you have done?"

Alex looked down at the sketchbook and paused to consider if he should share but then shrugged as he handed it to Edward. Alex had been looking at the planter in the center of the courtyard. It contained a tree, many flowers, herbs, and medicinal plants. Benches were facing it and away. Alex's drawing was not of a tree and flowers.

It was of a vortex of energy and light centered at the trunk of the tree and circling out, as if drawing energy from the earth, pulling it up, and, as it met with the light from above, creating loops and waves radiating out. It showed where the beams were different colors, the rays of the rainbow. All drawn as a detailed, intricate, and beautiful mosaic.

Edward smiled and looked at Alex with deep kindness and love as he spoke, "Alex, you have a beautiful gift. You do not yet realize this, but you will. You can see in a very special way, and because of this, you will help many. Thank you for sharing this with me."

Alex smiled. He wasn't quite sure what Edward was saying, but he liked that he said it. A lot.

Grandmother's compound was comfortable, and the boys had mostly relaxed into the easy energy of their hosts. Every day opened new doors of curiosity and discovery. Val was grateful for the ease of being there, though simultaneously conscious of the lack of progress in finding Lilah. She still wasn't sure how to process all that had happened. Finding Sissy's house and the unsent letters left her confused and frustrated.

What else should she know that she didn't? What else fell through cracks or got buried in time and confusion or ignorance? Val felt she was missing a step and a piece to bring it together. She hadn't felt this helpless since the day she left home at seventeen. But this time, Jake, Alex, and Lilah were depending on her. Cade, too. Val just couldn't shake the feeling that one wrong move might cause it all to spin out of control before she could put everything in place.

Val sat with her laptop at the window overlooking the back

courtyard. It was like looking at the world. The land was vast, and from the window, she could see the paths to the river, Clarity Mountain, and the Watcher.

Grandmother Flor watched her from the kitchen as Val answered emails, read reports, and busied herself with work. Despite the laptop in front of her, she wrote notes in a small notepad.

- *Talk to Elliot*
- *Make changes. -> What changes?*
- *Where is Lilah? -> Talk to attorneys. Make something happen!*
- *Melanie?*

Val's attention moved back to the computer and the documents she was reviewing.

"Do you like your machine?" Grandmother's voice had a way of luring her out of her thoughts.

"I like what it can do, but no, not so much. I used to spend a lot more time on it. I am not looking forward to going back to that."

"Then why go back to it?"

"I'm responsible for the success of my businesses and my employees."

"Your heart already left them. Time for your mind to catch up."

Val knew she was right. Her heart had left the businesses. The design firm stopped being of interest when the clients shifted from small start-ups to big corporate clients. What most identified as a sign of success she saw as a shift from passion to business. Yet that growth and success enabled the growth of the team and the focus on the product lines. Her passion shifted from the design and development to the people. As long as she viewed the employees as her responsibility to mentor and serve, the rest was tolerable. Most of the time.

Val told herself that her time in Star Junction would be a good opportunity to delegate more and encourage some of her identified leaders to step up and lead. She had gotten that far. Delegate and step away, so she had time for the kids. And life. "Maybe your magic box has some ideas after all." Val turned to face Grandmother with a perplexed look, but Grandmother had already vanished. Her email dinged. Elliot.

Val, just checking in. The ship is still afloat but dull without you. You already know this, but Jim may be an issue. Looking forward to you shaking things up again. Seriously though, how is it going with the kids? Have you made any progress finding Lilah? The suspense is tough. You need to be better at sharing details. I'm sure you're feeling that suspense too. I wish I could do more to help from here. Let me know if you didn't receive the package, and I will track it down myself! Be well, friend. Don't forget to breathe. And keep it light. Best regards, Elliot.

She couldn't help but smile. She knew Elliot loved a shakeup. Nothing like creating a moment of chaos to make a masterpiece.

Elliot loved watching Val in action. Good enough was boring. Why settle? He reveled in her mastery of fine-tuning. Val could spot the low pattern and raise it with grace. He had worked for accomplished CEOs who shook things up by shouting, ridiculing, cleaning house completely, and even demeaning people. But Val always seemed to see the higher target, and she did it for the artist, the project manager, and the clerk.

She could see clearly where they could be and what they were capable of. She would say very simple things to help them see it, too. There was no slacking off. She had no qualms about inviting someone to leave. Rise or leave—no judgment. If they wanted to stay, she would help them rise—every single one of them. But some she couldn't reach.

Elliot witnessed her commitment to her staff on his first day, and his ambition changed. This was someone he wanted to align with. His plan to build his résumé, create buzz, and bolt to bigger and better in two years vaporized. There wasn't better. Three years in, they shared drinks after closing a hard-fought deal. He confessed that she wrecked his plans of world domination.

She laughed. "What makes you think you aren't already?" They clinked glasses and laughed.

Val only regretted a few employee moments. The staff meeting just before she started this journey to Star Junction was one of them. She had finally had enough of Jim Steele's good-old-boy condescension and willful disregard of the company's mission and values, let alone her authority. Rather than calling him out in private, she did so in the meeting, reminding him of the values and suggesting that if he couldn't follow them, "perhaps" he was in the wrong place.

She didn't know why she didn't follow it by firing him. In truth she had known for months that he was struggling to align. She just hated that she had hired him in the first place. She let business mentors and, she thought, allies influence her decision. She tried to guide him, nudge him to align, remind him of the values and that he was, in fact, working for her. His condescending tones were comical in the beginning until she realized he believed his own talk.

Val's only regret from the meeting was that she called him out in front of his colleagues instead of in her office. Watching his body language, he didn't take it well. But then, hadn't that been what he had been doing to her since he started? Undermining her authority and planting seeds of doubt in others as she let him speak that way? Val knew the issue wasn't over. She left so quickly to come for Alex and Jake that she hadn't been back to the office and hadn't met with Jim to clear the air and manage fallout. Something in her gut told Val that Elliot's heads up was understated.

Grandmother Flor is right. My heart has left the business. Val sighed as she tried to shift her focus and considered what direction to take with Mr. Jim Steele.

Val took a break from the computer and walked to town. Walking had always been a good way of clearing her head. She stopped in to talk to Daniel at Bishop's Music to pay for the guitar she ordered and noticed the limited inventory and supply of empty boxes.

"Hi, Daniel, thanks so much for choosing a guitar for Jake. What did you choose?"

Daniel looked up. "Hi, Val! Let me grab it from the back." He returned with a vintage Gibson acoustic. "The sound on this one is so gorgeous it's sublime."

"That sounds like the perfect choice for Jake. Thank you." She walked over to the register with him. "Do you think you would be able to hold it a bit longer? I'd like it to be a surprise, but I don't have a place to put it yet."

"Normally that wouldn't be a problem, but I'm actually, well, packing up the store."

"Why?"

"So many of my customers have moved away. I just don't have enough to keep it open. Which means, well, I may need to move away too."

"Daniel, I'm so sorry. Is there anything I can do to help?"

"Get people to move back."

"I keep hearing that, but why are they leaving?"

"I hate to say this, but they need sustainable work. It's not like it used to be. People need money to survive, pay bills, and feed the kids. There's just not a lot of good work here."

"I didn't realize it was that bad. I'm truly sorry that you are planning to close your store. I hope that doesn't happen."

"Thanks, Val, I didn't mean to dump it on you. I'll have this for you. Just try to pick it up in the next couple of weeks—before the festival. I have to go to some interviews out of town."

Val left the store recalling when Daniel's grandfather owned it. She and her father went every week to visit, play, and listen to the frequent jam session by the musicians who played the festivals at the pavilion. It was hard for her to imagine that a place with such a rich history of joy and celebration would be lost. She ruminated but resisted the very strong temptation to go into problem-solver mode. At least not until she understood better.

When she returned to the compound, Val found herself rereading the letters she found at Sissy's and became more curious about Lilah and her father. Who was he? Where was he from? What did "Z" stand for? His writing and language felt different. It reminded her of how Grandmother Flor spoke, but perhaps even vaguer. Jake was snacking and listening to music with his headphones on.

"Jake."

He looked up and pulled the earpiece off his right ear.

"Did you know Lilah's father?"

Jake stopped his music, more because he didn't want to miss it than for the conversation.

"Um, not really. Kind of."

She smiled with raised eyebrows. "Care to help me understand that better?"

"Well, I met him a couple of times. At least, I think it was him. But they didn't tell me it was him."

"What makes you think it was Lilah's dad?"

"Because he's like her. Sometimes when I look at Lilah, I feel like she is made of light. Like she could just dissolve into the air and be everything that is there."

"Wow."

"I know, it sounds kinda crazy, but he felt like that, too. And the way he looked at me—like he wasn't looking at 'me' but something inside or beyond me. It felt weird but not bad." He laughed because that probably didn't make sense either. "That probably doesn't help."

"Maybe it does. Maybe that is what drew your mom to him. Right?" Val said.

Jake's expression became more serious and he asked, "Do you think he has Lilah?"

Val was taken aback. In all the conversations, Ms. Ramirez hadn't mentioned that. "I don't know. If he does, they haven't shared it with me. What makes you say that?"

Jake shrugged. "Just a feeling, I guess. I thought I saw him again after Mom died. He looked at me from across the street. I'm pretty sure it was him, but he didn't talk to me."

Val put her hand on his shoulder.

"I'm sorry you are going through this, Jake."

"If he has her, she is safe, at least. That's what I feel. But I want her back here. I'm her brother. She needs to come back."

"Yes, she does." Val knew that to be true—for herself, for Jake, and possibly for all of them, though she had no idea why. Val was in something she didn't know how to describe. A quest? Fighting to remember what her father had taught her so long ago and heal this family as best she could. A quest to reunite Lilah and Jake, and the rest of the family. She hadn't done anything that felt this important or profound in years.

Alex was helping Edward clean up the back room of the mart. He was "working" to earn treasures like art supplies and another adventure map that Edward said was Alex's next mission but only when he was "ready." Alex didn't know what was meant by *ready*, but whatever it was, he was going to show that he was, in fact, ready. So he showed up. Alex liked Edward and hanging out in the gas station because it seemed like there was always some new cool thing he hadn't seen before. Like his wolf totem. And the star charts and constellation maps that sparked his imagination and wonder. He couldn't wait to have one on a wall in his room or simply have a room again.

Alex missed his dad. They talked every couple of days, but Cade still hadn't said when he was coming. Alex missed his mom, too, but it had been so long since he had seen her. Sometimes she showed up in his dreams. That is how he remembered her because his actual memories were limited and getting faint. When it was just him and his dad, they could spend the whole day building forts or designing castles and laughing. They hadn't done that in a long time—not since Cade met Nancy and she changed everything.

Alex had tried to like her and earn her affection, but all he felt from her was hate. Once, he heard her trying to convince Cade that Alex needed to be sent away to a school for troubled kids. Alex had gone from being excited about everything—curious and thrilled to learn, explore, and discover life—to reserved, quiet, and fearful. He went from designing far-out telescopes so he could see galaxies to hoping he could make himself invisible so he would not have to be shipped away from his father.

Edward saw Alex drifting into thoughts and invited him to help on the floor. He gave Alex a stack of folded maps and brochures and asked him to sort them. They had gotten "knocked over and mixed up." Alex was glad to be on the floor with Edward for any reason. He sat on the stool and started stacking the different maps and brochures, and his mind moved to curiosity about all the places listed.

A woman wearing high-heeled boots, tight, shiny-black leggings, and a frilly gold-flecked blouse entered with a man who was dressed casually. A boy who looked to be about as old as Alex followed behind.

"Get the right kind this time. That other brand was disgusting," the woman barked as the man headed to the drink refrigerator.

He didn't respond. The boy asked if he could have something. A soda. A snack. A crystal. The adults didn't react. It was hard to tell if they even registered his requests.

But Alex did. He had moved off the stool and further behind the counter before the woman had even spoken. He didn't take his eyes off her, except to see the invisible boy. Alex closed his eyes slowly and took a breath, holding them closed for a few moments. Then he opened his eyes and looked at the child, wishing away the pain he saw—pain that was so much like his own. He looked at the father, and his heart beat faster. He swallowed noticeably, and the slightest frustrated sigh escaped him.

The woman finished looking at the jewelry and commanded, "Hurry up! We don't have all day since you got us lost." She looked at Edward seeking sympathy for their unintended detour.

He looked at her kindly but without validation.

She tried again in her sweetest voice, "Maybe you can help us figure out where we are? We were supposed to be on our way to the Deep Canyons Resort, but he made a wrong turn."

The man came up to the register to join her with sodas and a bag of peanuts. "You told me to turn right. I turned right. This is a cool area. No harm done."

She glared at him. "Honey, we are going to be *late!*"

Edward rang up their items and added a map. "There are no mistakes. We are never really lost but not always where we intend to be. If you continue down this road to the left, there will be signs to direct you back to the highway you seek."

The woman smiled sweetly as a thank you and turned away. Edward came from around the counter and approached the boy. "I have a gift for you, young man."

The woman quickly tried to intercept, "No, no, he doesn't need anything. He has too much already."

Edward continued to look at the boy. "Oh, that is good. This is not about need. It is a gift from the heart. It would be rude to refuse a gift given freely." He looked her in the eyes. "Would it not?"

She stepped back, sheepish for the first time. "Of course, that's very nice of you." She wasn't used to people contradicting her.

Edward picked up the mountain owl totem that the boy had been looking at. "Ah, this is an excellent one." He smiled and handed it to the boy. "The owl sees clearly and holds great wisdom. There is strength in wisdom. Trust that it will serve you at the right time," he said it just loudly enough for the boy to hear clearly and softly enough that the woman couldn't make it out. The boy bit his lip and nodded; his eyes still locked with Edward's.

"Well, okay, we really have to be going now. Have a nice day." She grabbed the man's arm and headed for the door. "Come on, Johnny. You are too slow."

Edward watched them leave the store and then turned to Alex. "Are you alright, young Alex?"

Alex nodded, looking down and swallowing.

Edward tapped the stool for Alex to sit again, and he used the one next to him. "What did you see?"

Alex looked at him with a pained expression. He didn't know how to speak it. Describe it with words.

Edward gave him time. "It will be helpful for you to learn to put words to what you see. It is safe to do so with me."

Alex nodded and paused through a swallow. "I saw the invisible boy. It was like he was being erased, and his dad was being changed. The connection between them was being blocked by *her*. Her tendrils, like an octopus. And everything was murky around them, like a hazy black cloud that was hard to see through." He stopped talking as tears began to form.

"And you've seen this before?"

Alex couldn't hold the tears back. "That was me. My dad couldn't see."

Edward placed his hand on Alex's shoulder.

***

The night before his father's accident, Alex started dreaming about Aunt Val, Jake, and the others. He dreamed that he would go with her but didn't know why. He also somehow knew that Nancy would be gone soon. The day after the accident, Cade walked in when Nancy was attacking Alex verbally and trashing his drawings.

"You know, you are just pathetic. These pictures aren't even of anything!" She crumpled them and put them in a trash bag. "It's no wonder your father had an accident with a son like you."

Cade's instinct finally kicked in, and the father in him returned. "What the hell do you think you are doing?" he demanded of Nancy.

She froze, stunned. She had been criticizing him and beating him down for so long that she never expected him to rise back up.

"How dare you talk to me that way!" Nancy's eyes glared back at him.

Cade saw through it all for the first time. Feeling clearer than he had since his wife died. "No, how dare you treat a child that way—especially *my son!*"

Alex stood frozen, watching the scene play out. It felt like a dream.

Nancy tried her other tactic, dripping honey. "Sweetie, we've talked about this. He needs more discipline, and a stronger—"

Cade cut her off. He was done. "No. He needs his father back and you to stop trying to deny him that."

Nancy stormed out of the room.

"Alex, forgive me. I love you, son. We are going to fix this, okay?"

Alex nodded quietly, stunned and more than a little afraid of the shouting.

Cade followed Nancy out. She spun around and glared at him. "You are a complete idiot—the weakest excuse for a man I have ever seen. I've wasted too much time on you. If you think I'm going to forgive you now after you embarrassed me in front of that pathetic creature? I have done nothing but help you, and you repay me this way?"

Cade glared at her in rage, but calm overtook him. He scoffed to himself with a sudden understanding of what he hadn't wanted to admit. He paused briefly, allowing the words to form. She fidgeted like her skin burned. When he finally spoke, Cade's voice was calm and cold.

"Thank you for showing me who you are and reminding me of who *I am*. The only forgiveness I want is from Alex. He is the only one deserving of my apologies or penance."

Nancy shifted again, playing a different card. "Cade, sweetie, this isn't you. I think you are confused from last night. Maybe you have a concussion. You don't want this."

It was her sweetest, saccharine plea. She touched his bandage and caressed the side of his head.

He stood motionless, looking straight through her, and then removed her hand from his head.

"I have never been clearer about what I want or need. It is time for you to leave. Never address my son in that way again. In fact, just don't ever come back."

Whatever power she'd had with him before was gone. She huffed and yelled as she stormed away, "You're going to regret this. I won't take you back!"

Alex watched it all from the window. He saw Cade look and act like his father again. He saw the tendrils of energy from her disintegrate and his father's energy return.

Cade turned and looked toward Alex, watching him, and nodded to his son. "I will not let you down," he said to the air. He repeated this to Alex many times throughout the day.

It was late in the day and the mini-mart looked great. Alex played at sweeping before they closed up.

"Mr. Edward, when can I go to the eye?" His heart was not in the sweeping of the store but in the fantasy of adventure.

"Before you can go, you must understand better."

"Understand what?"

Edward smiled. "Are you ready for a break?"

Alex nodded, and Edward gestured for him to put the broom away. "Let us step outside."

They walked around the outside of the store, and Edward pointed for him to stand in a spot and look. Alex wasn't sure what he was looking for. There was no way to see the Eye from here.

"Young wolf, stop fidgeting. Close your eyes. Plant your feet with deep roots. Slow your breath."

Alex settled into his body.

"Do you remember what the Eye looks like? Can you see it in your mind?"

Alex nodded affirmatively to all of these.

"Do you see the Eye, or does the Eye see you? Open your eyes now."

Alex opened his eyes and looked at the mountain. The Eye was there clearly, right where he hadn't seen it a minute ago.

"Wow, I don't understand. It wasn't there." Alex turned to look at Edward for an answer, and when he looked back the Eye was gone. Poof.

"The Eye is of the Watcher, the guardian spirit of the mountain. The Eye is not visible to all, nor at all times. How are you going to climb to it if you do not understand how to see it consistently? You will wander forever without end. The way for you to be ready is to understand this."

Alex stared perplexed. He closed his eyes and opened them again, squinted, turned his head, and still couldn't see the Eye.

"When you first saw the Eye, it was because you were open and full of wonder. You did not have an expectation. Now you have an expectation and can no longer see it. You are not the Watcher, the Eye is. To have an expectation is to have a demand that life conforms to your desire. The guardian is here to help and protect the mountains and land below. It is not here to satisfy your demands."

"I'm sorry. I don't understand. I want to."

"Yes, I know you do, which is why I am helping you." Edward smiled kindly. "What do you do when you want something from your father or want to do something or go somewhere different?"

"I have to ask if it is okay," Alex responded.

Edward's smile grew.

"Yes, you ask permission first?"

Alex nodded.

"Excellent. That is all for today."

"But I still don't understand."

"That is all for today. Our desires are not life's demands. It is time to go back to work and complete our chores." Edward sounded stern but smiled and winked playfully.

Alex let his shoulders down a little but agreed. He turned back toward the building but glanced over his shoulder at the mountain as he went, just to check again. Out of the corner of his eye, he thought he saw the mountain wink. He shook his head to shake off the notion. Not sure what to make of it, but knowing still that he wanted to go.

It was nearing dusk in the courtyard. Alex didn't bother to go inside when they got home. He just got out his sketchpad and watched as the light and shadows changed and captured the changes in his drawings. Edward had gifted him colored pencils, which he enjoyed experimenting with.

A soft breeze played with the leaves and a lizard soaked in the last bit of sunlight. A soft howling sound in the distance made Alex bolt upright.

"Is that a wolf?" His voice held both excitement and fear.

Edward smiled. "Yes, that is a young wolf."

"Wow, I didn't know they were here." Alex pulled his totem out of his pocket.

"What do you know about wolves?" asked Edward.

Alex shrugged. "I don't know, really. I've seen them in movies and read about them in books, but I've never seen one."

"What do you like about them? What do you feel as we talk about them?"

"I like how they look and they feel strong. Powerful, but they also, I don't know, love each other. That's why they are in packs."

"That is very wise. Wolf energy is very powerful. This is true. The wolf is strong and independent but not selfish. They are loyal. The animal spirits that join us in this life do so to help us. Sometimes to see clearly, or to show us how to love freely, move freely. Wolf spirit is one of strong intuition and awareness. The wolf in us is our pathfinder and a compass keeper. Family is first. The pack works together for the sake of the pack. Together they thrive."

"Do you think I will see one?"

"Young Alex, you have the wolf spirit with you. Just as your father does. When it is time, the wolf will call to you to listen. To know your own strength and trust your voice. Wolf wants to teach you. You will know when the time is right, for you will feel it in your heart."

Alex's eyes expressed his excitement and wonder, but he also felt a flash of fear. "But—what if I am afraid? What if I can't feel it or do what it says?"

"You are to trust your own heart, to trust the intuition that flows within you, to trust the strength of your soul. When the time is right, you will, and you will be fine. You are safe here."

"What do I do when it calls?"

"Talk to it."

Jake and Val entered the courtyard to say hello and check in on Alex.

"Jake, did you hear the wolf?"

Alex's excitement always made Jake laugh. He shook his head. "Aunt Val?"

"No. When did you hear a wolf?" She hadn't heard one since she was a child.

"Just a few minutes ago. Mr. Edward says they live here. I didn't know that. Did you know that? Have you ever seen them?"

Val smiled. "Yes and yes. I knew they were here when I was a kid. I didn't know they were still here. And, yes, I have seen them."

"Wow."

"Come on. Let's take the groceries in and get the dinner going. It is our turn to cook for everyone."

FOURTEEN

Grandmother Flor was sitting in the courtyard with the trumpet tree. The early morning sun created a soft glowing light around them. Val blamed her tired eyes for the optical effect. She quietly sat next to Grandmother. Together they watched the day become brighter. Grandmother Flor took Val's hand and continued in silence, watching the sun rise higher into the sky.

Val hadn't held anyone's hand in thirty years. Suddenly she felt seven again. Light. Innocent. Curious about all that was. She closed her eyes and sank into the way of feeling she thought was gone forever. She could see herself dancing with the drums that night her father called her to come home. She saw the flames flowing with her movements and her heart quickened.

Her hand squeezed Grandmother's tighter as she heard, "Hampui, Picaflor. Come back. Come home." She started with the words and opened her eyes, pulling her hand back. "Do not fear, daughter. You are only remembering yourself."

Val looked at Grandmother deeply. "I don't know what that means. I am myself. Val. The one who went away to learn other ways. The one who doesn't quite know what she is doing here or how any of it is going to work out. I'm not used to speaking in riddles anymore."

"Of course, you are. They are just different riddles."

Val let out a sigh of worry and frustration. Grandmother turned to face Val and motioned her to do the same. She held out her weathered hands, palms up, and invited Val to place her hands in them.

"You are right. You chose a journey for this life that took you far from what you knew. You made a choice at a young age to protect yourself, your memories, and all that your father taught you by burying it on the mountain because you feared it could be taken from you by your stepfather. You were warned, guided, and reminded often not to lose you, and you nodded affirmatively that you wouldn't. But you had already buried the *you* they spoke of.

"It is not such a mystery what is happening right now. You are remembering *that* you. You have come home to a place that will do everything it can to help you to remember and fully return. Picaflor wasn't a childish nickname. It was an invocation, an acknowledgment of the power of presence and joy you carried within from your birth.

"When William died, you felt such loss that in your child's heart you felt as if you were being punished. When Emmet came to your family, you learned to withhold all that you had once shared so freely. What you could not understand at the time is that what you withhold from others, you also deny yourself."

Val sat trembling. The power in Grandmother's hands held her there, the warmth permeating her body.

"I am not nine anymore or seven dancing around a fire. I'm middle-aged. I run companies and am successful at it."

"Yes, but a part of you is still seven, and she wants to teach you how to dance again, and smile, and play—and love. Just because we get older doesn't mean we are no longer all the selves that we have been, and all the moments we have lived. Every age of you still exists and has something to say or teach."

Grandmother moved both of Val's hands together and held them in her left hand as she placed her right hand on Val's heart.

Val felt a well of energy rise within, and her breath stuttered, a vague but sharp pain that surged through her chest.

"You want to know about the woman of the story, the woman who danced with the fire, because you were told that you were the girl who danced with fire. That answer is in you. You already know. When you release your fear and resistance, you will learn to trust the knowing inside."

Grandmother stood and kissed Val on her forehead. "Sit with the angel trumpets. They have much to tell."

Val looked up at the trumpet-shaped white flowers blooming from the tree, but all she felt was numb. She sat with the tree until after the boys rose, clamoring for breakfast. She realized how much she enjoyed hearing them make themselves noticed.

Alex was walking in the woods of the mountain. He could hear the creek nearby but couldn't see it. He followed a path that led up the mountain and should come to the creek soon. The light played dramatically with the leaves and branches, almost distracting and sometimes hurting his eyes. As he came around the corner, he saw a nook by the creek. It was surrounded by trees but was a perfect spot to stop and draw.

He sat on the ground and leaned his back against a boulder to draw. Suddenly he wasn't sure how much time had passed. The light had changed. The breeze stopped and everything was completely still. He looked at the water, which also appeared to be still. He wasn't sure why, but his heart started beating faster and he was afraid. Water wasn't supposed to stop.

He felt like he wasn't alone yet didn't see anyone else or hear anything. He put his stuff in his backpack as quickly as he could, the fear building and the feeling of being watched overwhelming. He tried to remember something that would help him right now. Maybe Mr. Edward told him something. Oh, why couldn't he think?

He zipped his backpack partway and put it on, looking around. Everything looked different. The nook didn't have an exit. Where was the path? He began to panic and couldn't catch his breath. He tried to push his way through some bushes and got snagged, his backpack tearing open and his shirt ripping.

Something in him said, "Stop!" And then he heard, "Breathe." He took a breath and closed his eyes, but he still saw and he heard, "Turn around."

He opened his eyes and turned. In an opening that wasn't there before, he saw a wolf watching him intently. Alex's heart skipped a beat and he froze. He stared at the wolf that seemed to get bigger and bigger. The wolf shifted its feet and prepared to pounce. Alex couldn't move. He was partly in disbelief. Just as he saw the wolf begin its lunge, he jolted away and awake.

He was in his bed, out of breath, sweating. "Phew."

Alex quickly got up and went to the kitchen where he could turn on a light and draw. He didn't know what else to do. He wanted to draw all of it, everything he saw. He felt if he could get it out on paper maybe, maybe he would start to feel okay inside again. He drew the creek, the nook, the trees… They all seemed so peaceful and friendly. Then he drew the part with the wolf, the trees, and bushes towering over him, surrounding him, the boulders he couldn't pass through, the branches that snagged him and stopped his movement.

The massive wolf stared at him. His eyes saw too well. The ears perked as if listening to his thoughts. What did he want? Was it like Mr. Edward said? Was it calling? As he looked into the eyes he drew, he got a chill and closed his eyes tightly. He put his elbows on the table and his forehead in his hands as his leg rocked under his chair.

"Young one, what has you up?" Grandmother Flor's voice was so soft and nurturing that he wasn't even startled by her sudden appearance. She felt soothing in a way he wasn't familiar with.

He lifted his head and looked at her but didn't have words. He didn't need them.

She studied him for a moment and then the wolf on his pad, and gently placed her hand on his back between his shoulder blades.

He turned around to face her and laid his head on her shoulder.

"The wolf comes to your dreams to help you, to teach you to express your heart and trust yourself. If you need to wail, wail. If you need to howl, howl. If you need to love, love harder, stronger, more, and trust. You are loved, child."

He wrapped his arms around her and allowed her love to release his tears. And for that moment, she felt to him like his mother, the way he felt when she held him. Nobody else's hugs had ever felt like that. He started to pull back with the question, but Grandmother Flor stopped him. "Yes, child, it is what you feel. You are always loved, supported, and protected."

Grandmother Flor was a chameleon. When nurturing, she was the very essence of pure love. When teaching, she was quick, clear, and sometimes sharp. She wove teachings into stories like others created a tapestry. Each word carried magic. Each sentence, a sacred spell for wisdom, understanding, and forgiveness. She lived with compassion, clarity, and a passion for all that was.

She knew life was the ultimate playground when we understood how to play. She loved teaching children how to play the instrument of their life. She was less patient with adults who were too attached to their stories. Yet without helping those adults to see and heal, the children would be in a harder place. She would not allow the children to be lost in the fog.

———

Jake and Alex were helping Grandmother Flor and Edward in the garden, mostly because they went outside to play with the dogs and find something more to do, and Grandmother was happy to oblige. Her hands were deep in the soil, planting seedlings and flowers. She and her son smiled at the help that just joined them.

"What are you planting?" Alex asked, wanting to know every detail of all that he saw.

"We are planting life, medicine, joy, beauty, and sustenance," she answered wistfully.

"Um, okay, but what?"

Grandmother laughed. "Would you like to help us add to our garden? I will teach you about the plants one day, but first you must get to know them."

"Sure!" they both answered.

"That is a very good answer." Edward was being funny. "We need holes dug over there and there." He pointed in the directions. "Start with the big holes for the trees. Then smaller holes for the herbs."

The boys stared blankly.

"Ah, yes, the shovel is there." Again, he pointed, this time to a shovel leaning against a tree. The yard was huge and it wasn't clear where he was pointing.

Jake and Alex went to get the shovel.

"You can take the plants with you, too."

The boys looked at the various plants, some just barely sprouting from small cups of soil, some in larger containers, and some so big Alex had a hard time lifting them. They thought maybe the plants would have labels or something to tell them which to take. They decided to do the holes first and walked in the direction that Edward had pointed. But they couldn't see where to go.

"Where do you want us to dig?" Jake asked with confusion.

"What are you planting?"

The boys shrugged. "I don't know. You said you needed holes, so we thought we would do that first because we don't know what goes where."

Grandmother Flor continued with her planting. Edward smiled at the boys. But neither of them provided any more direction.

"We aren't sure what you want us to do," Alex offered.

Grandmother Flor stood up and walked to the tray of sprouted herbs and flowers. She smiled at the tray and began telling the plants how beautiful they all were.

The boys exchanged glances.

Grandmother continued talking to the plants. "Who would like to live and grow in that section there?" As she pointed to the spot she had been working in, she watched the plants and responded, "Wonderful."

Grandmother gently gathered a few of the plants—rosemary, marigolds, and oregano—and carried them over to their desired spot. Before kneeling again, she looked over at the boys and gave them a knowing look and nod.

"Ask them; they will tell you. This is how you will learn."

The look on the boys' faces was something between bewilderment and terror.

Edward chuckled and decided to guide them a little more. He walked over to the boys and had them walk the area with him.

"Some people plant a garden using books and facts about what plants are supposed to grow where and with what. Some people plant gardens by what they want it to look like, regardless of the plants. But to plant a garden like ours, a living garden full of light and love and energy..." He paused and looked at Alex. "You have seen the energy. It is our way to ask the plants. Who knows better than the plant itself where it will thrive? We do our best to recognize our connectedness in all things."

"But how do you know what it tells you?"

"Ah, that is a good question. Practice. You won't know until you practice."

"But I don't want to choose the wrong spot and have the plant die."

"And if we do not get them all planted, they will surely die. The best way to learn is by doing. Give it your best, most open effort. It is okay to get it wrong. From that you will learn. You will learn to identify what it felt like when you heard it wrong and what it felt like when you heard it right. You will learn but only if you take action."

Edward stopped the conversation then and started whistling as he walked back to his plants.

The boys both shrugged.

"Okay, let's try," said Jake.

They walked over to the plants still waiting and asked which ones wanted to be planted over in the corner where they had just been. Each of them collected a few plants, coming back for the larger ones and the trees. Four trees. Sometimes Jake found himself whistling along with Edward, and sometimes Edward whistled along with Jake.

Val took a break from her work and joined them after a couple of hours, bringing cold water, lemonade, and snacks. "Aunt Val, Aunt Val! Do you see what we are planting?" Val looked over at the area and was amazed by how much work they had gotten done.

"Boys, that is amazing! How did you know what to plant?"

"We just asked the plants! Didn't they ever teach you that?"

"I think they did, once upon a time."

Grandmother Flor joined them. "Picaflor remembers." She looked at the section the boys were planting and gleamed with approval. "You have learned well, boys."

She gestured for all to sit and enjoy the snacks. "Today was good practice for the hike you wish to take. Learning how to listen and decide helps you to stay focused and keeps you from confusion. It will be important that you use this on your hike."

She looked at each of them, first Jake and then Alex.

"Does that mean we can go to the Eye?" asked Alex.

"If you are clear with your intentions and remember what you have learned, tomorrow would be a good day for you to go. It will help you to know why you wish to see the Eye. The guardian has a way of helping us to see. Be aware, you may find more than you imagine."

Alex's excitement drove Jake crazy, which made him a good teacher. Jake had forgotten how to have fun, to let himself get carried away with ideas and exploration. His only exception was music, but even there he hid. Edward told them to start the hike early and follow the map, which wasn't really a map at all.

"Start at the trail of the bear. Let the boulders lead you. Where the trees change, you will see a tree with three badges. Not more or less. It will lead you to the place that hides treasures. From there, you will find the remembering place and the Eye that watches."

To Alex he said, "Alex, listen to your intuition. You will recognize the signs you are given and will help Jacob to see. But you must also listen to his wisdom and let him help you to understand. Together, you will succeed."

And to Jake, "Jacob, a wise leader serves his people by listening to their thoughts and recognizing their gifts. Young Alex will see many signs along the path. Your experience brings the wisdom to understand what they mean. Let him guide you until it is time for you to speak what you know. Together, you will succeed."

Jake carried a small backpack with lunch, water, and tools that Edward provided. Alex had water, a sketchpad, and his wolf totem.

With a point in the right direction, they were off by 7:30 a.m. It was best to do the climbing early, as the day would become hot soon enough. The boys headed toward the mountain, searching for the trail of the bear. They came across signs that read: "Upper Lake Trail" and "Rainbow Ridge Trail" but didn't see any signs that said "Bear."

Jake was getting impatient and frustrated; his trust being tested. "Man, this is stupid!" he said.

Alex didn't respond right away. Suddenly he pointed. "Look!" About forty feet ahead was a large boulder that resembled nothing other than a bear. To Alex, it was clear as day. Just before the bear boulder was a path—not a marked trail taken by tourists but a path between boulders.

"This is it!" Alex walked faster.

Jake did too, though begrudgingly.

The boulders and landscape were varied shades of gray, brown, slate, red, and flecks of blue or green or white. Alex thought they were the most amazing rocks he had ever seen, but Jake had seen these kinds of boulders before and thought they all looked like, well, boulders.

"You don't think they're cool?" Alex asked in disbelief.

Jake rolled his eyes. "I don't know. I think they are boulders. Like normal. I never really thought about them being cool."

"You're lucky."

"Me? How do you figure?"

"Where I live there are just houses and roads. Our trees are little or cactus. It is mostly, I don't know, traffic and cars and buildings. And you have a sister."

Jake had never considered himself lucky before. Ever. In fact, he thought he was anything but. His mom died. He hadn't seen his sister in a year.

"You don't have a brother or sister?"

"No. Did you know about me?"

"What do you mean?"

"Did you know you had a cousin?"

"Yeah, I met you once, but you were a toddler. And I didn't know where you were." As they were talking and walking the path began to change, narrowing with more trees.

"I wish we hadn't been so far apart. I always wanted a family. I mean, not just in my dreams."

"In your dreams?"

"Yeah, sometimes I would see you in my dreams, and Aunt Val, and Lilah, well, I think it was Lilah."

Jake didn't say anything. He wasn't really comfortable with his dreams and had never told anyone about what he saw in them. But when he heard Alex talking about them now, and before with Aunt Val, they suddenly felt bigger and more real. He really wasn't sure how he felt about that.

"You're an interesting kid, Alex."

Alex looked back at him and smiled.

Jake smiled back. "Hang on a sec. I'm thirsty." They stopped to have some water and look around. Alex climbed up on a boulder to get a higher view.

"What do you see?"

"I see *everything*!" he said exaggeratedly and laughed. "Wait. I see where the trees are changing. Look up ahead!" Alex pointed up the path to a break in the path. The trees on the right were the same they had been seeing, a mix of scrub oak and juniper. On the left were pinyon pines littered with aspens.

"Let's go then." Jake was beginning to feel a bit of Alex's excitement, and before he could stop it, "Good eye," slipped from his lips.

Alex beamed as they continued up the path and followed the change in the one to the left. But as they started up this part, they stopped again.

"I don't know what it means, badges. What badges?"

Jake pondered for a minute and then replied. "Well, it is probably something that looks like a badge. You know, maybe round and with something in it."

They scanned the trees. They saw some with marks where the branches had been cut or fallen. Alex found a tree that had four round marks that looked like badges.

"Like these. These are badges! And look, they have pictures in them," Alex exclaimed.

"Yeah, those are like badges, but remember, it said not more than three. Let's go slowly and pay attention. You will see it. You've seen everything else."

Alex focused. He didn't want to miss the clues. He came across a big rock that looked like it was pointing ahead of them and slightly to the right, so he kept going. As they followed this bend to the right, there was the tree. Three badges complete with images.

Alex quickly got out his sketchpad. He knew he had to draw them but wasn't sure why. The top circle was slightly to the left and had what looked like an eagle flying; if it were a clock, it would be facing two o'clock. The next one down, slightly to the right, looked like the top half of the sun, like it was setting over a mountain. The third circle was farther apart and below the second. It looked like a bear paw pointing straight up.

Jake watched Alex draw them with patience and admiration. He looked around, trying to spot the next location. The path spread out and had many possibilities, but which one should they take?

"What do you think the pictures mean?" Jake asked.

"I don't know exactly, but I think they are like messages and directions. Like the eagle. Edward said that the eagle has clear vision and is super powerful. But I'm not quite sure what it is telling us."

"It looks like he is flying northeast. Which is probably that way." Jake took off the backpack to see what Mr. Edward had packed. "Ahh, a compass."

"The middle one looks like the setting sun, and the other is a bear claw. But which one is first? I mean, if they are directions—top first or bottom?"

The circles themselves almost looked like a path. Jake pointed out to Alex how they looked like a path that turned. They looked around at where they were. The different paths resembled the actual claws on the bear paw.

"I think we are in the first one, the bear paw. Look at the way the different paths go," Jake said.

"Then we should go this way because it is the way the eagle is pointing!" Alex pointed to one of the paths to the right.

"I don't think so. Not yet. If we go that way we won't be able to see the sun go over the mountain. Isn't that what you thought the second badge was?"

Alex thought for a minute and looked again at the claw.

"Look! The claws are all pointing to the left, like eleven o'clock. But the path looks hard and steep."

They decided to go further onto the path to see if it became clearer. As they started to climb, Jake looked back and could see the other paths clearly. The three on the right ended on the same cliff, but the next one over went on as far as he could see. They went back to that path, feeling it was the right one.

It was a long climb, and they grew tired. Alex started to get discouraged. Jake motioned that it was time to eat. They found a couple of boulders under a tree that provided shade and shelter—a perfect spot to sit and eat.

"Alex, don't worry. We are on the right path. It is the trail of the bear. Right?" Alex paused to ponder Jake's words, his expression lightening with understanding.

"So tell me about why we are doing this?" Jake urged.

"To see the Eye! The Watcher. Didn't you see the Eye?"

"What eye?"

"The one in the mountain! When Aunt Val and I drove in, we could see it watching us. Mr. Edward said not everybody sees it, but that he knew I would. You will see it too."

"We'll see." Jake looked around and he became quiet.

Alex got quiet, too. He watched as the breeze made the light dance with the grasses. "It's also because Mr. Edward and Aunt Val said that the Watcher is like a guardian spirit, like someone who watches over us. And I want it to watch over my dad too. I don't want any more bad things to happen to us."

"Yeah, me neither." He looked over at Alex. "I hope they are right. Hopefully, it is watching over Lilah."

Just then a hummingbird buzzed between them and circled. She flitted back and forth as if studying each of them and then hovered just in front of Jake. He couldn't help but feel lighter, and he smiled at Alex as he put what was left into the backpack.

When he stood he noticed the tree they were sitting under had a branch that looked like it was an arm pointing forward. He laughed. "I think you are rubbing off on me. You ready?"

With that, they continued in the direction the tree pointed. Jake heard beats in his head and had lyrics coming with each step. Mr. Edward's lesson in walking well came to his awareness. As they rounded the corner of the path, they saw the mountain. Its coloration looked like the bottom rays of the sun; neither had seen anything like it.

As the sun rose above it, the mountain shone in different colors. They took it in. Alex quickly sketched enough to remember. Jake pulled out the compass and shifted their path slightly to the left, northeast.

It wasn't far before Alex saw the big tree with the hole at the bottom. It was like a cave in a tree.

"Look!" He pointed excitedly.

Jake wasn't sure what he was pointing at, or why really.

"A place that hides treasures!" Alex ran to the tree and started drawing it. "I'm going to reach inside!"

"Wait! Just hang on a minute." Jake caught up and saw the big hole, but he also knew that things other than treasures could be inside. He picked up a long stick and told Alex to step back for a minute.

"You can't just reach into holes here. Sometimes animals live in them." With that, he carefully stood to the side and reached the stick inside the hole to coax out any critters. And one wasn't too happy about leaving.

"Whoa, what's that?" exclaimed Alex.

"That's a bull snake. Not poisonous." He reached the stick in again to make sure all was clear. Then they knelt down and looked together.

Alex scooped out a bunch of leaves, pinecones, and acorns, which Jake thought was odd. *Why are there acorns inside the pine tree? Maybe the kid is right.*

Alex reached back in and got his hands on something kind of sharp and pointy. He pulled it out slowly. It was a crystal cluster with purple and blue points. Both of their eyes got huge.

"It's amazing! Have you ever seen anything like it?" Alex couldn't contain his excitement now.

Jake wondered what it was for. He got up and looked around.

"Alex, come over here. What do you see? Where do we go from here?"

Alex came back to himself and thought about the directions. "From there you will find the Eye that watches all." He looked around the tree, on the other side, on all the sides, and then looked back from where they came.

"There!" He pointed at the mountain they had come from. The Eye that he had seen with Aunt Val was there, watching.

Jake looked to where Alex was pointing, but he wasn't sure what he was looking at.

"What?" He was frustrated, more than he expected. All of the sudden all of his frustration and anger and resentment and fear came rushing out. He worked so hard to keep it all in, to manage and control every expression. This felt like too much and he didn't know why. He was just on this stupid hike with his ten-year-old cousin. Why were so many emotions coming up? "What are you looking at? Nothing is watching us."

"Sure there is. It is right there. The Eye. It's right there." Alex pointed emphatically.

"I can't see it. This is stupid. I should have known."

"Yes, you can. I know you can."

"Look, Alex, I'm not like you. It's too late, okay? Just forget it. I can't see it." Jake pushed him away and turned.

Alex stood motionless for a moment just trying to figure out what to do. Jake couldn't give up. It was in the dream. He could see it too. Jake started to walk away and Alex, still holding the crystal, jumped at him and stopped him.

As Alex yelled, "Yes you can," he touched Jake's heart area with his right hand, looked him in the eye, and said in a voice neither recognized, *"You can."* And for a moment not measurable in time they were held there, Alex's hand on Jake's heart, and nothing else existed but them and the feeling coursing through.

Jake looked at him with tears in his eyes, heart racing, not sure if he wanted to punch him or run and hide. He finally looked back to the Eye expecting the same thing but hoping so hard that he would see what Alex saw. He took a breath like he had never taken before and let it out in awe. There it was. Watching.

He dropped to his knees crying tears he had held so long, and crying relief. He swore the mountain cried too, washing the tears away. Alex stood quietly, watching. Waiting. Frozen. He didn't know what had just happened. Something just took over, touched his hand to Jake's heart, and *zap*.

It seemed they stayed like that for ages, neither feeling time, just taking in this place and all that had happened. Jake heard an eagle's cry and looked to see one flying overhead. He returned to himself and looked for Alex. Alex was still standing in that spot, looking at Jake with uncertainty and fear. Jake was overcome with compassion and gratitude.

"Alex, you okay?"

Alex shrugged slightly, not sure what words to say.

Jake gave him a hug. "It's okay. Thank you. You helped me."

And Alex began to cry. He wrapped his arms around Jake. It was his turn to let it all out—the fear for his father, the pain from losing his mother, the anger and uncertainty. "Little man, you are okay. It is okay. Mr. Edward said this is the remembering place. I guess sometimes remembering means feeling what needs to come out."

The eagle called again. They both looked up as it dropped something that fell a few feet away from them. Jake picked up the feather admiring it.

"Wow, it's beautiful."

"It's for you. She gave it to you," Alex said with certainty.

"You think so?"

"Yes, Grandmother Flor said that when nature spirits gift us something, it is rude to ignore it. We should be grateful instead. And can gift something in return."

"Like what?"

Alex shrugged. "I didn't ask, but I think anything from our heart."

Jake pulled off the backpack and pulled out an apple. He looked up and turned in a full circle. "Thank you." And he set it carefully on the spot where the feather had landed.

The boys were quiet for much of the hike back. Silently processing all that happened, the adventure, the events, the feelings that escaped and arose and revealed themselves. Each accepted that the other had witnessed them and without plan or understanding held each other safely in that uncomfortableness. They were quiet as they walked lightly on the earth. They stepped without need of filler or busyness. More comfortable with the quiet between them.

As the boys approached the compound, Blu came out to greet them. They both stopped for a moment.

Alex turned to Jake. "Jake?"

Jake met his gaze. "I'm really glad you were with me."

Jake gave a reassuring smile. "Yeah, me too." And held out his fist for Alex to bump.

Edward was there by the door, whistling as he carved. He looked them over when they came close. "I see you had a successful journey."

They weren't sure how he always seemed to know things, but suddenly their quiet state erupted into excited energy.

"Mr. Edward, it was amazing!" Alex was, of course, the more expressive one. "We found all the markers and the Eye! Jake saw it, too. And look!" He held out the crystal they had found.

Edward smiled, pleased by the news.

Jake nodded with the slightest hesitation.

"That is excellent." He looked them both in the eyes and spoke while making eye contact with Jake. "And you have questions."

Jake nodded.

"Sit with them. Bring them to your music. See what answers you will find."

"But, I want to ask *you*," Jake replied.

"Yes, but ask the music first. It may surprise you."

Jake was beginning to notice something. Whenever Edward or Grandmother or Aunt Val suggested something that he didn't like—like waiting, or feeling into something, or asking the music, asking his heart, asking himself—he would often feel the most resistance or frustration when they were right. And he was surprised by his own answers. The answers he didn't think he knew or could come up with on his own.

His auto-response was: "If I knew the answer I wouldn't have to ask." But then he would inevitably find himself in a quiet moment, playing a guitar or humming or drumming, and different thoughts would find their way in. Quiet whispers that felt different from his usual thoughts.

They drifted in with the sound waves as he was immersed within the music itself. They didn't feel like answers as much as slivers of peace that took away the question marks and urgency.

Later, Edward found Jake in the courtyard with the guitar and Blu sitting at his feet enjoying the music. He'd laid the eagle feather carefully on the arm of the chair.

"I see you met the eagle."

Jake looked up and stopped playing, his hand going instinctively to the feather. "Yeah, it's okay to have it. Right?"

"You were meant to. The eagle dropped it for you." Edward sat near him with a reassuring look. "Tell me about your journey."

Jake paused, deciding what to share. He started with the easy stuff. "It was fun. Alex is a neat kid."

Edward nodded. "He is 'neat' indeed."

Jake looked at him and let out a breath. "And something happened. At the place of remembering, I think. I was frustrated and angry that I couldn't see the Eye. But Alex, I don't know, he was so sure. He reached out and put his hand on my chest, and everything was weird. Like we were in a bubble. And so much heat was coming from his hand. I could feel something happening to my heart. But I don't think it was my real heart, just, like—like breaking open. And then I could see the Eye. But I couldn't stop crying, not for a while."

"You had much to release." Edward's voice was kind and warm.

"But what happened? How did he do it?"

"He touched your heart with pure love. That is the greatest power of all."

"When I stopped, you know, crying, I saw that Alex was still standing where it happened. Scared."

"And you helped him as he had helped you."

"Yeah, I guess."

"It was a very important journey for both of you for many reasons—to enjoy and to walk well. To be at peace with yourselves, each other, and what is. Perhaps, the most important was to release the emotions and fears that you have been carrying. The anger. The resentment. All the things that eat at you and weigh you down."

Jake shifted, uneasy with his words.

"But how do you have bad things happen and not have anger? My sister is still missing. My mother dead. My father someone we don't want around. Am I supposed to pretend everything is okay?"

"No, you are supposed to feel. Express. Find words. Find music. Express more. There will always be experiences in life that are difficult, sad, and scary. This is part of the experience of life. It is important to have the emotions, notice them, acknowledge them, express them, and cause no harm.

"When we hold the energy of anger, we tend to only spread it instead of releasing it. Anger meets anger begets anger. We yell at someone who then yells at us or the next person. There are ways to express that transmute the energy instead of spreading it. One can turn it into something better. Lighter."

"But the problem hasn't gone away. My sister is still missing."

"Yes. Tell me, do you think it is easier to carry a river rock or a boulder every day?"

Jake cocked his head and fingered the eagle feather, still feeling agitated.

Edward continued, "How do you feel if you are the one carrying the boulder?"

"Tired and probably angrier."

"Young Jacob, it is not easy to learn this or to create this awareness for ourselves. Many never do. They spend their lives carrying every bad thing that ever happened to them as if in a backpack they can't take off. As if there will be a place to undo them all or someone will come and take them all away and erase our memories. This is not what is meant for us. We cannot feel good if we are drowning. We cannot rise if we weigh ourselves down."

"I don't understand. It sounds like you are telling me to just be happy."

Edward smiled. "No, forgive me. I am offering you another way of understanding. Your weight got lighter today because you allowed yourself to feel and release. You let go of the weight and still love your sister and still miss your mother. But for that moment, you loved them in lightness."

"Yeah. I did. It almost felt like I could feel them." Jake felt goosebumps as he realized it was true, and tears glistened from his eyes.

"Yes. You were in a state to receive. I've seen you watch us. Grandmother Flor, Lucy, even Val has returned to some of what she learned as a child. We greet every day with gratitude for what is. And every night we lay down the burdens and know grace. And this too is done with gratitude. Because we are meant to experience all of life but not to carry it."

"I'll try to remember."

"That is what the feather is for. To remember your lightness and how to soar."

Alex sat in the kitchen drawing as much of the day as he could. The purple and blue crystal sat next to his pad. He'd calmed from the excitement of the day and wanted to share the adventure. He studied what he was drawing and began to feel it all again. Grandmother Flor worked quietly preparing vegetables for later and baking something that filled the house with sweet aromas.

When his drawing slowed and his hand stilled, she spoke. "You had a very big day."

Alex looked up, lulled out of his daydream. But he couldn't seem to find words, so he nodded and bit his lip instead.

"And you are not sure of all that happened."

Again, he nodded. She took a seat on the stool next to him and took his hands gently in hers.

"Because of what you felt with these."

Another nod.

"And what do you feel now?" She continued to hold his hands gently but firmly.

"Warmth."

She nodded reassuringly.

"And I think it is energy, like with the crystals in the store. It feels nice."

"Yes. That is the healing power of love. Pure love. It is our truest state—who and what we are inside. But people forget. All we have to do is remember. In that moment on the mountain, you felt more love than doubt, and love heals armored hearts. Young one, you would be well-served to let it heal yours, too."

Alex leaned in and hugged Grandmother. "Thank you."

FIFTEEN

Star Junction had suffered. It had lost a lot of residents to "better opportunity" and ideas about wealth. Many of those residents discovered a different kind of poverty. Some returned, but some still wandered, lost and searching for a way to make it and a place that felt like home in the way Star Junction did. Leaving always felt so rational and made complete sense on paper, but somehow it never achieved the same state in reality.

Emmet had not been the only suitor who pulled people away. Those brought in by the work of the mill fell into three categories: those who were nomads just passing through, those who would try to settle for love or opportunity but who would eventually steal people away because they held a different target in their sights, and those who would be forever changed and would become family.

In truth, Star Junction was not a place. It was home. It was an energy that not everyone understood how to feel. It was sentient and loving and supported everything and everyone in its midst. Like any parent, Star Junction longed for her loved ones to come home.

She had never been overcrowded. Topping out at not quite four thousand people when Val was a child. Now she had less than two thousand residents, not yet counting Val and the boys. Many commuted to Exton for work as Sissy had.

A shutter banged against the window. Val looked over to see what was happening and saw the door open. She walked to it with a growing sense of dread. As she walked outside, the day was dim with an orange cast. Nobody was around. She looked over to the mountain and it was dark. She could barely make it out. She walked into town and found no one. It was empty. Desolate. No signs of life and a feeling of deep despair. Her heart began to race. She had to find the kids. She had to find them all.

She ran toward the square, but it was empty, and then she ran toward the mountain though it was cloaked behind dark clouds. She knew it was there. She continued. She called out, "What am I to do? Help me. How can I help?" The clouds parted, and she was in bright light at the top of Clarity Mountain.

She could see all the people who had left, all those searching for better jobs, higher paying lives, and intangible illusions. She heard, "Bring them home." Her heart sank with doubt and fear. "How am I supposed to do that?" She saw the empty buildings. She saw her company's sign. She saw gardens filled with vegetables and fruit trees. She saw a return of life. "Plant the seed of hope." And it all went dark again, her standing there, facing where the mountain should be. "Trust."

Val awoke with a start. "Why didn't I see it?" she wondered, beginning a moment of self-judgment from the overachiever. She shook it off, ready to start the day.

Val made her usual morning call to Ms. Ramirez. More often than not, she left a message. No news. No contact. No updates. Val was not the only one frustrated by the lack of progress with finding Lilah.

Jake came in and found Val working again. "You're always working."

Val looked up from her laptop. "Good morning, Jake."

He just stared at her, questions running through his mind.

"I do run businesses; it requires time on the computer."

"Probably be easier if you were there, huh?" His frustration was clearly expressed in his tone.

"Jake, I'm not going anywhere. I don't get a summer break like you do."

He rolled his eyes and looked away.

"Hey, we are not moving to California. Got it?" Val found her own tone becoming agitated.

"Yeah, okay." He put his headphones back on. None of it was about her working. He just couldn't articulate all that it was about. Another day without Lilah. Another day without answers. Another day without a plan.

Were they just going to stay in that limbo forever? Despite starting to like Aunt Val, he wasn't planning to trust her until Lilah was with him. Her words were empty until proven. He shook his head and pushed through the door to the courtyard.

Val let him go. *I can't keep chasing him down and trying to explain. I have work to do.*

Storms were brewing at the offices, too. Jim Steele had been causing dissension, which was made easier by her absence. She regretted not firing him before she left. Val tried to stay visible with emails and regular calls, but she couldn't feel into the issues as well from a distance. And they couldn't feel her presence and the calm stability that came with it.

As she scheduled calls with some of her team, her mind was on the dream that woke her and all the ways staying couldn't work. It was becoming clear, though, that she wouldn't be able to continue running both companies from Star Junction. Or she didn't want to. Something would have to give. Her business mind knew that she might need to break her promise to Jake. In the very least, she may need to go make an appearance at the offices and calm things down. In the meantime, Elliot was bringing the key players in for a private video call with Val.

Don't worry, boss. There won't be any mutinies on my watch. These are your people. —Elliot

Elliot had a way of steadying choppy waters. She hoped it was enough.

Jake came back in from playing Edward's guitar in the courtyard just as Val was concluding her emergency staff meeting.

"Thanks for the call, everyone. It's great to see all of your faces and touch base with how each of you is doing. I'm grateful for all of your amazing work and appreciate your patience while I am taking care of family matters."

"Boss, do you have an idea when you'll be back or here for a visit?"

"I, uh, I can't give you a date on that. There are balls in the air here that I have no control over. But I want you all to know I am a phone call away. Really. My open-door policy hasn't changed. The door just has to be a phone or video call. I know you are all busy. Again, I appreciate you taking the time today to be here. Now, go do what you do!"

Jake listened in the background. Val had barely ended the call when Jake spoke up, "So you are going back."

Val turned to face him. "That is not what I said."

"It's what you meant. You're going back, and you think we're going with you."

"Jake, I don't know anything yet. You are not the only one I am responsible for. I have seventy employees who rely on me to make the right decisions and run the company right for their well-being. There is a bigger picture here."

"Yeah, well, don't worry so much about me. I'm only with you because I have to be. I can take care of myself and Lilah. I did it before. I can do it again."

"Yeah, well, you're stuck with me, Jake. I said I will do my best, and I am. I never said I would be perfect. I'm the adult. I will make the decisions." She couldn't keep up with the energy swirling around them. Everything she said just came out and made it worse. She wasn't able to shift fast enough.

"I knew I couldn't trust you. You're just like the others who lie."

"I haven't lied to you. Not once. I told you I don't know, and I don't. Still don't. I want us to stay here if that is what you all want, but I haven't figured out how to make it work yet."

She took a breath in exasperation and began again, "You know what? We need to take a break from this conversation. Because it really isn't going well for either of us. I'm truly sorry that you feel the way you do."

This time Val walked away. She needed time to be outside and the front patio with all the aromatic herbs was the perfect place.

When the door closed, a couple of her notes blew to the floor. Jake was going to walk away but picked them up instead. The first one read:

- Can I move it here? How?
- Where is Lilah? Call Ms. Ramirez again. Schedule meeting this afternoon.
- Time for stronger action from attorneys?
- Sell companies?
- Find house
- Cade?
- Where is Melanie?
- Clarity Mountain...

The second note was a drawing of the mountain with what looked like a circle or spiral on top. Jake put the papers back with Val's notepad and tucked them under a bit so they wouldn't blow off again. He didn't know how to process his emotions and the information on the notes, but seeing them defused some of the anger.

Jake decided to practice walking well. That's what he told the others. Edward recommended the path behind the courtyard into the hills.

"You will find much music there," he said with a gleam in his eye.

As Jake exited the gate, Blu ran to join him. Jake looked back at Edward to see if it was okay for the dog to come.

Edward nodded in approval.

"Okay, Blu." Jake patted the cattle dog on the head. "Let's go."

It wasn't just a walk. Jake needed to sort his thoughts. About Val. About Alex, and Mr. Edward, Lilah, his mom. About everything. He liked everyone, but were they really his family? Going to stay his family? And what would happen when Alex went back to his dad? Was Val really going to stay here, or was he going to have to move to California? He didn't want to leave.

Lost in his thoughts, it didn't take long to reach the hills where sagebrush was joined by juniper trees and pinyon pines with a few aspens and currant bushes adding color. The recent rain brought an assortment of flowers—some big and vibrant, some tiny and clustered with perfectly adapted beetles spreading the pollen and savoring the nectar. Yellow, purple, orange and red patches decorated the path.

Edward's words about not carrying everything repeated in his mind. Blu stayed close to Jake while smelling all the scents she could. Jake found a boulder to perch on and watch Blu. It was amazing how Blu studied each flower, sniffing, licking, sniffing again. As he watched his canine teacher in silence, Jake began to notice little clicking noises. Grasshoppers!

Jake imagined they were having an in-depth conversation about all that Blu was discovering. This made him smile.

"They're talking about you, Blu."

Blu looked up at Jake and then continued her study. Jake slid down the boulder to lean against it, closed his eyes, and listened.

Tap, tap, tap, tap. A woodpecker got to work on a nearby tree. Buzz-hmmmm, took over as bees did their best to visit every flower. Mr. Edward was right. A lot of music was here. The wind played the leaves, and the branches danced a bit. Blu curled up next to him, her study complete for now. It was time for rest. She and Jake drifted off.

Lilah was playing in a sea of flowers. At first Jake wasn't sure what he was seeing. She seemed so far away. He started to run to get closer, Blu running next to him, but no matter how fast he ran he didn't seem to get closer. It was like he was running around her instead of to her.

"Lilah! Lilah!" he screamed for his sister. "Lilah, how can I reach you?"

He stopped running, breathing fast and hard and feeling every bit of fear and frustration and grief that losing his mother and sister could bring. Blu barked and nuzzled his friend. Jake dropped to his knees and allowed Blu to nuzzle more. Just then Lilah was suddenly in front of him, glowing as she did.

"Don't be sad, Jake. I am still here. It won't be long now. Do not worry about it all. Our family is real." She touched his face and disappeared.

Snap! Both Blu and Jake started from their sleeps and looked up. Someone was near. Blu sat up but did not move. Jake sat upright as he heard more snapping twigs and underbrush.

"Hello?"

He paid attention to Blu who was attentive but silent and at ease. He reached out to Blu and gave her a pat as he waited for whatever it was. The currant bush moved as if someone were pulling on branches. The someone was a fawn and its mother. Soon they saw the buck with eight-point antlers. Blu lay back down and watched.

Jake followed Blu's lead and relaxed his body. The deer family grazed and enjoyed their foraging, each looking at the boy and dog and continuing without alarm. Jake felt something change in him. His heart softened. The awe and excitement he would normally feel at the deer shifted to silent gratitude. For them. For seeing Lilah in his dream. For her message.

As he watched the deer, he saw the family and thought, *I can just let it be what it is, and I like that.*

On the walk back he found a rhythm in the sounds and a new song playing in his heart. He had a feeling that when he arrived back to the house, Mr. Edward would know that he had walked well.

Lucy found Val in the patio. She had come to coax Val off of the computer to join her on errands with the bait of showing her a house she thought she'd like.

"Hi, Val."

Val looked up to see her friend.

"What's up?"

Val smiled in an "I don't know where to start" kind of way. "Well, I have a problem employee who is creating dissension. And I just lost my cool with Jake. And I really wasn't expecting to ever do that."

"Val, you're human. You do know that. Right? Doing the best you can. And you're allowed to not always have the perfect response to everything."

"I'm not really sure about that. But at least my key employees are not swayed by the problem one. So that's a good thing."

"Hey, I came to tempt you away from your computer and have you join me for errands. And a surprise I think you'll love. I thought I'd have to drag you away, but you are already out here. So it should be easy to sway you. Right?"

Val laughed.

It was just as well. Though Val appreciated the tool that enabled so much to get done from so far away, she secretly loathed the thing. It took no time to say yes to Lucy's invitation. Val was even okay that Lucy was doing the driving.

"Where to first?" Val laughed at her own question. It didn't matter the order of things. She didn't even know what the things were.

Lucy smiled. Val noticed an envelope with Daniel's name on the dashboard. "Did you know that Daniel is thinking of or planning to close the shop?"

"Yes, many are. You've seen the empty buildings."

Val was surprised. She had noticed them but assumed they had closed long ago.

"Wow. How long has this been happening?"

"Our town has been shrinking for many years. We have lost many longtime families."

"But how? I mean, why?"

"You understand economics, business. You know the how."

"But I don't. I mean, Star Junction is different. Why here?"

"There are not enough of us to do the work. The work that will bring them home."

Val stared at Lucy, allowing her words to make sense. She didn't mean labor. She was talking like Grandmother, which meant she was talking about the mountain.

Lucy drove silently as Val processed the information. Val looked out the window at all they passed. They were not going to Daniel's. They were on the west side, blocks from the town center. They drove past the old warehouses, the rock house, the plant, the mill. They were all empty, but they were all standing. Beaten but not broken. Lucy didn't need to tell her what they were. She knew the buildings.

Val was stuck on how little sense it made for businesses to walk away from perfectly good structures and leave people without jobs. She thought she heard a hawk but realized that Lucy had put on music. It reminded her of the town festivals. Of dancing with her eyes closed. Of listening for her father's call.

"Val, it is good that you were called home. I am glad you are here."

"Me too. Even if I'm not sure I know everything that means." And she laughed again.

Lucy turned back toward town center onto Cedar Street.

Val looked at her quizzically. "Are we on a nostalgia tour?"

"I thought the whole town was a nostalgia tour," she teased.

They drove past the old house. Sissy's house. Val's old house. The one William helped build and carved love into. One house, two houses. Lucy pulled over and stopped the car. Val looked around, wondering what Lucy was showing her, and then saw the house across the street with the little "available" sign. It was the old Johnson house, but it has grown since then. Two stories, yard all around. A view of the mountain from the back.

"Really?"

Lucy smiled. "Really. It has been empty for three years. Let's go see."

Val hopped out of the car. Her mind raced with ideas and questions. One of the best streets in town with easy walking distance to center and to the compound. If they were going to stay, being close to family was important to Val. Just the thought of losing them again sparked an irrational fear that she didn't want to entertain. *Not if,* she thought, *since. Since they were going to stay.*

Turned out that one of Lucy's many jobs was as the local, somewhat informal, realtor. As such, she not only knew about available properties, but she had keys. Val walked through the door and surprised herself with a deep sigh. Her brain kept trying to stay in charge with rational thoughts like: *This is a nice space; it would be good for the kids. They would have room to grow.* But the tears clinging to the edge of her eyes said it all.

"Lucy, was it just waiting for us?"

"Yes." Lucy nodded with sincerity and reassurance.

They walked through the house, and Val ran her hand along the edges, the walls, the counters, the banister. Upstairs the bedrooms lined one wall with windows facing the mountain and the open yard with garden beds and fruit trees.

Val looked at Lucy in disbelief. "They really loved fruit—and somehow knew how to make them grow here." She smiled a magical smile.

"How do I buy it? I mean, I want to show the kids, but it feels like a yes."

"The kids will love it. And they will love knowing that they have a home."

***

Lucy dropped Val off at the compound and returned to her cafe. Val found Jake in the courtyard playing the guitar with Blu at his feet and the other dogs not far off. Alex was drawing at the table. Val sat down in the chair near Jake.

"Jake." He opened his eyes and stopped playing. "I want to apologize for the way I spoke to you earlier. I let a difficult situation influence our conversation, and I'm sorry."

"Okay." He looked down for a moment and paused. "I'm sorry, too. I just—I'm tired of not knowing anything. I'm tired of Lilah being gone. And I took it out on you."

Val smiled. "Well, I think we both got caught up in that energy. Thank you for saying that. Even though I am the adult, I appreciate it." She smiled again. "And I have some news. Alex, can you come over here?"

Alex picked up his sketchbook and came over to them. Two of the dogs followed.

"So it's been a full day. This morning I really wasn't sure what the plan would be. I've had a lot of pressure at work, more than usual, and partly because I'm not there. And unfortunately Jake got to experience me in a moment of pressure. But because of that, I realized I needed to take action. We've been waiting for something to happen or change, and that isn't how change works."

Alex was trying to follow all of this, but was growing impatient with the lead-up. "What action?"

"Lucy took me to see a house today, a house for us. I decided to purchase it."

"Really?" Jake was surprised.

"Jake, it doesn't mean that I won't ever have to go to California and deal with work, but it does mean that we will have a home here.

I hope that helps you feel more comfortable and maybe helps the trust, too."

———

Ms. Ramirez suggested they meet for coffee instead of at the office. It had been weeks of phone calls and office visits that revealed no progress. Val was open to changing the scenery. They sat outside and watched the town go by around the town center. Ms. Ramirez didn't want to have the conversation. She didn't know what to say, really. It was out of her hands. She was doing the best she could.

There just wasn't much information to give except that she was working on it. She was trying to track down Lilah. Trying to find the contact information and actually get through. It wasn't that she wasn't trying. It was more like she was banging against brick walls, calling numbers that never connected to people and leaving messages that never got returned.

This was not why she became a social worker. No. She became a social worker to help kids be connected to family, to have better homes and better lives, and it just didn't always seem to go that way. It was frustrating, but this case was the hardest because Sissy didn't die in the town or county she lived in.

Even if she had, Star Junction didn't really have a children's services department. They only had some families willing to take in kids, but there were more options in Exton and Hailstop. Unfortunately, these were not well-off places. Too many people struggled there, feeling they were trapped between worlds not really able to connect to one or the other. She almost lost her job over Lilah and Jake. This is something Val couldn't possibly know.

When people came to claim Lilah, with matching DNA but no paperwork, and no claim for Jake, she told them no for as long as she could. She was waiting for the papers that never came, the ones that were still on Sissy's desk at home because nobody went to look. Somebody else was handling it, according to everyone involved. She stood up to her boss and lost. Her boss handed over Lilah and called it one less case to manage.

This was after she had looked Jake and Lilah in the eyes and said she would keep them together. The look from Jake of scorn and betrayal cut through every ounce of professional armor. By the time she heard from Val, she was skeptical and assumed that Val was up to no good. Why had she waited so long? But now she knew that the same lack of follow-through that caused them not to know who to call also led to Val not knowing. Even though it was not her fault, she felt it weigh heavily upon her shoulders. It should have been her responsibility even though she was outranked. She "should have" listened to her gut.

Val saw Ms. Ramirez sitting there and took a breath. She didn't want to fight. Didn't want to alienate the person she hoped would be able to help them, yet Val couldn't help but feel a little adversarial.

Why was Lilah still not home with her brother? What on earth was the delay? They would even be in their own house within a couple of weeks. She wanted to be wise and calm and rational and a good role model, yet she felt this sense of urgency and panic.

What if she was too late? What if she couldn't get her back, couldn't find her? *Sissy, you have to guide me to her. I want to give her and Jake a home. Lead us to her.*

Ms. Ramirez saw Val coming and couldn't help but feel a rush of nerves course through her. She never understood why they were called butterflies. It felt more like invading ants.

"Ms. Ramirez, hello." They both smiled. Ms. Ramirez politely gestured to sit. "Do you have news?" Val asked.

"Thank you for meeting me here. I needed to be out of the office." She sipped her coffee and gestured that the other cup was for Val. "I hope you don't mind. I just got black for you, not sure what you like."

"Thank you. Black is fine. Honestly, I'm feeling a little on edge already. I am having trouble understanding what the delay could be. You have all the necessary paperwork and proof."

"Yes, we do. I'm sorry. It isn't that." She took a deep breath while trying to find the right words.

Val's expression was becoming exasperated.

"I am having trouble finding her. The contact information provided by the..." She paused, debating how much to say. "I am leaving messages and doing everything I can think to do."

"Provided by who?"

"The thing is, I didn't want to let them be separated. Lilah is with relatives. They came to claim her soon after. I denied them, but my boss said the DNA was all he needed to release custody."

"DNA?"

"Her father. I'm sorry. I am trying."

Val was stunned. She figured she had just been placed with some rich family or there was still resistance to her, but Lilah's father? Sissy's letter said that they weren't in touch. Then his letter—well, where did he come from? Where did he go? *Jake was right.*

"Her father was never a part of her life. We have to find them. We have to let them know that Lilah has family here now, and her brother needs her. And if I have any understanding at all of Lilah, she needs her brother too."

Ms. Ramirez listened and nodded. "I really am trying. I promise. I won't give up. I know you probably want to get back to California."

"No. Actually, I am buying a home here. This was their home and mine in another lifetime. This is where we will stay."

They sat in silence for a few minutes, not sipping their coffees. Val broke the silence "Were you aware that Jake's guitar was taken from him? He said by his first foster parents."

"That's not what I was told."

"But does it track? Could it be true?"

"Maybe. It turned out not to be a good placement. In fact, they are no longer eligible to foster." Ms. Ramirez tensed up. "Don't get the wrong idea. We have so many wonderful foster parents. They are just at capacity. And sometimes, the bad ones make it through the screening. But if they are on my watch, they don't last. I won't do that to my kids."

Val saw her passion for the first time. "Ms. Ramirez, forgive me. I did not mean to imply that you knew beforehand. I believe you care deeply. I just hope we can resolve this soon because Jake deserves better. In case I haven't said it, thank you for all of your efforts. And thank you again for the coffee."

Val mentioned the meeting to Lucy and Edward. They exchanged glances, and this time Val was in full attention.

"What? What does that mean?"

"We suspected she might be with her father." Was Edward's reply.

Val was tired and exasperated. She sometimes felt like everyone was playing a game she didn't know how to play, and it was exhausting. They could feel her anguish building. "What aren't you telling me? What does it mean? Please, I don't remember how to do this."

Grandmother Flor walked in. "Child, you have not forgotten. You are transforming. Transformation is rarely comfortable. Young Lilah is safe and in loving hands. She is a unique child, gifted to us. She will be returned when they know that she will be safe and cared for."

"They?"

"They." Grandmother Flor looked up and gestured to the stars. "You know we are of the stars." Val closed her eyes. Memories flooded in as a thousand stories all at once, washing through her. The stories of the Ancients. The stories of origin, the stars, God and creation. The stories that she had heard so long ago didn't fit into the life that she had come to know.

She stood quietly for a moment, absorbing slowly, allowing each word and every story to find its place in her being again. Filling in the gaps of a program, the text of her pages written long ago in invisible ink, waiting for the right light to illuminate their meanings. She opened her eyes and looked at the three of them and landed on Grandmother Flor's eyes.

"But how do I show them that she will? Do I need to convince them? Who do I speak to?" She paused again searching for the question that needed to form. "What do I need to do? What is being asked?"

"Only that you return those parts of yourself that you buried so long ago to the you of your heart. When you become whole again, you will know your answers. Become whole again, Picaflor. Embrace all aspects of you. The hummingbird and the hawk. The wolf and the deer. The girl and the fire. Remember."

Flor cupped Val's face in her still-powerful hands. It was a reassuring gesture that when combined with a nod of Flor's head held a commanding call to action. Now was the time. Val knew it. She had been putting it off, hoping to feel more confident before going. Hoping somehow to find her footing and center on ever-shifting sand. William had spoken through Flor. She used his words and nicknames.

"You have become a strong woman out in the world, but you will not feel your own strength or truth until you call the child of you back. Heal with her and let her show you the way."

***

The dusk was a magical time here that seemed to last especially long this time of year. The cooling breeze brought relief from the heat as the sun took its time leaving the horizon. The boys were throwing horseshoes with the other kids, laughing and playing in a moment of levity that came as both surprise and relief. Even the adults laughed at the playful antics of measuring closeness to the pole and the reasons for missing.

Val watched from the edge of the yard, just outside the house really. She smiled when others caught her standing alone. She smiled at their levity through her tight shoulders and clenched jaw. She smiled and nodded in agreement of the goodness of the joy. She smiled when Alex looked for her, somehow knowing he was checking on her. She smiled.

It was a practiced smile, a coat of armor aimed to convince others of her presence and participation despite her dedication to staying just outside of any true connection. Her body fully engaged, her mind ready for any drill and poised to perform, and a masterful barrier made of charm and deflection.

"Why do you stand here?" Val jerked from her thoughts. It was usually Grandmother Flor sneaking up on her.

"Mr. Edward, you startled me." As if to erase the question, she added a smile and even lifted her right index finger as if to scold.

He reflected her exact smile, and she looked away, biting her lip as memories of relationships flooded through.

"Why do you stand *here,* Picaflor?" Her hands began to tremble as she closed her eyes and fought to maintain composure. She wanted to say, "I'm enjoying watching," or, "It's fun to watch the kids. It's good for them."

But all she could do was tremble as she avoided answering, avoided looking at his eyes, knowing there was no composure to be had in them. And what was the point of composure, anyway?

He put his hand gently on her back between her shoulder blades and softly continued, "Life can never be outside of you, Picaflor. Do you not think it is time to start feeling again? To trust and enjoy life?" He paused again as her whole body trembled in a way that terrified her. "William taught you well about your heart. It is time to open it again. This is why you have come."

She couldn't stop it. She took in a gasping breath and opened her eyes as she turned to face this gentle teacher, her beloved uncle. As she turned, she thought she saw Grandmother Flor across the yard, but everything else seemed to have stopped, faded into the background like an old photograph.

She saw the boys playing as though in an alternate space. She saw herself at eight, playing with the others. Little Val stopped and looked directly at this Val before vaporizing into light.

Val finally found Edward's eyes and the voice to say, "Why is it so hard?"

Edward just smiled and gently held her there.

"It is not hard; you are just out of practice. It will get easier when you remember."

She let him hold her there and let herself feel. Her trembling became a flow of vibration that coursed through her body. To the others they were watching the fun. To them, there was only this. The resurrection of Picaflor.

CHAPTER

SIXTEEN

From Picaflor's Journal:
How to climb Clarity Mountain:
Ask permission.
Talk to the plants and rocks and wind.
Talk to the animals too.
Thank them for their help.
Play with them all.
Have fun.
Dance with the sun.

Grandmother Flor gifted Val a bundle for her journey: a collection of sacred herbs and tobacco, flower water, smudging wands, a lighter, and a thermos of a special herbal tea "to help her see." As Val put it in her backpack, she added water, snacks, offerings of flowers and teas, and her old journal and hand-drawn maps. She didn't know why she chose what she chose. At this point, she was no longer thinking about when or how. Clarity

Mountain would not wait. The boys would be entertained by their own adventures and well-guided by this family of wisdom keepers.

As she had done thirty years before, she left the house before dawn and began her quest. Slower than she used to be, she reached the base of the trail after twenty minutes and paused. *Remember to ask permission.* Val removed a handful of bay laurel leaves from her bundle, held them in her hand, and prayed. She asked permission of the mountain and the help of Spirit and all her allies to guide her clearly on her path. *"What am I to do? Show me, how do I heal and reclaim the part of me who knew this mountain well? Thank you for guiding me."*

Val began up the path and into the first thick. Memories had already started. Memories of her last hike when she came to bury her bundle, when Emmet was about to move her family away from their home and everything they had ever known. He didn't know it, but Cade was the reason she made it up, and down, the mountain that last time. His presence helped her to stay on course.

The anger and fear that she felt toward Emmet, and consequently life, were ripping her insides apart. Those emotions led her off track on that journey and cost an extra hour of climbing. If Cade hadn't been there, it might have been longer. Her desire to protect and care for him forced her to surrender sooner and ask for help. *I should have told him,* she thought, but perhaps he wouldn't have understood at the time.

Emmet's voice played in Val's thoughts. "You better watch out," he'd say with a pointed finger and spiked breath. "You think I don't know about your precious little hocus pocus mumbo jumbo bullshit." He would stumble toward her until his face was just inches away.

She held ground. Val always held ground. William had taught her to never turn your back on a predator or a disturbed person. There is power in seeing them, no matter how much they try to dissuade you.

"One day you will come home and all your mojo crap will be gone. Then we'll see how special you think you are." His hand gestured toward her and then wandered down her chest and midline, his fingers circling her breasts before moving back up to her face. "Hmph."

"Emmet, come enjoy your dinner while it is still hot. We made your favorite." Grace's words had a certain tone and rhythm that seemed a lullaby to Emmet. He became agreeable with Grace and the idea of eating; he was hungry, after all. But before he turned, he leaned in even closer to sixteen-year-old Val, her eyes fixed fiercely in defiance of this man having anything to do with her life. Behind her eyes was determination that he would not succeed. She would bury her treasured bundle for safe-keeping. She would protect her father's legacy.

The memory was filled with rage and blame. All heroes needed a villain, and victims a perpetrator. Grandmother Flor's voice whispered in her mind, *"Is everything as you see it?"* She searched the memory for the answer.

"Father, please help me see through different eyes, to see through any lies. Show me what you see." She didn't see Emmet but herself— angry and resentful at the replacement of her father. Disappointed at this adult who didn't know the ways, who couldn't teach or be or love as her papa was and did.

As she walked, she saw a slideshow of their interactions. Her at age ten, being ten—not responding to him, not listening to him, not warming up. Letting Emmet know without words that he wasn't necessary. She was obedient for the most part, but in the way of a caged animal at the zoo. She saw him shift from trying to demanding.

Amazing how we don't know our power. Her child-self thought she was willing Emmet away, but the only part of him that left was the part that wanted to earn her love. And that was something she hadn't been willing to give. As if her papa had it all and took it with him when he went, she didn't feel like she had more for a new father.

As time went on, Emmet's behavior proved her withholding as correct. The more demanding and menacing he became, the more certain she was in her defiance of him. Her refusal to love him. She was a child, and he was a grown man responsible for his actions. He should have known better.

He should have found ways to do better, but he came from others who also didn't know. The ways of Star Junction were not the same as the ways of the world, yet they could have been. Star Junction was a place where people didn't have to remember the old ways because they never stopped doing the things that the "world" seemed to have forgotten so deeply as to never have known at all.

Suddenly Val realized she had stopped walking. She looked around to see she was immersed in a densely shrubbed area with no clear exit.

"But I was the child! He was the one who should have known better. He should have known how to be better. It wasn't fair!"

As she made her declarations Val leaned against a boulder and felt the slow shifting of energy, a dawning of awareness. "I just wanted my father. I needed him." She imagined Emmet's face the first time they met. Not through the eyes of the little girl who missed her father but through the eyes of experience and wisdom.

She could see the man full of insecurities expressed as nervous mannerisms. A man in disbelief that this beautiful woman would consider him, who figured he would never find another woman who would. He was nervous to meet Val and Cade. A seemingly strong man terrified to be responsible for a family and more terrified that they would see his fear. He had no idea how to be around children.

Val let her body slide down the boulder and sink into the earth, softening as she remembered Emmet in the beginning. She could see him trying and able to succeed some with Cade, who was younger and a boy. Emmet did teach Cade some of the "boy" stuff she had never felt drawn to, like oiling his baseball mitt and working on the car. Emmet seemed to delight in his babies as if in complete wonder at the very possibility of it. He would hold them awkwardly, afraid they might break if he held them too close, as if they would evaporate or disintegrate upon contact with his chest.

Val had never been able to see Emmet's humanness before. He had been the villain so long. Could he have just been a man, who started out with hopes and fears like she did but got lost in the fears, and the anger? Could Val change the label after all these years? Tears came to her eyes with the realization of the grudge she held and the barrier she built. She looked up and around her. "I am beginning to see. Forgive me."

Val heard a noise and turned to see a fox about thirty feet behind her. It returned her gaze and then continued through an opening she had passed.

"Thank you, friend." Foxes could be wise or mischievous. She wondered which he was being. She walked back to the opening and looked through.

"*Can you see through?*" Val heard the question in her heart. She was pretty sure the question wasn't referring to her eyes or the opening in the path. *I'm working on it*, she thought back.

Val laughed a little at how much easier it had been when she was a child. She closed her eyes and asked for help with the direction. The wind rustled the leaves in the opening. She thanked them and walked through.

Picaflor's Journal Entry:

Papa said, "People do not always act like the truth of what they are. Sometimes they get confused and forget that they are made from love." And I should forgive their true selves. He also says that doesn't mean I have to let them hurt me. Just forgive them in my heart. And it would be a nice thing to pray that the light return to their hearts and they remember themselves.

Val knew she would have to go deeper to reach the top. She hoped to have memories of her father on this climb, all the teachings he shared with her, about how to listen, to ask, and to see. As she reflected and listened to birds playing, it came to her that she was the memory. Every time she asked for help, every listening, every release was the enactment of his lessons. He was there with her whether she realized it or not. A wave of emotion came over her. "Thank you, Papa."

"Time to play, Picaflor. You have been fierce for too long. Return to balance and be playful like the hummingbird. Drink in the nectar."

Val paused in that place a bit longer. She offered water to the earth and the hearty little flowers sprouting up from the sandy dirt and then took a drink herself. She remembered her father's voice when he spoke to her.

It was easy to be playful around him. Easy to laugh and giggle and imagine wondrous and magical things. The more magical, the more he loved it.

Oh my god, she thought. *Emmet didn't stand a chance.* She chuckled at the awareness and got up to continue. She could see a clear path, for now. And just as she did as a child, she turned back and thanked the boulder that she had leaned against, thanked the ground for holding her, thanked the trees for the shade.

"Everyone is our teacher, child. Every person we meet, every experience we have. When you are uncertain, ask, 'What did I learn?' And you will begin to understand their purpose in your life?"

Val continued to find her way up the mountain. Each step met with memories, questions, and sometimes answers. *I learned to be fierce.* The carefree child who flitted about with playful agility and wonder learned how to plant her feet, see through people, and fight with piercing focus and strength of will.

Would she have ever known that such strength and determination lived within her if life had not turned the way it did? Would she have succeeded the way she has? Met the people who guided her, taught her, and became her allies? Would she have ever left Star

Junction and learned about other ways of being in the world? Started a business? Loved the people she loved?

The answer was clearly no. No. If Emmet had not played the role he did, she likely would not have learned or accomplished all that she did. But what would she have done? Become?

If Emmet had not played his role, Val would not have had sisters, or Jake, or Lilah who she had only met in her dreams yet knew as a gift. She took in a deep and stuttered breath and let it out with the old story. Val could point her finger at Emmet and blame him for much, but could she also find the place to thank him? To know that the gratitude she felt for the people in her life and the success she had has a connection to his presence and actions?

She had viewed Emmet's decline into alcohol abuse as proof of her position and justification for her coldness, but in this moment, she also saw it as the toll he paid for his role. How hard it was on his being. How it broke him down until he wasn't able even to be Emmet anymore. He had lived a hard path.

"Forgive me, Emmet. I didn't see it. Thank you for playing that role in my life. Please know, I forgive all of it."

Instead of blaming him for killing the magic, she could thank him for teaching her to develop her fierceness, her strength, and her footing. Not to condone bad behavior, simply to have compassion for the souls who play the tormented ones. And her father's reminder came back, "Return to balance."

Be fierce and loving, playful and productive, strong and joyful. Strength without compassion is a lie. In this moment she knew it was time to let go of the anger and the blame. She was the warrioress who was sent to train in the world and return with the understanding and tools she needed at home. When she reached the top, she knew what her offerings would be.

The circle of perspective was ready to welcome her. As she reached the top and made her way to the circle, she felt it hadn't changed a bit. Val removed her backpack and arranged her supplies. The flower water was first. She sprinkled some in her hands, clapping them together so that the water splattered and sprayed out with each clap.

Then she cupped her hands and breathed in the fragrant elixir of carnations and cloves deeply—once, twice, three times, exhaling fully each time to clear her senses. She poured a little in the shape of a cross at the east marker and entered barefoot to feel the dirt.

In the center Val kissed and placed the flowers, herbs, an apple, and a cookie. Grandmother Flor had often told her, "Mother Earth loves sweetness."

"Thank you for receiving me here, for guiding me and protecting me on the journey. Is there more for me to know on this visit?"

She stood facing east with her eyes closed. Then south. Then west, which by now had the sun lighting her face. Then north. As a child she felt the wisdom of the directions without understanding how it worked. The shift in perspective created a shift in perception.

Val walked to the point of each direction and then faced the center. As she reached the north point, a hawk landed by the center, close to the southern line. Val watched the hawk. It looked at her, moved closer to the center, and then focused back at her. She took a step toward the center too. The hawk just looked at her, so she continued, slowly. It looked away for a moment then back at Val and bounced. She smiled.

"What are you telling me?" She reached into her pocket and pulled out some dried meat. "Is this what you want?" It bounced but didn't take it. She was kneeling now, just a foot or so away from the center. She looked at her offering. Then put her hand over different items, the apple, the herbs, the cookie, the flowers.

He bounced.

"You want the flowers?" She gently separated and held out some flowers. The hawk took the stalks in its beak and launched. As it circled overhead, it dropped a feather for her. She smiled in awe. *"Thank you, friend."*

Her prayer for the children, for healing, for understanding had been heard and received. Her offering was accepted, a gift given and received. It was time to find her apacheta, the stacked rocks marking the spot to dig. Val closed her eyes to visualize the spot, trying to recall the memory.

She looked in the direction the hawk flew and saw the cluster of boulders and trees. *Is that it?* She wondered, feeling that it was. She approached and saw the opening between the boulders. Inside the little cubby she saw the double-apacheta, intact, as if they had glued the stones to stay in place.

"Wow, amazing. Thank you." She pulled out the spade she brought and began to dig. The earth was hard at first. Val paused and prayed aloud. "Thank you for protecting my sacred bundle. Will you help me to reclaim it now? I am ready to use it again."

She moved the spade slightly north and it went into the earth easily. The dirt began to fall away in easy-to-remove clumps. And then, there it was—her bundle tightly wrapped up. And Cade's wolf resting on top. She gently removed her bundle and wrapped up Cade's wolf with one of the cloths.

This is for him to reclaim. She buried it carefully, packing the dirt to protect it. She started to get up but stopped to remove the top rock from her apacheta and lay it at the base.

Val brushed the dirt off of the cloth as much as possible before gently laying it down and untying the strings. "Here goes," she said to herself as she opened the bundle and cried.

They were as she left them. The hummingbird William had carved for her, the doll Grace had made with Grandmother Flor, a hawk feather, and a crystal. She had forgotten how beautiful the hummingbird was. Her father's work. Her father's expression of love for her. Her heart. Her essence.

She picked it up and held it, brought it to her heart and closed her eyes. She could see it come alive again in her mind's eye. The colors of the stone illuminated and radiated light out from its wings, throat, heart, green, red, blue, violet. Her heart fluttered and she cried more at the surprising feeling.

When it felt right, she reached down, eyes opened and picked up the doll. Her mother's gift. It was feminine on one side, masculine on the other. The headdress made of hummingbird tail feathers fanned out like rays of the sun. Feather sequins decorated the energy centers of the body. She played with it as a toy as a child, loving it completely but not fully understanding the meaning and power it held.

The feminine side showed the right hand on her heart and the left open, palm up beneath it. The masculine side showed the left hand on the heart and the right hand holding a staff with markings. The work was intricate and detailed.

"Did mom really do this? I don't remember."

In that instance she flashed upon a memory of Grace visiting Grandmother Flor weekly for a number of months. It was cooking or some other visiting excuse. She could see them making the doll together. Deep gratitude washed over her. She realized just how many angels she had working magic in her young life.

As she sat, she noticed sensations of opening passageways. She didn't know how to describe it or identify it—a very distinct yet unnamable feeling. As if she were removing the coverings over artifacts weighed down by eons of dust and debris, moving boulders from the opening of a cave, or perhaps finally just unlocking the doors and letting them swing open as the cleansing breeze washed through. Remaining on her cloth was the tri-point crystal uncovered on the last hike with her father and the hawk's feather gifted on the first when she was five. She placed her new feather alongside it, this one with a bit of orange-red tinge from the tail.

Val knew when she started her climb that day that she would spend the night on Clarity Mountain. She didn't know why as she used to make the hike in a few hours. But it wasn't just the hike. She knew she was to be there for more.

As she set up a small fire, more for the offering of herbs and sacred woods than warmth or food, she saw herself in her story. She saw the self who was angry at the loss of her father. Saw the self who punished the man who couldn't replace him by withholding love and acceptance. Saw the self who didn't know how to do it differently. And the one who punished herself to spite her stepfather.

She now saw her act of burying her treasure as cutting off a part of herself. She also saw her temptation to blame herself and call it the wrong choice. "I shouldn't have." Grandmother Flor's words reassure her, *"There are no should haves or shouldn't haves. There is only what is and what was. If it happened, it was meant for you to learn and grow."*

She sipped the tea that Grandmother gave her and watched the small fire. Val saw her sixteen-year-old-self burying the bundle. She could feel the fear and anger and confusion, the anguish underneath the surface of calm and strong. *"It's okay, Val. It's okay. Thank you. I love you."*

Her sixteen-year-old-self looked at her and smiled before disappearing into the smoke. Sitting in the spiral of time, she repeated this process over and over, with herself at nine, and ten, and eleven, and all the years, all the ages of childhood, and all the life moments after leaving Star Junction, after leaving her family, all the times she chose safety and protection, all the times she found her way through what felt impossible and never-ending. Seeing, feeling, acknowledging, forgiving, asking forgiveness, witnessing, loving each part, each moment that brought her to who she was right then.

When her younger selves stopped coming forward, Emmet appeared. "Forgive me." He was young and clean shaven and his eyes bright.

"I forgive you, Emmet. Thank you. Please forgive me, too. I love you." And she was surprised by the truth of that statement. Then Grace appeared and Sissy and the others.

She was not the victim of them avoiding her. As isolated as she felt, singled out and alone, she knew she played a part in it. She just didn't know how or why. A part of her had given up and started giving differently of herself. She showed up with her head, ready to jump in, solve problems, figure out solutions, share wisdom or advice. She could see it now. She could feel it then but didn't know what to do with it. How to fix it. How to fix her. Life was so good on paper. Now as she could feel her heart reopening as tears flowed, washing the heavy coating of time away, she could also see her resentment and jealousy of the ones who got to stay together. In that too, she heard herself say, "I'm sorry, please forgive me. I love you."

Val slept quietly between dreams. The fire finished with its work. She could hear rustling from time to time, perhaps in the distance. Sound had a way of teasing the ears up here. In the quiet you could hear everything; you just couldn't quite tell where it was coming from. The rustling could be from trees in the canyon. Trying too hard to figure it out could be a little disorienting.

She closed her eyes. "If it is for me to know, act, or understand, let it be clear. I trust I am safe and protected here," she said quietly in her thoughts to reassure her mind of what her heart already knew. "If I am to move, I will." She again felt gratitude wash over her, the warmth of the earth embracing her body more comfortably than she imagined it could with her curves.

"I don't mean to disturb you."

Val realized the voice came from outside of her dream. She opened her eyes to see light bright enough for her to squint. She changed her position and worked to adjust her eyes so she could see the man standing a few feet away.

"Forgive me." As he realized the angle and position of the sun and perhaps brightness, he moved to the side and lowered himself to sit. "Is that better?" He smiled.

She sat up and nodded, a little disoriented but not frightened. Val didn't think she had ever encountered another person up here that she hadn't come with. She could see now that the sun was just breaking on the horizon. *He must have had a flashlight.*

"Good morning," she said warmly and with a hint of a question in her expression.

He smiled again, and she smiled, feeling a little awkward. Wondering if he was going to speak. "I'm Val."

He nodded with a smile and looked toward the sunrise. They sat there watching it quietly. She relaxed into the moment again. Perhaps he wasn't there at all, or she was still dreaming. Though the light had been almost blinding, her dreams usually had more action. The dawn created a soft pink and peach cast over the horizon with layers of blue and purple hovering as long as they could. And then they were in daylight.

"We are so glad you have returned." His voice was filled with warmth and something else she couldn't quite identify. He was still watching the horizon. Val wasn't quite sure how to receive his words.

"We?" She turned to face him and he did the same.

"Yes, we. We had hoped that you would return." He smiled warmly to pause. "And reclaim yourself, your connection, shall we say?"

Val was mesmerized and speechless. She was accustomed to Grandmother Flor's way of speaking, but this was far beyond it. "Solana admired you so. She had faith that you would return and take care of Jacob and Alex and…"

"Lilah." Suddenly Val realized who he was. Sissy's real name was Solana, the sunshine.

"Yes. Soon. You have done well to remember. We have been praying with you all this time. You know this now. You have never been alone."

Val couldn't help the tears from forming. Tears of love and relief and joy and recognition. She knew the truth of his words because of the feeling of the tears. A truth gauge.

He continued, "I can feel the questions building inside you. You need not ask. The answers are already taking form and are there for you to receive. We love you, Picaflor." That last part came in William's voice, which gave her goosebumps.

She realized he was about to leave as he became like light itself. "Wait, who are you?" She had to ask, had to be sure.

He smiled again "You can know me as Z. It is what your sister called me."

Z changed from form to light as Val sat watching. She took a deep full breath and felt a *thank you* whisper from her depths.

Val stood atop Clarity Mountain and looked upon her beloved town. Out of the corner of her eye, she saw a flicker and looked to see it closer. Something on the old warehouses was catching the morning sun and casting light beams. Val smiled in wonder and knowing.

"Papa, what are those buildings for?"

William looked to where his daughter's little hand was pointing.

"Those are industrial buildings. Those two are warehouses, the one further down is the mill. I thought you knew that, Valerie."

"Yes, but what are they *for*?" She put her emphasis on the "for" and shrugged slightly, opening both hands in front of her as if holding a box that she wanted to open.

"Oh, you mean, what are warehouses used for?"

She nodded her head emphatically.

"These warehouses are used for many things. They have been used to store the wood from the mill and the furniture built by our artisans. They are used for business. When a company makes products, they need a place to store them before sending them out. And they need places for supplies. What else can you think of that a warehouse could be used for?"

"Ummmm, all of my drawings!" she said with satisfaction.

William smiled and laughed with joy.

"Yes, you could use it for all of your beautiful art. That is an excellent idea, Picaflor." Then he reached to tickle her. She shrieked, and they both laughed.

———

"I see it now. Thank you."

Walking through the trees had a way of bringing one to presence. For some they seemed silent and neutral or towering ominous obstacles. Not for Val. She walked among the trees and knew she was walking with Spirit. William taught her young to listen differently so she could hear the whispers. To just sit with them quietly or to play with them singing.

Until the day she left to pick up Alex, when she sat in her yard under the walnut tree, she had forgotten about talking with the trees. Today as she walked among them, she said, "Forgive me for forgetting."

The trees gently shook their needles and leaves with an imperceptible breeze.

Val smiled. "I missed you too."

She stopped walking for a bit, deciding to sit with them. Just sit and feel and be. She closed her eyes and breathed deeply in as if pulling all the essence she had missed for so long back to her. Filling her lungs with the very essence of life itself, slowly, intentionally, consciously. She noticed tears trickling from her eyes and felt them as the joy or relief of returning home.

She could hear her father singing her song and opened her eyes. Sitting on a branch not ten feet away was a beautiful, mature hawk, watching her and waiting like it would for prey. Val felt goosebumps spread up and from her spine.

Their eyes locked, and they both remained motionless except for the racing of Val's heart. She heard a sound not too far away, an animal or someone breaking twigs while passing through. Val's eyes couldn't help but look for the cause of the sound, but she saw nothing. When she looked back, the hawk had vanished. "Thank you."

Val returned to Grandmother's compound around 10:00 a.m. The hike down was quick, though she did not hurry. At first it seemed that nobody was home. Val was vibrating. The energy and ideas were coming so fast she wasn't sure where to start. So she stopped for a moment, slowed down, and set her backpack on the table to remove her items.

The hummingbird, the doll from Grace, the feathers and crystal. She was itching to talk to Grandmother Flor, but the home was silent. She closed her eyes and decided to shower before taking any action. When she came back from her room, she heard Grandmother humming in the kitchen.

"Grandmother."

"Hello, child, welcome home."

"Thank you." Val couldn't contain her energy and excitement.

"You had a good journey?"

"I did." She exhaled her words. "I did. I met Lilah's father. And I have an idea that might help the town, but I need to talk to Lucy and to call my business partners."

Grandmother Flor smiled at the life flowing through Val and responded playfully, "Then you should do those things. Talk to Lucy and call your partners."

"Yeah." She laughed. "Okay." She began to leave the room but turned back. "Grandmother, thank you," she said it from the heart and Grandmother received the expression with a gleam in her eye.

"You are welcome, Picaflor."

Lucy was prepping for the lunch crowd when Val walked in. "Hey, how was it?"

"I'm not even sure I can describe it all, at least, not right now. But great. Lucy, the empty buildings—the warehouse, rock shop, mill— are they in working order? I mean, they looked solid from the outside, more than I would expect from abandoned buildings."

"Most of their issues are cosmetic. Nothing substantial, though I can't speak toward the mill equipment. That would have to be checked."

"And how hard would it be to take ownership, get permits, and establish a business here?"

"What do you mean?"

"Well, in some states, some cities, it is very challenging and takes a long time to get permits, licenses, and insurance, not to mention expensive."

Lucy laughed. "This is Star Junction. The buildings are available, and the town wants businesses here."

"That's what I wanted to hear!" Val gave Lucy a huge hug. "I have an idea to help the town and the family."

Lucy just looked at her in awe and slightly amused.

Elliot picked up before the second ring "So I actually get a call!"

"Hi, Elliot."

"How's it going? You good?"

She smiled as she answered, and he felt it. "I am the best I have been in a long time. And I am calling with a project and a proposal of sorts."

"Shaking things up?"

"Absolutely. Check your email. I'm sending the details now. Elliot, it's time. You've been hanging out with me, and it's been fun. I've been grateful. And now it's time for you to lead. I want you to run the service side of the business. I won't be moving back to California. This is home for the kids, and home for me. Again. I've drawn up the business proposals and contracts, but I wanted to do this with a conversation. You are too good not to take over that side of things. I'm putting my house on the market there, which you already guessed. The other part of the shakeup is that I am going hands on with the design and manufacturing of products, and we are moving the facilities here. There are empty buildings perfectly suited, and there are people in need of jobs.

"Holy crap, Val. You do like to shake things up."

"And?"

"And I love watching what happens when you do. I'm honored to accept your proposal to take the helm of this ship. But it won't be as much fun without you."

"Well, you won't be rid of me—not completely. But I suspect you will do just fine at shaking things up on your own."

"What about Jim and the others?"

"I'm sending announcements, calling the ones I need to, and singing your praises. And Jim will be fine working for a company he is more aligned with. And, Elliot, you are in for a ride. Thank you."

Elliot didn't want her thanks. Not really. She always expressed appreciation and respect. But Elliot enjoyed working with her too much. It really wasn't as much fun without her.

SEVENTEEN

lex was in the courtyard drawing the angel trumpet flowers. The dusk moved too quickly to capture the way the light filtered through, but even in the dark, the flowers seemed to glow. The moon was high already and a stillness settled over it all. Something moved, and Alex looked to his left to see what it was. He couldn't make out anything in the dark, just the glow of the moon and trumpets, but he could sense something or someone.

"Hello?" He looked around more, wondering where everybody was and how it got so late. "Who is there? I can't see you."

The figure seemed to be circling him. He put his pencils away, but some dropped. He trembled. He caught two little flashes of light, reflections from the moon, and knew they were eyes. He closed his eyes tightly and clutched his sketchpad to his chest.

"It's okay, Alex. You can do this," he said to himself. He took a deep breath and opened his eyes. He put his sketchbook down and stood as tall as he could as the figure continued to move around him.

Alex turned to face it. "I know you are here. Let me see you." He wasn't sure it would work. He turned as the figure circled again. In his head he heard, "I am safe."

Alex asked again, "Why won't you show yourself? I am ready." The figure stopped as did Alex who swallowed the lump in his throat. Just before it tackled Alex, the moonlight illuminated the wolf.

Alex awoke with his pulse racing. This dream felt so different from the first. But still, he was pretty sure the wolf attacked him. Why? For the first time, he didn't want to draw it. There wasn't anything to draw.

Val noticed he wasn't drawing at breakfast. This was a first. "Hey, bud, no drawing today?"

"Eh, maybe later." He played with his food and swung his leg under the chair.

"What's going on?"

Alex just looked at Aunt Val, not sure how to bring it up.

"Another dream?" she asked.

He nodded.

"It was a wolf again. But it was different. I mean, it didn't chase me. And I wasn't so scared, but it still circled me and tackled me. Why does it want to hurt me?"

"It doesn't sound like it wanted to hurt you. It sounds like it was letting you know that it is with you."

"But it jumped on me."

"Did it bite you? Were you harmed?"

"I woke up."

"I know it seems confusing. But sometimes what we perceive as a threat or attack isn't that at all. Sometimes Spirit gets our attention in startling ways. The wolf spirit is getting your attention to help you find the strength within yourself. Seems to me that the wolf has been getting your attention since we first arrived. Mr. Edward saw that and gifted you the totem to help you."

"Yeah, it's all kinda cool, but I'm not sure I understand."

"Well, you don't have to understand it all. Just trust your heart. And trust that we are all here to listen and to help however we can."

She paused to consider her next words. "Alex, you've been through a lot. And I know you have to be missing your dad. It's okay to have feelings about it all. When we don't express our feelings, we block a lot of the good stuff too. We had a deal. Right? You tell me all of it, even if you think I won't like it."

She nudged him and smiled. He rolled his eyes and smiled a little. He liked his aunt Val, but he didn't know how to process it all.

"Right?" She nudged again.

"Right," he agreed.

Val put her arm around his shoulder and her hand on his head.

"Things will come together. I love you. Your dad loves you so much it scares him. You are loved by everyone here."

"Why does it scare him?"

She found the crack. "It scares him because he doesn't want to lose you like he and you lost your mom. And he doesn't want to make more mistakes that hurt you."

"But he didn't hurt me. Nancy did. He just—he just kinda wasn't really him."

"Yeah. He knows, and he doesn't want that to happen again. He's probably afraid to disappoint you, let you down again. I would be. Grief is hard. We think as adults we should be able to manage it because we rationalize. We understand that things happen in life, and we should just be able to keep going as if it is all okay. And then we realize we can't, because it hurts and we don't understand and then we feel guilty and put this extra pressure on ourselves to get on with it. But in truth, we're sad and feel like our worlds are upside down. Being an adult doesn't make it easier. It just makes us more skilled at pretending. Because business must get done. Sometimes we all lose ourselves, or parts of ourselves."

"When my mom was still alive, everything was like a happy dream to me. That probably sounds weird. There was so much color. I think I kind of lost the color. It all became sort of gray. My dad was the most colorful of all of us, but then he wasn't. I really want him to be that again."

He was fighting what was coming. His breath became choppy as he tried to pull it all back in. She pulled him a little closer as he surrendered to the tears.

Blu stretched her body in the sun as only a content dog could. Alex watched her as she stretched her paws out, rolled onto her back to scratch it a bit, and then lay with her belly exposed and eyes closed.

Jake watched as he strummed the guitar. "I think she is posing for you," he said to Alex. He felt lighthearted somehow, strumming a playful tune to match the mood.

Alex smiled and embraced the idea. He turned the page of his sketchbook and began. The other dogs became curious and joined Blu. Alex was very accommodating, and by the end, the drawing included Blu, Leelo, Foxy, and Flex—the whole pack.

Val came out to see how they were doing. "You two want to go for a ride?"

Val pulled the car up to the house. She'd told the boys that she was getting a house, but they weren't as excited as she hoped they'd be. They had become attached to Edward and Grandmother as well as Lucy and Lucy's kids. Yet even they knew something would have to change.

Jake still harbored doubts about Val sticking around, and Alex didn't know if Cade would move them back to Phoenix. They were restless in the car as they had been restless the last couple of days. Things felt much like pressure building in a keg, yet nobody could quite reach the tap.

They perked up when they realized the house was barely half a mile from the compound. Jake turned around in the seat and saw his other house. He looked at her bewildered.

She met his gaze. "Trust?"

He didn't know the answer to that, but he was trying. He shrugged his shoulders and opened the car door.

"What if we don't like it?" Alex asked. He was filled with more worry than usual and wasn't himself.

Val just smiled at him.

"Let's go find out." She headed up the steps to the front porch, and Alex beat her to the door. His eyes were already soaking in every detail. Jake was more reserved. He didn't want to get attached, and his old house was literally within view. They were surprised that there was already some furniture. Some of Val's work had been ordering furniture and supporting the local shops for supplies.

The boys looked around with wide eyes. Alex was the first to break. "Wow!" he exclaimed as he saw the living area with comfy chairs, couch, TV and the essential accessories. They even seemed to like the kitchen, which was to the left of the living space. To the right was an office big enough to double as a guest room. The boys stared at the stairs.

"Okay, here's the deal. There are four bedrooms upstairs. The master bedroom is mine. I put sticky-notes with question marks on the doors with the rooms I think go to each of you. But it is for you to negotiate. Ready?"

Alex nodded. Jake shrugged.

At the top of the stairs to the right was the corner bedroom opposite the master. The note on the door said "Jake?" They opened the door and saw a room big enough for a king-size bed, desk, dresser and musical items.

Val knew this, but Jake only saw the two windows, a big closet and the trees outside. He liked it, which he showed with a shrug and a slight nod. He smirked when Val turned the other way.

The room next to Jake's had Lilah written on the note. It had a big picture window with a nook to sit in, a modest walk-in closet and plenty of room for a young girl. "I thought you and Lilah might want to be next to each other."

Jake nodded but was quiet. He was trying not to think about Lilah still being gone, still not with him. He wanted to trust Val, but what if she couldn't get Lilah back?

"Okay, Alex, are you ready to see this one?" She pointed at the door.

He opened it before she finished the question. It was almost a mirror to Lilah's room, but with etched windows above the main that created cool effects when the light filtered through. Alex was mesmerized. His excitement quickly turned to worry.

"What's wrong?"

"But what does this mean? Is my dad coming? Am I going to be here or with him?"

"When your dad comes, you will decide together what to do next. You are always welcome here. And your dad can take the office downstairs. Or you can get another place together. We don't have to have all the answers yet. Right?"

"Okay. Thanks, Aunt Val." He hugged her.

"So should I have the bedroom furniture delivered?"

The boys nodded. A sense of anticipation and hope filled the air.

"When will we move in?"

Val looked at her watch playfully. "How about this weekend?"

Jake scoffed. "What if we didn't like it?"

She smiled at him and nudged his shoulder. "Well, I'm really glad that you do."

***

Monsoon season brought the play inside after dinner at the compound. The boys sat on the floor between the couch and the table. They were engaged in a mean game of dominoes with Lucy's kids as thunder rumbled in the distance. Grandmother Flor looked at Edward and excused herself.

"Wow, is that thunder? Will it get closer?" Alex always asked questions with a delightful combination of excitement and wonder.

Edward smiled. "Most certainly. It will be very close."

"Cool!"

Jake shook his head and rolled his eyes at Alex. "You're a weird kid, Alex." Jake smiled when he said it.

"Yeah, but it's a good weird."

Val watched with wonder at how easily the boys interacted. Even with the age difference, they'd become friends. Thunder rumbled louder and longer. Flashes lit up the sky outside. Grandmother Flor returned with candle lanterns. Another flash and they could hear the rain pouring from the skies.

"Right on time," said Edward to his mother. They lit the candles just before the lights went out.

"Boooooommmmmmmrumbleruuummmbbbleemmmmbbbm-mm," said the night.

"Wow! Why is it so loud?" There was alarm in Alex's voice.

"It's alright, Alex," Val assured him.

"But I've never heard it so loud!"

"The sky is talking. It has your attention, yes?"

Alex's eyes got wide, and he nodded to Edward's question.

"I had forgotten how loud the thunder could be here." Val found herself pulled into a memory yet still present in the room. It was a feeling of wonder, awe, being outside of herself. She looked over at Grandmother, who met her gaze and nodded without moving her eyes away. "My father used to tell a story about how they built the mountains."

"What? You can't build a mountain, Aunt Val!" exclaimed Alex.

Val smiled.

"Yet there is a story about doing just that. When the ancients first arrived, they knew they had found a beautiful place. It was rich with trees, plants, animals, and water. After they were here for a bit, they thought about how nice it would be to have a place that was higher than the rest—a place to be able to see everything below it, including the great canyon in the distance, and contemplate and appreciate the abundance they had, the many gifts of the land. They decided to have a ceremony, like one of the festivals we have now, to ask divine source to call forth such an elevated place. They waited for the stars that night and began the fire.

"They had a great medicine woman who was said to dance with fire and call stars from the sky. That night she called upon the stars as the fire danced with her. Some of the ancients had already begun to forget themselves and let fear lead their thoughts. One of the men of the town had done just that. He also became jealous of the woman and tried to stop her work. He confronted her and poured water on the fire. She stopped and looked upon him with kindness.

"'My brother, do you not remember?'

"He raged, 'You must not act in this way. You have no right. You should be ashamed.'

"But the woman would not return his fear or anger. She looked upon him with love and continued, 'Fire and water can also work as one. Only with the elements can the earth be changed. Both for cleansing. Both for transformation.'

"Right at that moment the sky rumbled and a bolt of lightning struck the fire pit and lit the fire again. Thunder sounded and rain began to fall. The ancients stood motionless in awe of the sight until the medicine woman spoke again, 'With both water and fire we cleanse, we forge our world and find our path. The earth is the mother that nourishes us, the foundation for our feet, the host of all that grows. The plants that feed us and give us shelter and clothes. The animals that join us on this journey. Tonight, the earth transforms from our vision.'

"The earth shook. The woman pointed to the boulders behind her. Just beyond the path between them she began to pile dirt. Everyone except the man added to the mounds. He stood motionless. Anger growing in him. Helplessness welled up in his exasperation. 'Sister—who art thou?'

"Tears fell from his eyes. She came to him and touched his face. 'It is only I. I am thy sister, thy friend. I am the one you asked for. I am thee. Brother, we are in the dream. Fear not.' She took his hand and he let her. The rest of the townspeople had stepped away, watching from a distance. 'There is only love here. Joy to be expressed.'

"With that, lightning struck the mound and continued for what could have been days. The people were tired, and they went to bed after cleaning up the center. It was dark now without the stars or the lightning, and none could see what happened to the mound. The next morning in the light of the sun, the people saw what they could not the night before. From the boulders led a path to the mountains that we now call 'Clarity Mountain and the Eye of the Mountain.'"

The kids all sat mesmerized. Grandmother and Edward smiled.

"But you can't just make a mountain!" exclaimed Alex.

"Why not?" asked Grandmother.

"But what happened to the woman—and the man?"

"Yeah, you didn't tell us."

Val paused for a moment with a soft smile. "Hmmm. If I remember correctly—Grandmother, please correct me if I am wrong —the woman and the man climbed the mountain that night. The man liked the view so much and loved his community with a love beyond words that he chose to watch over it always. He became the Watcher, the Eye of the Mountain. From there, he has a perfect view." She paused while they took it all in. "It's funny, I had forgotten that story until now. It is really beautiful. The town's love came together to create a means for clear vision."

"Yes, and so much more. You told the story well, Picaflor."

"Why do you call her picaflor?" asked Alex.

"Picaflor is the name her father called her to remind her of the joy inside. Picaflor means hummingbird," answered Grandmother Flor.

"I call Lilah hummingbird because she is always flitting around." Jake seemed intrigued that Lilah would have the same nickname as Aunt Val. "But you are so different than her."

Val couldn't help but laugh at that.

Edward responded, "Ah, if you had known your aunt as a child, you would understand."

Jake just looked at him quizzically.

The conversation continued but Val's attention went inward, suddenly remembering the story Lucy told her about the girl who danced with fire—and that the girl was supposedly her. Telling the story of the woman who danced with fire to help build a mountain. Her adult brain felt the story entertaining, but now it nagged at her. What was the meaning of dancing with fire? As much as she loved being here and watching the boys experience this place, she still had moments of feeling unready and less certain. How could she be respectful of the stories and the way of life and still be her rational self? She just might not be ready to believe the magic again.

She looked up to catch Grandmother Flor watching her with a smile. *Ahh, caught you,* she thought. *Or is it that I caught you?* Was the distinct thought she heard in her head in Grandmother's voice. She let out a tired and somewhat nervous sigh that she turned into a yawn.

"Well, I think it is time for me to turn in. Boys, you too."

Grandmother laughed in agreement. "Yes, storms have a way of helping us to sleep." And she laughed gently again.

Val put her hand to her heart and nodded to Grandmother. She could not debate or explain away anything that Grandmother Flor said. If she had learned anything, it was that Grandmother always saw beyond the words and there was no way to hide. Maybe tomorrow she would ask Grandmother to explain.

Val was lying on the floor of the Star Pavilion, gazing at the stars. No one was around. Music was coming from far away. The constellations seemed to brighten and dim one at a time. The Milky Way lit up like a highway. Then there was a flash of light and thunder. She looked over to see fire burning in the pit. Thunder became the drum. Wind rushed through and circled around her pulling her to the fire. She got closer and the fire got brighter. The drums beat faster and the wind played like a flute. She reached her right hand out and circled the fire. A flame followed her path. Her heart started to race, and she breathed deeply and closed her eyes. Her body moved with the music. She danced and twirled. But she couldn't see, so she finally opened her eyes.

And awoke. She looked around the room. All was quiet. No fire. A little of thunder rumbled in the distance. "And what is being forged tonight?" she wondered.

The storm only delayed their move by a couple of days. Val got up before dawn to handle work tasks before the boys got up.

"You guys ready?"

Alex looked up from his drawing like he was not quite done. Jake shrugged.

"Okay, you have ten minutes. Then you need to get your stuff!"

Val dropped the boys off at the community center to help Lucy prep for Friday's Fire Dance and Festival. Val wanted the time to oversee the last of the deliveries and finish setting up their rooms. Plus, she had two conference calls to fit in and papers to review. As Val opened the doors to the new house, emotions overwhelmed her.

She closed her eyes, hands to her heart. "*Is this what you meant, Papa?*" She stood in the doorway, in gratitude and awe. She could not have envisioned the change in her life, yet it was exactly what she had longed for—family, community, and inspiration.

"*Picaflor, little Valerie, you are a warrior. Love is your power. Joy the net you cast to bring us all home. Don't forget the joy.*"

"What is the Fire Dance?" Alex asked Lucy while helping at the center.

"The Fire Dance, or Festival, is a traditional celebration for our town. We have many ceremonies throughout the year, many celebrations of life and prosperity, abundance, and each other. As you know, every Friday we have music at the pavilion to remind people to play, dance, and sing. To let the troubles of the day and the week go. To let go of all the worries that weigh them down.

But we have special ceremonies to mark seasons, solstices, eclipses—essentially transitions and transformation. The Fire Dance is one of those. This very powerful time marks big change. So many people prepare offerings of music, food, dance, stories, herbs, or art that is specially prepared with gratitude and love of life in mind. And we share our offerings with each other and dance together."

"But what is the fire?"

"The fire cleanses. When we are ready to let go of the things or ways that burden us, we offer them to the fire, and it cleanses and transmutes that energy."

"So that's what the offerings are? Bad things?"

"Not exactly. People are encouraged to offer the fire what they wish to be free of because being ready to release a burden is a service to all. But the festival is also a celebration of life and abundance and community. The second offering is of light, not to burn in the fire but to share for all. Some people make food to share. Some share crafts or stories or services. Jake, Grandmother Flor would like you to share your music at the festival."

"I don't know. I don't usually have people around. I'm not ready. But I know she wants me to."

"It isn't what she wants. It is what she sees. It is important, and could be very helpful for you and Lilah."

He examined her closely.

"Okay." He really didn't know what to think, but if there was a chance it could help, he didn't care if the whole world came. He would play.

"What should I offer?" Alex asked with enthusiasm.

"What is in your heart to share? Sit with that for a while and the answer will come."

Part of the festival meant providing food, supplies, and help for community members. People brought the items they were no longer using or could spare, extra fruit or vegetables from their gardens, and offered time for handy work or cleaning for any neighbors in need. Lucy and the boys and other volunteers were helping to organize the shared items and connect the people offering services with those in need.

The last of the deliveries arrived. Val pushed herself to get done everything she could do, short of decorating. She saved that to share with the boys. When Lucy arrived with Jake and Alex, Val met them at the door. She hugged Lucy in gratitude and excitement. The boys were wide-eyed with curiosity.

"Okay, guys, are you ready? The decorating of your rooms is up to you."

They went to Jake's room first, as it was the first at the top of the stairs. The furniture included an adjustable desk, dresser, and a king-sized bed.

"No way!" He was overwhelmed. He didn't want to believe it would happen, that he would ever have more than a drawer and an old, beat-up twin bed. He looked at her and kind of smiled with his wry look. "You know I don't have enough clothes to put in those drawers."

She smiled back. "Don't worry. We'll work on that, too."

He surprised her with, "Thank you, Aunt Val."

It was the first time he had called her that since she picked him up. The first thank you. The first real smile.

She put her hand on his shoulder and smiled. "Hey, you better check the closet." He walked to the closet on the other side of his new bed, checking out the navy and maroon bedspread with a stepped cross motif or Andean cross on it. He opened the door to see a few clothes and an acoustic guitar.

"Really?" he asked, stunned.

"Yes, I had Daniel pick it out for you."

He had tears well up in his eyes, but he worked hard to control them.

"Wow."

"Wow, that's cool, Jake! Can't wait to hear you play it! Can we see my room now?"

They all laughed and turned to head to Alex's room. His had a queen-size bed. "Whoa!" And a twin-size bunk bed on top, plus the desk and dresser, a bookshelf with one shelf full, and an easel and art cabinet with more supplies. On the wall was a picture of the Eye of the Mountain.

Alex gave Val a huge hug. "Thank you, Aunt Val! It is so awesome."

As Alex was checking out his stuff, Jake hovered by the middle room, the door not quite closed. Val nodded to him open it. It was fully furnished too. A full-sized bed, pink flowers on the soft yellow and blue walls, a dresser and play area that would one day become a desk, and a bookshelf with one shelf full. A faceted crystal hung in the window creating rainbows as the light shined through.

"But you don't even know if she is coming."

"Jake, there is no other option. We have to have faith and trust that Lilah will be here. You will be reunited with your sister."

He wanted to believe her so badly.

Val assured him, "I feel it with everything in me. She will join us."

"I like her room. I think she'll like it a lot."

"Hey, can we go outside? The yard looks awesome!" Alex had great timing.

Jake flicked him with his hand. "Race ya."

And they both took off.

Val laughed. "I thought I said no running in the house!"

Fruit and nut trees mixed with aspens, laurel and juniper to create a diverse space and areas for shade. The raised garden beds were currently filled with weeds and trumpets, but they would make great vegetable and herb gardens. Best of all, the yard opened out to hiking trails in the mountains. They all loved it.

Val wanted it to feel like home. She could already picture the garden, teaching the boys how to grow food, how to cook, and how to tend to the land. And they could walk to town, to the ceremonies, to Mr. Edward, Lucy, and Grandmother Flor.

Alex had spotted no fewer than a dozen "awesome" rocks, a couple of lizards, and a horned toad in the whole eight minutes they had been in the yard. "When can we check out the trails?"

"Soon." Val took an easy, deep breath, breathing in the house, the boys, the feeling of family that she had missed for so long. They had a couple of days until the festival, a couple of days to get used to the house, start cooking here, and begin making it home. Val still had lots of work to move the business, set up shop, and make it all come together, but this moment was for breathing.

EIGHTEEN

Alex daydreamed while doodling, trying to decide what to do for his offering. It was the day before the festival, and he hadn't started. He was watching birds outside the window and playfully asking them, "Do you know what it should be?"

He was having trouble focusing. When Val took a break from work and noticed he was still in the same place she last saw him, she checked in.

"Hey, Alex, what's got you lost in thought?"

He shrugged. "I keep thinking about Dad. Do you know when he is coming?"

"Hmmm, no, he hasn't said. But if you are thinking about him, maybe you should give him a call and check in."

"Can I?"

"Of course, you can. Go talk to your dad!"

Alex became increasingly uneasy as he told Cade about all the updates, the house, and preparing for the festival.

Cade responded with, "That's great, bud," and, "I'm sure it will be fun," but there was no energy in his words. He sounded muted and distant, and Alex became terrified he would lose him again.

"Dad, are you okay?"

"Yes, of course. Don't worry. I'm just busy." But that wasn't the problem. Cade was terrified. Despite the work with the counselor and completing all of the conditions for his probation, he felt paralyzed and unready for the responsibility with his son. Cade was holding back or holding on, the strings of experiences proving hard to cut. Star Junction scared him. What if he got there and still couldn't be a good enough father? What if he got there and couldn't support them?

"Dad, I miss you. When are you coming?"

"I'm not sure yet, but it will be as soon as I can."

"You already said soon! You keep saying soon. I need you."

"Alex, I know you miss me. I miss you too. Please try to understand. I will be coming when I can. I love you."

"I know, Dad. I love you too."

The conversation left Alex concerned and on edge. It was a repeat of the last call. What if Cade didn't come to get him? Or made them move back to the city? Alex couldn't imagine living anywhere else again. He was finally starting to feel like he belonged somewhere.

Val watched Alex's demeanor change after the call. "How's your dad?"

He looked up at her with worried eyes. "I don't know. Why isn't he here yet? He should be here. If he really loves me, he should be here." He walked away with his sketchpad and went out the back door.

Val gave him space to work through it. She got back to work on the plans for the business move. Paperwork was her least favorite thing, but she was confident she'd have it done in a couple of hours. She got lost in it instead.

"Where did Alex go?" Jake's question startled Val from her work.

"What do you mean? He's in the yard drawing."

"No, I saw him head up the trail about an hour ago."

Val bolted up, "What?" She ran to the back yard. "Alex! Damn, I thought he was just drawing. It's over a hundred degrees. Did you see if he had water?"

"No, I'm sorry, Aunt Val. I didn't realize he'd go far. I thought you knew."

"Jake, don't worry. It's not your fault. I need you to get three water packs and your shoes on. We need to go find him. I'm calling Cade" she said as she grabbed her phone.

"Hel—" Cade tried to answer.

"Cade, what did you say to Alex?"

"I told him I love him and that I wasn't coming yet. That I wasn't sure what we were going to do."

"Little brother, pull it together."

"Val, I just need more time."

"No, you don't need more time. You told me that your obligations of community service and payment were all met. Whatever you think is holding you back, you're wrong. It's time for you to come be with your son."

"I just don't know what is right. He's doing so well with you. What if I screw it up again?"

"Cade, listen to me. He doesn't need you to be perfect. He just needs you here. And quite frankly, you need you here. Whatever you're afraid of, it's time to face it. You are not going to find your way out of hell there. The way out is here with your son. You don't have to know the rest."

"Yeah, alright, I'll come next week."

"No, you'll come now. Your son needs you. Right now. I have to go find him because he left after your call—without water on a one-hundred-plus-degree day. Get your ass here!" Click.

Val had only spoken to her brother like that once before. It lit his fire both times.

The heat rose from the boulders in perceptible waves. Alex had followed the trail for a long time while thoughts and fears wove webs in his head. *Alex! Pay attention.* He heard the words inside his head, commanding him from his thoughts. He looked around and realized he had come much further than he meant to. Sweat burned his eyes. He scraped his arms pushing through the brush to get into a shaded nook that was almost a semi-circle.

He should have brought water. He didn't even know he was leaving. He saw a flash of light on the trail when he was drawing in the yard, and his curiosity got the best of him. He put his sketchbook down and went to check it out. But now, he couldn't find what it was. He was just hot and he wasn't sure how to get back.

What was Aunt Val always saying about listening? Or maybe he could try walking well. Would that lead him back to the trail? The shade felt good, but it wasn't water, and it wasn't cool. Tears dripped from his chin and he wiped them. Mr. Edward's voice came to his mind.

"Offerings are meant to show gratitude and love and surrender to a higher power. We give something of ourselves or of value to us. Some people tithe at church, some plant flowers and water the land. Some make art or other treasures and gift them. An offering can be anything of our hearts, even pure tears or a heartfelt *thank you*. If you are ever in need, ask for help and offer your gratitude."

"I'm sorry. I'm not sure how to do this. I didn't mean to come this far alone. Please help me get home." He pulled his wolf totem out of his pocket and placed it in front of him. A shaft of the sun worked to light the green in the malachite. "Thank you for helping me." He watched the hot air shimmer off the boulders and the quaking leaves of the aspen tree. It all felt hypnotic and he dozed off.

An eagle cried out in the distance. Alex began to wake, not quite remembering where he was. He looked around and froze. He slowly rubbed his eyes, wondering if he was still asleep or hallucinating. Just at the other side of the semi-circle, not five feet away, lay a wolf. The wolf lifted her head a little to look at Alex and then laid her head back down. Alex's breath quickened in disbelief and shock. The lump in his throat felt as big as a baseball. He swallowed with a lot of effort.

"Hey there—" he said, quietly noticing the wolf's ears perk toward him. "Good wolf, right? Yeah, you're a good wolf."

He looked around to see if there was any way past the wolf, though he wasn't sure why. He sure couldn't outrun her.

"Mr. Edward, well, all of them say that you just want to help me. Right?"

The wolf looked at him while he spoke. "I didn't mean to leave. I was just upset about Dad."

Alex tried to remember to breathe in between sentences or words or thoughts. Maybe the wolf would like his voice. He noticed his totem had fallen back onto his lap, and he held it tightly.

"I just want him to come here. I miss him. He's my dad. You understand. Right? He's my dad, and he should be here with me." He lowered his shoulders and relaxed a little. He and the wolf just gazed upon each other, and Alex started to feel okay. "Okay then, maybe you can show me the way back to the trail. I bet they're worried about me."

The wolf sat up and Alex smiled.

"Yeah?" Alex got up too, slowly, still not quite sure whether he was safe or if it was real. The wolf turned to head out of the nook. Alex followed, but not too close.

"Hey, where are we going? This doesn't look like the path." But it was greener.

The wolf led him to a hidden stream and began drinking.

Alex lit up. "Water!" He moved as quickly as he could without startling the wolf and kneeled down to drink. "Thank you, I was really thirsty." He coughed some of it up from drinking too fast.

The wolf waited, and Alex tried to drink some more. He cupped the water and poured it over his head.

Then the wolf continued. Her markings were beautiful—black, gray and tannish white with blue eyes.

"Were you the one in my dreams?"

The wolf didn't respond. They just kept walking through the brush. The day was waning, and Alex wasn't sure where he was. He stopped for a moment to look around. It looked different. The wolf continued and Alex followed.

"Which path did he take, Jake?"

Jake pointed to the path on the right.

"*Papa, help us find him,*" Val prayed aloud. Just as they started up the right-hand path a hawk flew right in front of them to the other path. They looked at each other and both moved to the other trail.

They walked in silence for a while, both focused on any sign of Alex.

"Alex!" was the call every few minutes.

Jake broke the silence. "What's Cade's problem?"

Val looked at him. She felt annoyed at first, torn between understanding and protecting her brother and her own annoyance at him not being here. She contemplated her answer.

"I imagine it's the same issue that we all face from time to time. Fear."

Jake tried to understand, but it didn't make sense to him. "Alex is a cool kid. Uncle Cade should be here."

"Agreed. I believe he is on his way. So let's find Alex, okay?"

Jake nodded.

"Alex!" They climbed fairly quickly and found some shade from trees on this path. They reached a plateau and took a pause to drink some water. Val carried the extra pack for Alex.

Alex was certain now that they were heading down, he just wasn't sure if it was the right down. The sun shifted in the sky and began to lower. Alex tried not to notice but was glad it was cooling off a bit. A rock slid under his foot and he slid with it.

"Hey, wait! I need to rest." And he sat right there with the rock, tied his shoe, and closed his eyes for a minute. He didn't notice the wolf turn back toward him until he felt the wolf's nose push against the side of his head. His eyes shot open. The wolf nuzzled him again, pushing up as if to make him rise.

"Okay, I'm coming." The wolf looked in the direction she had been leading him, glanced back at Alex, and then went back to the edge of the path where it turned.

"Alex?"

Alex shot up, "Jake?"

Val shouted, "Alex, where are you?"

"Aunt Val, I'm here! I'm coming." They rounded the corner to see him getting up, and something disappearing into the brush. Val and Jake ran to him.

"Alex! Are you okay?" Val looked him over.

Other than a few scrapes and a lot of dirt, he appeared okay. She took the extra water pack off her back and gave it to him as she wrapped him up in her arms and then grabbed Jake and pulled him in, too. Val closed her eyes as tears streaked her face.

"I'm sorry, Aunt Val... I didn't mean to leave like that. I'm sorry. Please don't cry." She just held them there for a minute and neither one tried to break free.

She let out a deep breath and loosened the embrace. "First, I'm crying because I am happy you are okay and we found you. And because I was just reminded of how grateful I feel to be here with both of you, to have both of you in my life. We are family." She looked at each of them in the eyes, and they both nodded and teared up. "Let's go home and let everyone else know that you're okay."

They started to walk and Alex said "Wait!" As he turned around to look back at the wolf. He couldn't see it.

"Thank you!"

"Who are you talking to?" asked Jake.

"The wolf. Didn't you see it?"

Jake started to roll his eyes, but they all looked back and a wolf stepped out of the brush.

Alex beamed. "She showed me the way back to the path and to water."

"Well then, I owe you a thank you as well. I am grateful for your help." Val had been through too much to question it.

Jake wasn't sure what to make of it, but he nodded anyway.

The phone was ringing when they arrived home. "Hi, Lucy, we found him. He's fine and has quite a story to tell." Lucy laughed with her on the other end of the phone.

"Grandmother would like to have you all for dinner." Val looked at the boys and how tired they were, but Grandmother's invitations didn't get refused.

"Thank you. We'll come, of course, but it'll be an early night. I'd like them to get some rest for tomorrow."

"Of course! It is about tomorrow."

As they all got cleaned up to go to the compound, Val checked her phone. She had eight messages from Cade.

What is happening?

Did you find him?

Please tell me when you find him.

Shit, what is wrong with me? I should have been there.

Any word?

Val?

I'm on my way.

Just, please, tell me when you find him.

Val responded: *We found him. He is fine—just tired. We will be at Grandmother's for dinner. Do you remember? They are at the end of Constellation Drive.*

As she typed it she wondered if she knew of any other streets with that name.

Grandmother Flor sat at the end of the dining table and Edward faced her. The kids filled in the sides of the table with Lucy and Val. On the table were two tureens filled with Grandmother's Festival Stew. It didn't matter the weather outside. This was the traditional dish the night before every festival. It smelled of goodness—fresh herbs, onions and garlic, other vegetables and, well, the rest was a secret.

The boys were trying to figure out if it had meat. She also made her soft bread. Essentially, generously thick flatbreads that were so light and fluffy nobody could get enough of them. They worked perfectly with the stew. After they offered their gratitude and began to enjoy the meal, Grandmother spoke.

"I am grateful that you have all found your way home and are here to share our traditional meal."

Alex interrupted, "It's really good, Grandmother."

Jake kicked his foot under the table to stop him from interrupting again, but Grandmother just nodded to Alex.

"Thank you, Alex. There was a time here when things were much simpler and options fewer. Today, we can go to the market and find almost anything we desire to put on our table, but there was a time when our choices were only the food we could grow, gather, or hunt and the generosity of neighbors sharing. As you can taste, we never suffered with that. This is the stew I was taught by my grandmother, and perhaps she by hers. The ingredients are simple and delicious. As everything is when it is made with love."

She paused there and conversation trickled back in. Jake asked for more bread. Val for some of the chopped herbs.

Val finally found words, "I had forgotten about this dish. About this tradition. Thank you for including us. I can almost feel Papa and Mama. I can almost hear his joyous laughter."

Grandmother's eyes gleamed. "Yes, he is joyous, as you say. William was always an excellent teacher of levity. And this night should be. Please, all, be in joy."

"Our celebration begins tonight, and tomorrow the whole town will join. Perhaps each of you would like to share what you are doing for your offering?" Edward had a way of inviting conversation.

"I thought I would draw something, or maybe paint. But I don't know what yet. I haven't thought of anything." Alex shrugged and looked back to his plate.

Edward responded, "Anything that is from your heart Alex. What do you wish for the people, the world, or even yourself? How can that be expressed? And do not forget to write down what you wish to let go of. That is what you will burn in the fire."

Alex nodded that he understood and Edward's attention shifted to Jake.

Jake realized they were looking at him. He quickly swallowed and took a sip of water. "I'm working on a song. I hope that is the right thing."

Grandmother smiled brightly. "If it is from your heart, it will be perfect. Music is a wonderful vehicle for love."

Each had their turn as they finished the meal. Val noticed a text message and excused herself to look at it. *I'm here—but I'm not ready. How do I climb Clarity Mountain?* She looks over to Grandmother and Edward.

"I'm going to get some more water, anybody want some?"

"And I will bring dessert!"

The kids' eyes lit up with Grandmother's declaration. Once in the kitchen, Val shared the text from Cade.

"He wants to climb Clarity Mountain tonight before Alex knows he is here."

"And he must." Grandmother's tone was firm.

"But it's dark—and he only had one lesson thirty years ago."

"Child, he will be protected. You know if he is called, he must go. You cannot always be his protector. Some things he must do for himself. He wants to face his son whole again—and he must, if he is going to stay."

Val nodded knowingly. "Have him come here in an hour. We will be finished by then as the boys must sleep well and be rested for the festival. We will greet him and send him with guidance and supplies."

Edward and Lucy excused themselves from the table as they were all finishing, and Val and the boys were preparing to leave. They returned carrying wooden crates with plant cuttings and seedlings as well as smudging bundles and goodies from their garden. Val felt a little overwhelmed.

"What is all this?" she asked with joy.

Grandmother answered, "These are from our garden to yours. To begin cultivating abundance, joy, and beauty. And the boys will be good helpers. When you are ready, we have three young trees for you to plant."

"Thank you, Grandmother," came from Val, Alex, and Jake in unison.

"Now you must go and get rest for tomorrow."

Cade followed instructions and waited outside until Val and the boys left. It was the hardest thing for him not to run up to Alex. When he saw his son, his chest constricted; he held his breath to keep from calling out.

Val's car drove away and Cade heard Grandmother, "You can come in now."

He swallowed and let out a big breath like he was preparing to lift a heavy weight. He walked around to the door and felt eight years old again. Grandmother Flor held open her arms and allowed him to melt. As he trembled, Edward spoke.

"Son, it is wise of you to answer the call of the mountain. You have climbed it before?" Cade nodded.

"Once, with Val, just before we moved away."

"Yes, and you learned on that climb. You watched her and learned?"

Cade just nodded. He didn't know what to say.

"And you buried something there."

"Yes." Cade spoke quietly. All of the words he had rehearsed and questions he planned disappeared in the night. He let them lead, needed them to lead.

"A gift from your father."

"Yes."

"It was a very powerful gift, son. Retrieving it will help you to remember."

"I hope so. I don't want Alex to have half of a father." Speaking the words broke his voice as his hands attempted to stop the tears.

"Alex has a good father who is learning and has healing to do, like all of us. Your father included."

"William? That's hard to believe from all of Val's stories when we were kids."

Edward and Grandmother laughed.

"Of course, because you were children. It was not for you to know the struggles of the parents' journey at that time."

They paused and sat in silence together. Cade was beginning to relax a little and breathe again.

"Son, we are so glad to have you home."

Cade teared up again. "I wasn't sure I had a home anymore. I'm so grateful that you have been here for Alex and Val and Jake. And me —I started to think my memories were just dreams."

"Perhaps they are both." Grandmother Flor had a twinkle in her eye. "We have prepared a pack for you. A flashlight, water, snacks, offerings. Special tea for when you reach the top. Listen to your heart. Pay attention. And if something arises for you—memories, emotions, old stories—be willing to lay them down and let them go. That is how Clarity Mountain will help you."

"Son, you will know what to do when the time comes," Edward spoke reassuringly. "We will show you to the path, and we will see you tomorrow. It is the Fire Dance Festival. You see? You have timed your arrival well. Alex will be very excited to see you. Together you will share stories."

Cade put the backpack on and held the flashlight in his hand. "Thank you."

———

Dear Cade,

You were always the best big brother. You saved us so many times. Can you forgive me for needing you to? Because of you, Jake has a man he can look up to. Just thinking of that brings tears to my eyes. I can never thank you enough. What a lucky boy Alex is. I know you are struggling too, but I also know you will do anything for your son. You know he is a lot like you. Right? I can hear it when he answers the phone and see it in the pictures you showed me.

Cade, I'm writing because I don't know if I will see you again. Or when. The doctors aren't providing too much hope. But they don't know me. I am so glad we came back to Star Junction. Just being here makes me feel like I can survive anything. I had forgotten just how special a place it is. For the first time in forever, I feel like I am home. Jake and Lilah—you will love Lilah—have a chance here. Maybe you should consider it too? Alex would love it here.

I thought a lot about what you said about Val. You're right. I know you're right. I am sending her a letter too. I tried to call. I really did, but the words just didn't come out. If I don't get to see her, hug her for me, okay?

Love, your little Sissy Sunshine

Val got up early to get some work in before making breakfast and summoning the boys. As she walked down the hall, she found Alex already busy at his easel painting, and it was a show. Val was grateful for the floor protector under the easel.

"Good morning, Alex." She startled him. He turned to see her, almost out of breath from his painting. "Whatcha doing?"

"I figured out what to do for my offering. I've never painted before but I couldn't stop thinking about it since the wolf helped me."

Val smiled and let out an impressed sigh. "Alex, that's a beautiful offering. You're an amazing kid. Keep going!" She smiled and walked away, tears in the corner of her eyes.

Val walked past Jake's room and heard music. His music. *"Phew. Papa, it has so much love."*

As she walked down the stairs, she swore she heard the message, *"This is just the beginning."* She let out the kind of little laugh that signified either nervousness or the transformation of disbelief. With both boys already up, it was time to make breakfast.

"Boys! Breakfast is ready!" Not that they couldn't smell it. Pancakes, eggs, bacon, and fruit. Lots of fruit. Something about living in the heat, fruit seemed like the best treat in the world. She wasn't quite sure why she chose pancakes. It's more of a treat kind of breakfast. But then, it was a special day. And maybe, just maybe, she was feeling Cade. She used to make him pancakes after Emmet left for work.

They, the kids and Grace, had many secrets from Emmet. She smiled at it now. Funny how it all felt so serious then, keeping secrets and getting away with stuff to try to feel normal. The boys came running down the stairs and burst into the kitchen. Val burst out laughing. Partly at the enthusiasm. Partly because Alex had paint on almost every section of his body. The boys stopped in mid-burst.

"What?"

Val tried to shake her head. "Nothing." But then Jake looked at Alex. Then Alex looked at his reflection in the stainless-steel fridge. They all burst out laughing.

"Oops!"

"It's okay, Alex. I'm pretty sure it will wash off. You may need new pajamas, though!" They laughed again as she served the food. "Wash your hands."

Alex shrugged the "oh yeah" shrug and went to the sink. Jake laughed as he took his first bite.

"These are really good, Aunt Val."

"Thanks, Jake. I used to make them a lot."

"I'd like to learn."

"Yeah? Okay, next time."

"I know how! I make them with my dad," Alex chimed in.

"Well, he should know how to make them really well because I'm the one who taught him!"

"Really?"

"Truth."

With that Alex took his first bite. "Okay, these *are* really good, but I think my dad's are better."

Val laughed. "Alright, we'll test them out when he comes."

"Deal!"

Val watched the boys enjoying their pancakes and asking for more. It felt like a great start to festival day, yet part of her heart was with Cade on the mountain. It didn't feel like worry, that would have been Val a couple of months ago. It felt more like a part of her was there with him, supporting him.

She hoped he was able to return in time for the festival. "*It should be plenty of time,*" she told herself. She took in a deep breath and turned her attention back to the boys.

"What are you offering, Aunt Val?"

Wow, she hadn't really gotten that far. Weird. She had been so focused on them and moving the business and finding Lilah. Then it came to her that it was all part of the offering. All of it. She had been living the offering. Then she remembered to play.

"How about my pancakes?" They all laughed.

"You can't offer those," Jake replied.

"Why not?"

"Because there won't be any left!" the boys exclaimed in unison as they both reached for more.

"Well, I will know the offering when it is time." That felt truer than she knew.

Val and the boys arrived early to help with the setup. The Star Pavilion was already glowing, and Val was taken back in time.

"Papa, how does it glow like that?"

William always laughed. "It glows with all the love of our town. It radiates all that we put in it." Picaflor said, "It's so pretty."

Adult Val still had a little trouble grasping the glow as love, yet she didn't doubt it. Just walking in the area of the round structure felt magical. She saw Grandmother Flor watching her and smiled. Grandmother reflected her joy and gratitude. Val put her hand on her heart. *"Papa, it's better than I remembered,"* she said in her heart.

Lucy took Jake to show him where he could warm up and how to help the other musicians. Alex found Edward and showed him his painting. Edward teared up and laughed with joy. The painting showed the Star Pavilion with a fire, stars, the mountain, the Watcher, and his wolf, all in a swirling vortex of energy and stars.

"Young wolf, this is a beautiful offering. Thank you, Alex. Thank you." He gave Alex a big hug.

Alex was almost embarrassed at the strong reaction. He was hoping for, "Wow, that's great," but the tearing up and emotional responses felt a little overwhelming, but good too.

They all kept busy helping Grandmother Flor direct traffic. The food tables were ready to go. Plenty of chairs were set up for people to relax and eat or enjoy the music. The wood was all prepared for the fire. It was almost start time, and Cade still hadn't returned.

Val asked Edward if he knew to come to the center. "Ms. Valerie, your brother is making his journey. He knows to return here. Worry will not help him."

"You're right. It's not really *worry*. Just wanting to see him and see Alex with him."

"They will be a pack again soon."

Val smiled in agreement and nodded.

Alex saw them and came over.

"What time does it start?" he asked.

"Soon!" Edward looked around and gestured to show all the people. "Very soon."

The gathering place was already filled with people. It felt a little surprising considering how quiet the town had been for the summer. Even the Fridays had been subdued. The musicians were finishing their setup, and the food tables were overflowing with offerings for the feast. The smells were intoxicating. Everybody had come out. Val spotted Daniel at the stage and went over.

"Daniel! You're here." She couldn't hide her hopeful joy.

He turned and returned her smile. "Val, yes. I decided to wait it out a bit longer. Are you really moving your business here?"

"Yes, I am. I really am." She smiled, feeling a little awkward. She was reminded again of just how fast news spread in this town. "I saw it from the mountain and had to try."

"Thank you. Just that decision has created buzz. People are talking. They have hope again. I don't even know everything that you do, but I know if you are taking over three buildings with the intention of creating opportunity, I have hope for our town. Our home. And I won't abandon my home." Val gave him a hug.

"I am so glad you are staying. Let's keep that hope." As she was talking to him, she saw a figure in the distance. Her smile only got bigger. "Oh! I have to go. Play your heart out tonight!"

Daniel nodded. "I will."

Val hurried back to Alex and Edward and signaled to Edward.

"This will be a historical Fire Dance," he declared.

Alex wasn't sure what they were talking about. Val moved behind him, put her hands on his shoulders and gently repositioned him. He rolled his eyes at the weirdness of his aunt.

"What are you doing?"

She held her hands there. Edward moved to the side.

"This is just weird." He started to shift and shrug her off. Then he saw the man moving toward them. He froze as he tried to form the words, "Dad? Dad!" He started to cry.

Val leaned down to him and whispered, "Go," in his ear. And Alex ran toward the figure.

Cade was dirty and haggard, but when he saw his son, he forgot his exhaustion and ran to meet him.

"Alex!" He lifted his son up and pulled him in. Alex wrapped his arms and legs around Cade.

"Dad!" He couldn't control the sobs. All the emotions poured into Cade's shoulder.

"I'm here, Alex. I'm here, and I'm not going anywhere."

Val made her way closer but waited for Cade to signal they were ready.

"Hey, I hear it's festival day."

Alex nodded against his shoulder.

"Shall we join the others?"

Alex lifted his head. "Yeah, I want to show you my offering." He hopped down.

They walked over to Val. Cade reached for her and pulled her close.

"I hope you never have to talk to me that way again."

"I better not have to." They both laughed.

"I missed this. Thank you, Val—for Alex, for teaching me how to climb Clarity Mountain, for the apacheta, for keeping Dad alive for me. Thank you."

She hugged him in the way of their youth.

"Cade, thank you. You helped this all begin with a phone call. We are family and I am so glad to be acting like it again." She kissed his forehead like she did when he was a child. He laughed and did the same to her. "How was your climb?"

"Best thing I've done in a long time. It really helped me to put things in the right perspective and discover or maybe reclaim a few things." He held up his wolf totem that William had carved so many years before.

Val put her hand on her heart and took a breath in, biting her lips a little.

"And there's more. It's the weirdest thing, but I think I talked to or heard from or saw—or whatever you call it—I don't know, but I think Melanie is coming. I just kept feeling her. We haven't been in touch for years."

"Wow." Tears welled up in Val's eyes. "That's wonderful."

The music started. They found Lucy and moved closer to the stage. Jake came over to see Cade. He loved his uncle and was glad he showed up. Things were starting to feel like they might work out.

"Wow, Jake, look at how tall you are."

Jake shrugged his shoulders. "Yeah, I guess. I'm glad you're here, Uncle Cade. Seriously."

Cade gave him a firm hug. "Me too, Jake. I'm glad we're all here. Thanks for looking out for Alex."

They did a triple fist bump like they'd done countless times before, even though it hadn't been often. Cade had been the most consistent male figure in Jake's life, and it was a relief to Jake that he seemed to be coming through.

"Jake, when do you go on?" asked Val.

"In a bit. The first group plays for a while, and then they'll call me."

"You feeling okay about it?"

"I don't know. I mean, I guess so. If it will help, I want to try, you know?"

"We're looking forward to it. You'll be great," Val encouraged.

"Val!" Val turned but didn't see anyone. "Val!" The voice moved its way closer. "Val!"

"Elliot?" She finally spotted the direction of the voice calling her name and the source. Elliot was making his way through the crowd of people. At six-foot-four, he stood out.

"Val!"

"Elliot, what are you doing here?" Elliot caught up to her and looked around.

"I had to see it for myself—this magic place that is stealing you away."

She was surprised and couldn't help but be flattered and amused. She was going to miss Elliot's daily presence and balancing humor.

"Besides, Cleo missed you. She's in the car with the AC on."

"You're crazy, but okay. Thank you. Welcome to Star Junction! My hometown. My home."

"I can see why you like it." He looked directly into her eyes and spoke sincerely.

The others struggled to contain their curiosity. The boys were not the only ones clearing their throats and fake coughing.

"Elliot, please let me introduce you to my family. My brother Cade, his son Alex, my nephew Jake, Mr. – er, my Uncle Edward, Lucy, and this beautiful town." Her hand indicated each, and each nodded. "Family, this is my business partner Elliot. He is taking over the client services division so I can focus on the product development and production here."

Cade reached his hand out. "Elliot, nice to meet you. Val speaks highly of you."

"Cade, pleasure."

Alex followed his father's lead and reached out his hand. "Thank you for helping my aunt move things here."

"Alex, I'm glad to help. I'm excited about the future."

Val was beaming with joy. She hadn't felt embarrassed in ages.

"Oh, you guys are too much!" She wondered if she was blushing.

Jake took his turn, looked Elliot square in the eye and shook his hand firmly. "Hello."

"Jake."

Val was watching Edward closely. This felt like silliness.

Edward just nodded to Elliot with a sly smile, and Lucy offered, "Glad you could join us. It is a very special day."

"Is that food I smell? I'm starving!" Elliot declared. He always knew when to shake things up. They all pointed over to the food tables, and he excused himself. "Oh, I brought all the papers for us to go over, and sign in person. All business, all the time." Val laughed and beamed. Signing the papers and making it official was her offering, just in time.

Over the speakers they heard the call for the next performer. That was Jake. Alex and Cade both gave him fist bumps. Val gave a nod and wink. "Go get 'em."

He smiled and headed to the stage.

Edward looked at Val with a gleam in his eye.

She looked at him quizzically and finally asked, "What is that look?"

He smiled and patted her on the back. "It is good to see you again, Picaflor." Val couldn't help a slight head bow and tilt. She smiled self-consciously and looked up at him out of the corner of her eye. He was right. She did feel like Picaflor again. Playful, loving, full of joy. She smiled deeply and then looked at him directly.

"It is good to be seen again, to be Picaflor."

Lucy smiled too.

Jake was nervous. He had never played in front of people other than the family. He really didn't know if he could. He didn't look up. He walked to the stool on the stage with his guitar and didn't say a word. He sat motionless, barely breathing. The townspeople were kind and waited quietly, but the silence became awkward. Daniel stepped in during this pause and introduced Jake.

"We'll get started in a minute," he announced. He leaned down and whispered in Jake's ear, "You've got this, bud. We're all family here. Just play like you do in the store."

Then Daniel sat on the stool behind Jake and started tapping time lightly on a drum to help Jake find the music. Jake closed his eyes and listened. He could hear Grandmother's voice talking about the gift of sharing from our heart and the powerful force that could be. He started. His hands found the strings, his fingers the notes and the chords and the rhythm of it all. He played a mesmerizing instrumental that entranced the people. His hands stopped, and he looked up at the townspeople.

"I, um, I want to play a song I wrote for my sister Lilah to call her home. Thank you."

She dances like a hummingbird, the flowers all delight. Sweet nectar from the sun is picaflor's flight. The light dances through her angel wings, and picaflor sings. Dear picaflor, dance with the world. Spread your joy and love. Fly with Spirit. Delight the stars above. My picaflor, please find your way home tonight.

Elliot walked up to see the look on Val's face. They all saw it. "What is it?"

She looked at Elliot, and Cade, and Edward and answered, "That's my father's song—the one he sang to me as a child, or, part of it." She put her hand to her mouth and then her chest with tears of disbelief and joy.

Before anyone could respond, a car pulled up to the edge of the crowd. It seemed out of place, and they all looked at the same time. Ms. Ramirez got out of the driver's seat. They were paralyzed. Goosebumps covered Val's body. Elliot put his hand on her back to comfort her. Ms. Ramirez walked to the back seat door and opened it. A beautiful young girl with curly, flowing golden hair got out.

"Oh my god—"

"It's her! It's Lilah from my dreams," Alex exclaimed.

Ms. Ramirez and Lilah started walking toward them. Jake saw from the stage, jumped down, and ran toward his sister.

"Lilah!" he called out.

"Jake!" Lilah yelled her brother's name. The girl who was said not to talk by Ms. Ramirez. She jumped into her brother's arms and he spun her around until he dropped to his knees crying.

"Lilah! I tried so hard to find you. Don't ever leave again."

Lilah put her hands on his face.

"I know Jakey. It's okay now." It was almost as if she were absorbing his tears and pain. She turned to Val and walked over and held up her arms to be hugged. Val picked her up and hugged her. "I knew you would come for us, Auntie! Thank you."

Val hugged her so tightly and breathed in the breath they had all been waiting to breathe.

"Lilah, I am so grateful you are here, and happy to meet you."

"Me too." Lilah didn't rush, but wanted to meet them all. She got down from Val's embrace and hugged Alex. "Thank you for dreaming with me, Alex." Alex already liked her. He looked at his dad and smiled. Lilah was greeted by Cade, Edward, and the rest. Ms. Ramirez watched from the car. Val looked over, put her hands in prayer position, and nodded to her.

More music had started in the background. It was dancing music. Val could feel herself lifted with the drums. She took Alex's hands and started dancing. Soon the whole family joined. Elliot found his way back to her and took her hand. They danced, and the world fell away. "And dance with the sun," repeated in her heart. It was great fun. As they came back to themselves and the earth, the music calmed.

"We've been very blessed this festival," Grandmother Flor spoke, and the town quieted. "You have all been generous in your offerings and open in your gratitude and expressions of joy. This is how it is meant to be always, and how it used to be." She paused as if listening for the words to come. "Have we not learned how easy it can be to forget ourselves and each other, to forget our wholeness and our source? And now, we have also learned how easy it can be to remember.

"The ancients foretold of a time when people would lose themselves. And they foretold of the time of renewal, an opportunity to rise again. Star Junction has new life, but our work has just begun. Each of you has a role to play. Each of you, vital. The light one has returned to help us. The luminescent hummingbird. You remember that there are many junctions for the stars, and they are all calling for the time of renewal. Remember now. Remember well, with joy in your hearts and love throughout."

Lightning struck the mountain and provided drama and a light show for Grandmother's message. The mountain was awake. The Watcher watching.

With that Grandmother disappeared from the stage, the music began again and the fire burned. The townspeople came to the fire and fed it the things they wished to free themselves of and the prayers they had for others. It received them all. Every scrap of paper written on. Every vice shed. Every burden of guilt or shame one wished to release as a whisper or a scream. The fire consumed and transmuted them all for those who were ready to move forward.

Z and Grandmother Flor watched from the distance. "This is a beautiful festival, Eliaflore. Your efforts have been very effective."

Flor looked to Z. "Yes, Zekiel. The seeds of remembrance are beginning to grow. Our patience and hope rewarded."

The fire awaited them. The young girl started, her golden hair glowing with the flames. She let the beat of the drums and the crackle of the fire guide her movements and danced with all her heart and joy. Val saw Lilah dance and joined her. Lilah smiled when she saw Val and held out her hand. Their movements synched, and the fire brightened.

Val's joy and wonder defied her understanding. She looked up at the stars and invited them to dance, too. Grandmother Flor took Val's free hand. The trio danced together, raised their arms to the sky and sang their love. In unison they spoke: "Ancient Ones, Spirit of Life, you are needed here. You are not forgotten. Please return. Help the rest to remember. It was said that there would be a time to begin again. To return to our knowing and the truth of all things. We call to you now. The time is now. Return the stars to guide our path and we will once again feel what it is to be a junction of the stars. Let thy light be revealed now." Together they tossed resin into the fire and the fire sent their message to the skies in a fountain of sparks.

The council of ancients circled the portal watching the beloved souls creating stories on her. The Earth Mother deserved better. Fortunately, there were those who stayed true to the ways. Who felt the connection through their hearts and witnessed nature's support and love. The Ancients saw the progress made, how the energies were returning closer to balance. How the seeds planted long ago, the efforts of devoted souls over generations were signaling clearly. The time was now. One at a time, each of the council reached an arm to the center of the portal opening and dropped a star to the earth. "It is time," they said. The stars were named: Illumination, Communication, Love, Compassion, Forgiveness, Connection, and Joy. The stars fell one by one to the fire where the three danced, each star creating a light show of colorful sparks spreading their essence across the land.

The End

Acknowledgments

As I sit pondering my acknowledgements I wonder how far back to go. I mean, my gratitude and list of people starts long before the act of writing this book and those that follow. It's been a lifetime of learning, growing, and experiencing life. Joy and sorrow. Success and failure. Love and loss. I am grateful for all the teachers who have graced my journey.

Let me start with "I did it, Mom & Dad!" It took me a bit longer than imagined...but I finally claimed the writer in me and now have a book to show for it. And a few more on the way. I hope you are smiling from the clouds. I'm grateful for every bit of my time with you both and our family. Of course, I am grateful for my brothers, Mark & John, and all of the extended family.

Scribe Hive Publishing LLC. I am thrilled and grateful to be a part of this talented group of women. Grateful to have a "hive" for support, encouragement, and oh so many laughs. I'd like to think that I would have completed this book and stayed the course on my own...thankfully, I didn't need to test that. Each and every one of you has a part in this victory. You are my Hive. Together we thrive. Kim, Rhonda, Jill, Diandra, Alvagh, Crista, Kathleen...

For the journey of writing this book, I have many to thank for all types of support from encouragement to a couch (or bed) to sleep on while I traveled "in search of" a place to land. The journey took me to

Oregon, Nevada, Utah, northern Arizona, and California — and led me to this story. My gratitude is for the universe, for the awe inspiring places I hiked through and camped in, and for all the generous and amazing people in my life. A handful housed me during this houseless, nomadic period: Deborah & Jim, Gala & Bill, Beth & Brian, Liz, Kathleen & Edgard, and Susan & Reuel. I am eternally grateful. But the list doesn't stop there.

Early in the process of writing the book I realized I needed to find a way to support myself and the book. I decided a great option would be to take a seasonal job somewhere close to the fictional setting of the story. I landed at the North Rim of the Grand Canyon. The location made it challenging to join the online class I had joined, but couldn't be beat for beauty and inspiration. About ¾ of the way through the first draft, and at the end of the "season", I said "yes" to a 48-state road trip with my new beau. It was the best decision of my life. I promise I will write more about this someday. But for now, I will leave it with my deepest gratitude and joy for David Weissmann aka: DogDad.

This story wouldn't exist if I hadn't joined my dear friend Melissa G's "Flight of the Hummingbird" program. I took this course during my road travels, complete with 5x3ft canvas and paints. A vision quest with art, the course was to invite Hummingbird energy into the painting. The course worked great, not only did a beautiful hummingbird appear on my canvas, but this book found its inspiration and form.

The book wouldn't be what it is without the highly talented editors involved. The early guidance and encouragement of Kathleen McGowan helped me take my zero draft to viable working draft. The wisdom and expertise of Laurie Scheer guided the shape of the story, including leaving out the parts that belong elsewhere. And Amanda Brown makes copy editing look easy. Thankfully.

There are people who encouraged me so long ago it feels like another lifetime. I don't know if you'll know it's me, but I'll name you anyway. You were invaluable to my confidence and my growth. Karen Wallace and James Callner of West Valley College (Saratoga, CA). Your mentorship so long ago still holds significant space in my being.

And, for my lifelong friends and extended family. You all know who you are. I love you. I am grateful for you. And, there is another. My dear friend's mother, Carol Woodard. Decades ago, with the confidence of youth I announced that I was going to be a writer. Instead of dismissing me she asked "when you write your book, will you put me in the acknowledgements? I've always wanted to see my name in a book." Or something like that. Honestly, I have carried this with me for those decades...knowing that one day, I would be able to include her.

About the Author

Serra Wildheart is an author and co-founder of Scribe Hive Publishing LLC. Her experience spanned industries from Tech to Wine until the call to write spoke louder than the rest. Serra brings the heart of experience — success, grief, joy, and picking up the pieces when it all crashes down — and alchemizes it to soul stories. She loves exploring and credits her travels to Peru, Europe, and throughout the United States for coloring her world. But mostly, she writes stories from the heart with the hope to touch your soul. When she is not doing that, she enjoys cooking, hiking, painting, and hanging out with her dogs and beloved DogDad.

Serra is currently writing books two and three of the Legends of Star Junction series with plans to release in 2024 and 2025.

About Scribe Hive Publishing

Scribe Hive Publishing LLC is dedicated to publishing great reads. Learn about our authors, available titles, and more at:

www.scribehivepublishing.com